RETURN TO GRACE

BETHANY SURREIRA

D1714244

COPYRIGHT

First paperback edition December 2020

Cover design by Bethany Surreira
Editing/Proofreading by Amanda Cuff, Savage Hart Book Services
Formatting by Ashley Munoz

ISBN 9798562165343 (paperback)
ASIN B08N47FKRV (ebook)

www.bethanysurreira.com

❀ Created with Vellum

For Sabrina and Alexandria.
You, my girls, are magic.

PROLOGUE

"That right there is my favorite sound in the entire world," Paul said, watching his daughter, Leah, run through the meadow giggling.

"Man, ain't that the truth," Brad said, shifting positions and crossing his arms over his chest. "Who knew being a dad would soften us up?"

"Soften? You're the biggest softie I know!" Paul responded. "Shall I let the ladies in on what happened at senior prom?"

"Um, no. Let's not go there," Brad said, a slight blush forming on his cheeks.

"Fill us in on what?" asked Lucia, Paul's wife, as she walked across the field to where they were standing.

"Nothing," Brad yelled quickly. A chorus of laughter erupted at his declaration.

"Boys will be boys," Tammy said, and linked her arm through Lucia's, leading her toward the weeping willow tree in the corner of the meadow. "Come on. Help me set up the blanket under the tree."

As Lucia pulled the pink lemonade out of the picnic basket, she glanced up at Caleb and Leah playing in the meadow. She tapped Tammy on the arm and nodded for her to look at the kids.

Leah twirled round and round, her pale-yellow sundress twisting in the wind. She wore a delicate headband to keep the wisps of hair from falling into her face. She flitted around from flower patch to flower patch like a little bee, trying to find the perfect flowers for her crown.

"Caleb," she called out. "Wanna be my king?"

She motioned to the crown she had started to make for herself, and Caleb stood up and ran across the meadow to her. Before he sat down to make his own crown, he put her sweater over her shoulders.

"You don't want to catch a cold now," he said, smiling at Leah while their mothers smiled back at them.

"Ahh, young love," Tammy said to Lucia. "Should we start planning the wedding now?"

The meadow was on Dooley Butler's family farm, and while he hated to admit it, he always seemed happy it would be his one day. He loved teaching all the kids how to ride. "A cowboy in New England," was what Paul and Brad always called him, then they'd tease him about needing a cowgirl by his side.

That particular Sunday, after everyone finished setting up the picnic, Dooley came barreling out of the barn with a bucket of beers. His goofy grin was on full display, as always.

"Howdy, fellas! Anyone want a beer?" he asked, as he tried not to roll down the hill.

"Took you long enough," Brad teased. "I thought maybe you met a girl or something."

"Funny you mention that. I actually did meet a girl. Her name is Becky and she's working with my mom in the garden. Trying to help her with some hybrid flower to win over the judges at the Spring Festival."

"What? Why didn't you tell us?" Tammy asked, swatting him on the arm.

"Well, it's still really new and I wasn't sure if it was going to go anywhere, so I didn't want to jinx myself," he admitted.

"Makes sense," Paul said. "What's she like?"

"See for yourself," a voice called out from the barn.

Out came a petite brunette carrying two bottles of champagne. She had a smile that matched Dooley's, and they looked like the two missing pieces to a puzzle.

"Hi! I'm Becky," she introduced herself, handing a bottle to Lucia. "Dooley told me you ladies like pink lemonade, so I thought I'd spice it up a bit."

"Thanks! It's so nice to meet you. Dooley has told us nothing about you," Lucia said, teasing Becky back.

"Hey, now! Good things come to those who wait. We can't all meet the love of our life at an airport," Dooley shot back.

"An airport?" Becky asked. "Now this, I've got to hear."

"That's a story for another day," Paul said. "It's very nice to meet you, Becky. I'm Paul Abernathy and this is my wife, Lucia. Our daughter, Leah, is over there making crowns with Caleb, Brad and Tammy's son."

Brad walked over and put his arms around Tammy's waist and nodded. Everyone was happy to see Dooley finally have someone. His heart of gold matched his goofy personality, and he deserved to find someone, too. Dooley gave Becky a peck on the cheek, and her skin darkened a shade of pink.

"Let's eat!" Dooley shouted. "I am starving."

"It's good to know that Sunday mass causes you to starve," Tammy said and laughed. "We've got sandwiches today, kids. Chicken salad, egg salad, and tuna salad. Take your pick. I also packed some fruit, veggies and dip, and chips. And of course, brownies for dessert. Dig in."

"You're the chef, right?" Becky asked.

"Cook. I've never had any formal training, but I do own a small place in town," Tammy responded. "Dooley really has told you a lot about us all."

"That's only cause I love ya." He winked.

The group continued to eat and laugh and drink. Those were the days they lived for. Unconditional love between friends who had become family. The ladies packed up the food and blankets, and the men threw away the trash. As the men were walking back, Brad started to sweat and sway a bit.

"You okay, buddy?" Paul asked.

Shaking it off, Brad kept walking toward his wife. "Yeah, man. I'm fine."

Paul looked at Dooley and then over to Lucia. His eyebrows furrowed and his concern read clearly on his face. Brad was a stubborn man, and they all knew it, having grown up with him. Still, he said he was fine, and Paul wasn't about to push him.

"See you later, Dooley. It was so nice meeting you, Becky. We'll have to have you over soon," Lucia said.

"Definitely," Becky answered.

Dooley and Becky retreated back to the barn, and the rest of the group headed in the other direction toward their homes. Caleb and Leah, as always, peddled up ahead on their bikes, laughing and singing. Their crowns were still atop their heads.

"Brad!" Tammy screamed.

Caleb and Leah stopped and turned around to see Brad lying on the ground, clutching his chest. Tammy cried over him while Paul ran back to the barn, yelling to Dooley to call 9-1-1. Caleb dropped his bike and ran over to his parents.

"Dad! Dad! What's happening? Why is he on the ground?" he cried.

Tammy couldn't answer through her tears, and she grabbed Caleb to hold him close. He shoved her away, yelling, "Help him! Dad, can you hear me?"

"I love you, buddy," Brad said to Caleb through forced breaths. "I love you so much."

"I love you too, Dad. Help is here."

The ambulance flew down the gravel road to where Brad lay,

but he was already gone. Despite the speed at which they arrived, they weren't able to revive him.

"Heart attack" and "pre-existing conditions" and a bunch of other words that Caleb and Leah didn't understand kept coming out of the paramedic's mouth. Tammy sat in the dirt and held Brad's hand while Lucia held her. Paul and Dooley held each other and cried. Their best friend was dead. Becky stood next to the kids and tried to comfort them.

Caleb cried as he looked at his dad lying on the ground. How was he going to live without his father? He was only eight years old. How could he take care of his mom now?

"It's okay, Caleb," Leah said and hugged him tightly. "I'll always be here with you. I'll never leave you. I promise."

1

OKAY, SO IF I COULD JUST GET THROUGH THIS VERMONT PROJECT for John, I'd be all set. And if I could secure Portugal, then I was definitely a shoo-in for the international division. I had worked my ass off to be considered, and I wasn't about to give up hope.

"Leah?"

But that was a lot of time and a lot of work. It was totally worth it, but I could say goodbye to my social life! Not that I ever did much to begin with. My job had taken over the majority of my life already.

"Hello? Earth to Leah," Sara called, tapping on my desk. "What's going on in there? Daydreaming about Josh again?"

"Hi, sorry. What's up?" I responded, ignoring her question. I honestly couldn't remember the last time I daydreamed about Josh. Was that bad? Probably, but I didn't really care right now.

"What were you zoning out about?" Sara asked, always the nosy one.

"I cannot believe this project is almost done," I said. "I feel like I've been working on it for years."

"Feels good, huh?" Sara replied, and sat on the corner of my desk, weaving her fingers through the edges of her silk scarf. She had a way of making herself comfortable no matter where she was.

"You have no idea," I replied, trying to hide my confusion over Josh.

"One day, I'll be as good as the almighty Leah Abernathy. I bow to you, my queen," Sara teased, and dodged my swatting hand inches from making contact with her leg.

"You never stop, do you?" I laughed. "Now go away. I have work to do."

I turned my chair back around to face my desk. This project wasn't going to finish itself! A landscape of a picturesque Vermont winter stared back at me and I smiled. I hoped to visit one day if all went well with my proposal for John, the owner of the resort I was working with. My cell phone buzzed the second I stopped daydreaming and actually started to get some work done.

Josh: Hey, babe! I'm running late tonight. Still at the office working on this deposition.

Takeout at your place? I'll pick up.

I sighed, mulling over my response. To be honest, I didn't much care that he was running late, but I felt like I *should* care. It should bother me that I hadn't seen my boyfriend in ages because he was too wrapped up in work, right? Rather than dwell on that emotion, I texted him back.

Leah: That sounds wonderful. I'm still at work anyway. What did you have in mind?

Josh: Anything but pizza! LOL!

Leah: Funny. I'm going to Giuseppe's on Friday with Sara. How about Chinese? We haven't had that in a while, and I could go for some dumplings.

Josh: Sounds good to me. Your usual then?

Leah: Yes, please. I'll see you in about an hour?

Josh: Give or take. Why don't you pick out a movie or something?

Leah: Okay, see you soon.

I tried to focus on my work, but I couldn't seem to get back into the groove, so I packed up my things to leave. It had been a while since I had a quiet night in with Josh. With all the hustle and bustle of both our jobs, if we weren't out at a dinner or a meeting for work, we were grabbing a quick bite to eat before heading to our own apartments. Work was higher on the list of priorities for both of us, and while it left little room for typical romance, it was what we had agreed on. It had always worked for us, but lately, I was starting to wonder if we were outgrowing that arrangement.

"See you tomorrow, Sara."

"Later, Leah. Tell Josh I said hi," Sara responded.

I smiled in acknowledgement and continued to the elevator. I pressed the down button and wrapped my scarf around my neck. I wasn't sure if I was more excited to see Josh or to eat Chinese in my sweats, but either way, I couldn't wait to get home.

New York City winters were brutal, but I almost always opted to walk to my apartment instead of hailing a taxi. And since I had plenty of time to kill before Josh was set to arrive, I could take my time and enjoy the sights. The city around Christmastime was beyond magical. It still didn't hold a candle to the Christmas Festival back home, but it did the trick. I smiled, watching as all the tourists lined the streets to get a glimpse at the massive Christmas tree in Times Square. I had lived here for seven years now, and I still wasn't tired of its beauty.

I popped a ten-dollar bill into a donation bucket a man was holding and sing-songed, "Merry Christmas!" before making my way down the sidewalk.

By the time I got to my apartment building, I had already sung about ten Christmas carols to myself. I even sang my favorite, "O Holy Night," twice. Thanks to the fresh air and Christmas cheer, I was on cloud nine when the door to my building opened.

"Good evening, lovely Leah," the doorman, Walter, said with a smile.

"Good evening to you, Walter," I replied.

"Your gentleman is upstairs waiting for you. He arrived only a few moments ago," he told me.

"Thank you," I said with a wink, trying to ignore the feeling of disappointment that tugged at me. I didn't want Walter to know that, deep down inside, I wasn't really sure I wanted Josh waiting for me.

I decided to take the stairs instead of the elevator to get a little extra time alone before I saw Josh. The thought made me feel guilty. Something was up with me, but I didn't know what it was. I sucked in a deep breath before I reached my floor.

"Hey, babe," Josh crooned when I came into sight. He was leaning against the wall by my apartment door, his jacket thrown over his right shoulder as he balanced our food in his left hand. How did he make holding Chinese food look so sexy?

I lifted myself onto my tiptoes and kissed him hello. He smelled almost as delicious as the Chinese.

"Hey. The food smells amazing. This was such a good idea," I said as I unlocked my door.

"You want me to grab the plates while you get settled?" he asked, following me inside.

"You can grab one for yourself if you'd like. You know I like to eat straight out of the carton. I'm going to go change real quick," I said. "Did you want to watch that Christmas movie about the family who adopted a dog and then went on a road trip? Sara said it was cute but not too cheesy."

"Whatever you want is fine with me," he said, placing the plates and silverware on the coffee table in front of us.

I turned away from him and rolled my eyes, heading toward my bedroom. Hadn't I just said no plate? You'd think after two years of dating he would know that I always eat my Chinese food with chopsticks. I took a deep breath and shook off my negative thoughts. What had gotten into me lately?

After changing quickly and throwing my hair up into my signature messy bun, I rushed back into the room and plopped down onto the couch. I moaned at the sight of all the food in front of me. Josh laughed and handed me the container of lo mein.

"How was your day?" he asked. "Are you getting excited about your presentation with John?"

I swallowed a huge bite of lo mein and paused briefly before answering. "I am. I'm also a little nervous. I've never worked with a client of this caliber, and I've never had a project this big before. This could make or break my career, and I'm not sure I'm ready for either of those options," I said, shoving another bite into my mouth.

I was lying; I was ready for the next step. But instead of telling the truth, I said what I knew he wanted me to say. He wanted me to tell him I wasn't ready so he could build me up and tell me how great he thought I'd do. Then he'd pat himself on the back for being such a great boyfriend despite the fact that he couldn't even see I was making myself smaller in order to build up his ego.

"Sexy," Josh teased and wiped a lone noodle from my cheek.

"Sorry, I didn't have time to eat lunch today. I'm famished," I said, not caring what he thought as I slurped up another noodle.

"You're cute even if you eat Chinese food like it's the Last Supper," he said.

I winked at him and grabbed a dumpling, but I wasn't feeling as chipper as I was pretending. For some reason, our banter was feeling forced all of a sudden.

"Your presentation will go great. I know it. There isn't anyone more qualified to help bring his vision to reality. You should have more faith in yourself. You're only twenty-five and bringing in these kinds of clients is a huge accomplishment. Be proud of yourself," Josh said.

There it was.

"Thank you," I said and kissed him on the cheek.

He was always so good at making me feel like I was at the top of my game, and I always let him. When it came to work, I fought hard to keep up momentum and please all my clients. Josh was my main motivator and exactly what I needed to keep moving forward. I knew all my hard work would pay off with him by my side. I was afraid that was where it ended, though. If only he was what I needed in all departments.

"Are you even watching the movie?" I asked.

"Nope. Too busy watching you eat."

"Ew, that's so creepy. You're lucky you're cute," I said.

Josh laughed and collected his plate and empty containers. He grabbed mine on his way out of the room and put the dishes in the dishwasher. He was always on top of things.

"Hey, do you want me to take your garbage on my way out?" he offered. "It'll probably stink up the place."

"Oh, you're not staying tonight?" I asked. *Shocking.* I wasn't sure why I even bothered asking anymore. If we ever ended up getting married one day, we'd probably be sleeping in separate bedrooms.

"No, I have to be at the office early tomorrow and I still have so much work to do tonight. I'm sorry, babe. Another night."

"I understand. One of these days, we'll have nothing to do and we can actually spend more than a few hours together," I said. "Who am I kidding? No, we won't."

We laughed, knowing our jobs always came first and our social lives second. And maybe love came after that. It was surprising that we had even lasted this long.

Josh put on his coat and grabbed the garbage. He leaned over the arm of the couch and kissed me on top of my head. *What a romantic send-off.*

"I'll text you when I get back to my place. Don't forget to lock up," he said and walked out of my apartment.

I sighed, getting up to lock the door before making my way back to the couch. I grabbed a blanket and curled up so I could watch the rest of the movie alone. Sometimes—no, most times—I preferred it this way. No distractions. I could zone out and let the actors take over my thoughts. Just as I pulled the blanket up over my shoulders, my cell phone buzzed. *Sara.*

"Hey, girl. What's going on?" I asked from underneath my blanket shelter.

"You sound…cozy. Did Josh just leave?" Sara asked.

"Yup, he said he has more work to do for the deposition tomorrow. I guess this one is really important and will have a huge impact on his career. If he wants to make partner—"

"Then he has to leave his amazing girlfriend to go home and work. Blah, blah, blah," Sara interrupted. "I'm telling you, girl, it's *always* work. Don't you get tired of being second to his job? I mean, I'm not saying you should always be first because his career *is* important, but come on!"

"Oh, stop. You know it's not even like that. And it's not just him. I'm always staying late at work to finish something up. You know I did that even before we started dating, so don't start with me." I laughed despite the fact that her words were burrowing their way past my excuses.

"I'm just saying! I know this relationship is my fault, but I think you need to talk to him. Or, at the very least, take a long look at yourself and where you see this going because this isn't normal. And I would really hate to see you waste your life in an unsatisfying relationship just because you're comfortable."

"Sara, I truly appreciate you looking out for me, but I'm fine. Josh and I are fine. This is what works for us. And I do like my alone time after he leaves so I can unwind from my own busy day," I said. Honestly, at this point, I wasn't sure if I was trying to convince Sara or myself.

"I love you, girl, but I could shake the shit out of you," Sara teased. "You're gonna marry this kid someday and end up sleeping in separate beds. I can just see it now."

"Oh, shut up! But seriously, I was just thinking that same thing." I laughed, not at all surprised that we had the exact same thought. "You're just bitter because you're alone."

"Well, yeah. Maybe a little," Sara said.

"Speaking of which, how did your date go last night? I can't believe I forgot to ask you about it today at work. I'm assuming by your lack of enthusiasm that it hadn't gone as you'd hoped?" I asked.

"It wasn't all that bad. He was…nice. But we had nothing in common except that we come from similar backgrounds. He's the son of mayoral candidate George Reid. You'd think that having a father with that type of background would push you to become someone of importance.

Nope.

He literally dropped out of college to work for some start-up company, lost all of his investment, and now lives back home with his parents. He doesn't work *at all* and has no desire to start looking for a new job or go back to school. He actually told me he was thinking about becoming a professional online poker player or trying to make money playing video games. I swear, I thought he was joking, but he was completely serious."

"Stop! Oh my gosh, that reminds me of that kid in college. What was his name? C.J.?" I replied.

"Yes! I totally forgot about him. But at least he graduated. I don't know how, though."

"Do you remember those god-awful cargo shorts he would wear? Shit, I'm going to Hell for this. Whatever, it was forever ago anyway."

"If you're going to Hell, then save me a seat on the train. And yes, I totally remember the shorts. And the stupid matching pants. Why on earth did he always wear a jersey of some sort?

Seriously, a basketball jersey over a long-sleeve T-shirt is not the way to win over the ladies," I replied.

"He was funny, though!"

"If I'm not mistaken, Sara, didn't he ask you out?" I asked. "I feel like it's all coming back to me now. He wanted to take you to that all-you-can-eat Chinese buffet, and you told him you couldn't because you had to wash your hair every night for the next two years."

"I completely blocked that out of every corner of my brain. Leave it to you to unlock those doors. If it weren't so late, I would say I'm coming over so we could drink and reminisce, but I'm beat," Sara told me.

"Next time. I'm gonna watch a little more of this movie before I shower and go to bed. I'm not looking forward to waking up for work tomorrow."

"Me neither, girl. Me neither. But I'll bring you a latte. If you're lucky, I'll even throw in a lemon poppyseed muffin for you."

"You are too good to me! All right, I'll see you in the morning."

"Sleep well, my friend. Text me in the morning if you want anything else," Sara offered.

"I will, thanks. Night."

I had no idea what I did in my lifetime to deserve a friend like her, but I was so thankful to have her in my corner. Even if she did pry a little...or a lot. Okay, ALL the time.

After I finished the movie, I brushed my teeth and took a quick shower. I couldn't stop thinking about what Sara had said about me and Josh. I knew that no relationship was perfect, but was this really not normal?

2

"Happy Wednesday, folks. I come bearing lattes," Sara said flatly as she sauntered through the office. Her usual bubbly grin was masked with a forced smile, and she stopped when she reached my desk. She handed me the to-go cup I knew was filled to the brim with the piping hot chai latte I had been dreaming about all morning.

"Two days in a row?" I asked, delighted to have a second cup of caffeine.

Sara winked as she sat down at her desk. Anyone else in the office wouldn't have noticed a difference, but I knew her so well that I could tell something was off. I grabbed my phone and sent a quick text, asking her what was wrong. Her eyebrows rose when her phone pinged, and she grabbed it and replied immediately.

Sara: Meet me in Boardroom C in fifteen minutes.

I watched the clock nervously. Sara wasn't one to bring anything from her personal life into the office, but she was acting strange and I wasn't sure what to make of it. Had her ex-boyfriend Ricky shown up again? I thought he was in jail, but who even knew anymore? Could she have lost her trust fund?

Not like that would have even mattered since she was one of the hardest working women I had ever known.

My thoughts trailed on until I saw Sara head to the boardroom. My heart sank as I made my way to my best friend. I wasn't sure I was ready for what she might have to say.

"Sara, are you okay? What's going on?" I asked nervously.

"What the fuck, Leah?" Sara exploded. "I'm so over this place. I've put my blood, sweat, and tears into this company, and it's almost as if Cameron just keeps me around to be the office eye candy. Tell me why Karen has been here all of six months, yet she was just offered Leisure Services for the Caribbean team."

Holy shit. I was not expecting that at all. Sara was always the calm, cool, and collected one. She never let things get the best of her, and she almost always saw the positive side of every situation. That didn't mean she wasn't aware of the negativity around her; she just preferred to live her life without the added drama.

"What are you talking about? I didn't even know there was an opening on your team. Why didn't you tell me you were gunning for it?" I asked.

"I didn't know it was an option. I just found out through email that Karen was taking over the position. Apparently, Bill is retiring early and moving to the Carolinas to spend more time with his grandkids."

"I don't even know what to say. It's too late to do anything about it since she's already accepted the position, but I do think you should talk to the board and let them know you're interested in advancing. This way, the next time they have an opening, maybe you'll get a heads up," I told her. "I'm so sorry this happened. You definitely deserve to move up in this company."

"I'll wait a few days before I draft an email. I'm too upset right now, and I don't want to say anything I might regret. You mind reading it for me and giving your thoughts?" Sara asked.

"Of course. I have to get back to my desk. I have a conference call in ten minutes and I'm not prepared at all, but let's get back to this when you're ready to talk more."

"Thanks, girl. You're the best," Sara replied.

I smiled and nodded at my best friend. It wasn't pure luck that we both ended up in the same freshmen year algebra class at New York University. I truly believed it was fate. I had never had a friend like Sara before, and her friendship was a warm welcome coming to the big city from such a small town.

I got back to my desk and rifled through my folders until I found what I needed for the call. VERMONT was stamped neatly across the top. This would be the last call before my big presentation, and I needed to get everything right.

When I first started in travel, I only helped people book vacations. Over the years, I had become the go-to girl for expanding business and bringing in new clientele. But this was the first time I had single-handedly helped another corporation create their own travel destination.

I had known I wanted to get into the travel business ever since I was a young. With a degree from New York University in tourism and hospitality, I knew I was in the right place to follow my dreams. Although my job was to create a reality for other people's dreams, I had yet to leave the United States and see the rest of the world for myself.

My phone chimed loudly, and my assistant's voice rang through the speaker.

"Ms. Abernathy," Casey said. "John is on the phone ready to speak with you. Should I put him through, or would you like to use the phone in one of the boardrooms?"

"Patch him through, please. Thanks, Casey," I replied. It was go-time.

"Leah Abernathy," I answered in my usual work tone.

"Hello, Leah, how are you today?" John asked.

"I'm great, John. Thanks for asking. I trust all is well with you?"

"Always is, my dear. How's everything coming along with my passion project? Are you ready for Friday?"

"I am! I'm excited to share my ideas with you. You and your team have been so much fun to work with, and I'm looking forward to seeing you all again."

"Wonderful to hear. So, let's briefly dive in on the final touches for the larger cabins."

What was supposed to be a quick call turned into a two-hour pick-apart of the smallest of details. I wasn't annoyed in the slightest, though. I lived for this. For me, travel wasn't only about the final destination, but also what I could gain from the trip— the experiences, the memories. I wanted everyone to love seeing the world. And I was lucky because my job allowed me to interact with the owners of these establishments and not the travelers themselves. That was Sara's department.

I continued to work on the project through lunch, proud of myself for remembering to bring food this time. Before I knew it, Sara was standing at my desk, letting me know the workday was done. *Shit, already?*

"What a day!" I said. "I've been working on this project for so long, I feel like I'm actually living at the resort in Vermont."

"Rub it in," Sara responded, rolling her eyes. I couldn't tell if she was really annoyed or not.

"Shit, I'm sorry." I grimaced. "I wasn't even thinking."

"No worries. I'm just teasing you," Sara said.

My phone buzzed loud on the top of my desk. I already had a feeling I knew who it was and didn't have the energy to deal with any of that.

"Ugh, I don't even want to answer this right now," I said and tossed my phone back onto my desk.

"What? Who is it?" Sara asked.

"Josh. I just don't feel like talking right now. I don't even know why. I haven't talked to him all day, and I was sort of okay with that," I admitted.

Sara made the "zip your lips" motion and looked at me.

"Don't even say it, Sara."

"I'm not saying a thing. You want to go to McNally's Pub and grab dinner and some beers?" she offered.

"Yeah, let me text him at least. I owe him that." I had never ignored Josh's calls before, and honestly, I didn't know why I was today. I had just been so confused on what the hell the two of us were even doing together anymore, but the thought of walking away stressed me out just as much as staying.

Leah: Hey, babe. Still at the office. What's up?

Josh: Same here. About to leave. Was wondering if you wanted to grab a bite to eat downtown.

Leah: I can't tonight. I told Sara I'd go out with her for dinner and drinks. It's been a really long day.

Josh: Understood. Tomorrow? I can try to get out earlier.

Leah: I have my presentation with John and his team on Friday, so I think I'm gonna stay in and work on that tomorrow. But I can meet you for breakfast Friday? I can go into work a bit late if I need to.

Josh: That sounds great, babe. It'll have to be early, though, because I have that dissertation at eight-thirty. Do you want to plan to meet me Holly's Diner at seven?

Leah: Perfect.

Josh: All right, love you. Have fun tonight and say hi to Sara for me. You two stay out of trouble!

"Geez, you writing a novel?" Sara teased, and put her coat on. I stuck my tongue out at her and sent off one last text.

Leah: Haha. I'll tell her.

I locked my phone and threw it into my bag without even telling him I loved him back. I tried telling myself it wasn't intentional, but a little voice nagged in the back of mind that it was. I had definitely woken up on the wrong side of the bed every morning this week.

"He says hi and to stay out of trouble," I told her.

"Us, get into trouble? Never," Sara said with a mischievous smile. "Never."

I know what you're thinking, Sara, and it's not happening.

"All right, let's head out before they run out of shepherd's pie like last time. You'll owe me two weeks in a row of Giuseppe's if they're out," I threatened.

"Ouch! Okay, let's go. Wouldn't want the princess to die of pie starvation over here," Sara gently elbowed me and laughed. "Cab or subway?"

"Cab," we both said in unison.

———

It was still early enough that the crowd was pretty quiet. We definitely didn't mind a little music and conversation, but it was nice to have some quiet every now and then. Especially after the day we both had.

"Hey, ladies, can I start you off with something to drink?" the waiter asked, his eyes fixated on Sara.

I knew Sara almost better than she knew herself, so I jumped at the chance to order beers before she could ask for shots. I hoped dinner would be a nice way to unwind and wouldn't turn into a sobfest or an all-night rager. That wouldn't solve anything.

"We'll have two Sam Adams Winter Lagers, please, and a basket of fries," I said, noticing the waiter hadn't taken his eyes off Sara. "Do you still have any shepherd's pie?"

"What?" He dragged his eyes to me reluctantly. "Oh, sorry, apple pie? I'll have to go to the kitchen and check. Two waters?" he said.

"No," Sara said annoyed. "Two beers, a basket of fries, and do you have shepherd's pie?"

"Got it," he answered, his cheeks turning a deep shade of pink. "Yes, it's been a slow dinner crowd tonight, so we have plenty. I'll be right back with your beers, and I'll go put in that order of fries. Did you want to place your dinner order now or wait a few?"

"We'll order when you come back. Thank you," Sara said. She was all business tonight, and this poor guy hadn't stood a chance. He walks away like a puppy with its tail between its legs before turning back to Sara. *Thank goodness I ordered beer.*

Sara and I were the same age but we couldn't have been more opposite if we tried. She was the daughter of a high-powered attorney and a politician and had a trust fund bigger than most people's entire household salary. She came from old money and attended only the best schools in the city. Her first apartment was a penthouse on the Upper West Side.

I was a lowkey country girl, and Sara was a high-maintenance city girl and didn't care who knew. She carried her socialite ways into the office, and it only enhanced the projects she worked on. The only similarities between the two of us were our insane work ethic and pure hearts of gold. And judging from the way she treated this poor boy, I knew the news of Karen securing the position Sara had wanted was weighing heavier on her than I had originally thought.

"Okay, then. So this is how tonight's going to go?" I asked.

Sara scoffed at me and popped a pretzel into her mouth. She chewed on it as if it had offended her in some way.

"Look, I don't mean to sound like a bitch, but it's completely unnecessary to gawk at a patron. Come on, man! I'm just trying to get some dinner, a couple of drinks, and some good conversation. Is that too much to ask?" she spit out.

"Nope, carry on," I said. I knew it wouldn't end well if I tried to rebut, so I kept my mouth shut and let Sara do the talking.

Sara smiled at me with her famous I-can-do-this-all-night grin. *Please, do not let this be a long night, Sara...*

"So, I want to talk to the board about a promotion. Or at the very least, a higher level of clientele. I'm really annoyed that Karen was offered the position and no one even bothered to ask me. I know we talked about it already this morning, but I can't wrap my head around it. I've been working for Cameron for almost four years. FOUR!" Sara shouted.

"I know, I'm so sorry," I told her. "Is it even worth talking to the board, though? Do you think you can schedule a meeting with Cameron? Instead of losing your shit, just let him know you're interested in moving forward in the company. Maybe he has other plans for you. I get that he's kind of an ass, but he might have something else up his sleeve."

"Here you go, ladies," a young, blonde waitress said, placing a basket of fries, a pitcher of beer, and two beer mugs on the table. "On the house. Enjoy."

"Wait, what?" Sara asked.

"Our friend over there is a little embarrassed. Either that or he's afraid you'll kick his ass and get him fired," the waitress replied, nodding over to the waiter who took our order.

"Oh my gosh, Sara! Look what you did," I said and laughed. This wasn't the first time she intimidated someone like this, and it most certainly wouldn't be the last.

"Shit. Is this what the rest of my life is going to look like? Free beer and fries from scared boys? No wonder my dating life is such a joke," she said, looking back to the waiter who was half-hidden behind the bar. "Tell him thank you, but I know how hard you guys work for your money. I appreciate the gesture, but we'll pay."

"I'll let him know," the waitress said with a smile.

Sara and I giggled and watched the waitress give the waiter the message. The color drained from his face, and he rushed back into the kitchen.

"I guess that made it worse," I said to Sara, and started scarfing down my fries. I hadn't realized how hungry I was until they were brought to the table.

"Shut up," she said, swatting at my arm. "We can't all be perfect like you."

"Oh yes, that's me. Leah 'Perfect' Abernathy. Glad you finally realized that." I laughed.

"Can we change gears and talk about you for a minute or five?" Sara asked.

"Yeah, of course," I said with a mouth full of fries. "What's up?"

"Josh," she said flatly.

"Here we go again. You're the one who introduced us and now you have a problem with us dating? After two years, mind you," I said.

"Okay, first off, I've known him almost my entire life and he's just barely more mature than he was in the twelfth grade. Second, I thought it would be a fun fling for you. I never thought it would last. I mean, you two hated each other at first. I was mortified when we all went out and you literally sat there and scowled at him for the entire two hours we were at the bar. I'd never seen you take so many shots of whiskey. I thought for sure I was gonna have to carry you home."

"I was nervous. He's a good guy and you know it," I defended him.

"Oh, I'm not disputing that. I'm just saying I think your relationship is one of convenience and not love. And I think you know it, too. I also think you're not the least bit upset at me for pointing it out," Sara said, then took a big gulp of her beer.

"I could never be mad at you, and I do appreciate you looking out for me, but I've already told you that this works for us. I don't understand why you get so upset with him about things," I said. Sara's words had started to hit home, and I found myself defending him instead of being truthful with my own feelings.

"Leah, I get upset because I know your worth, and you deserve to be loved so much harder than this. A relationship should never just be comfortable. There should be fireworks and intensity, good and bad. You call *me* first when anything happens to you. You don't tell him anything he doesn't *need* to know. All of that is a huge problem. This is a man you say you love, and yet you tell him the bare minimum. He's basically just a friend with benefits who has the same career goals as you."

"What the fuck, Sara? Who cares if we don't see each other or talk to each other every day? He's a driven man and has his sights set on becoming a partner. I support that fully. I have big dreams, too." I continued to defend him because I felt bad he wasn't here to do it himself, but even as I said the words, they felt hollow.

"Stop defending him! You just hit the nail on the head and you don't even realize it. He has his sights on becoming a partner in his law firm, but he doesn't show you that he has his sights on becoming a partner in your relationship. Tell me something, Leah, and be honest. Are you in love with him?"

"Of course I am," I said quickly. Sara stared hard at me until I sighed. "At least, I think I am. I thought I was until this interrogation started."

"I'm not trying to tell you how to live your life. Okay, well, maybe I am a little," Sara said, causing us both to laugh. "But in all seriousness, you deserve better. Not because he's a bad guy, but because he's not *your* guy. You deserve someone you can't bear the thought of being away from. Don't lose sight of what you really want because of what you have right now."

I started tearing up. I hated how well this bitch knew me. Sara was almost always right when it came to giving me advice—and vice versa. I grabbed a napkin and started blotting away the tears that were falling from my eyes.

"I thought this dinner was supposed to be about you, and that you'd be the one bawling your eyes out," I said, throwing my tear-soaked napkin across the table.

"Yeah, well, things change," Sara said and threw it right back.

———

WE FINISHED our food and drinks and paid the waitress. The poor waiter from the beginning never came back to our table, keeping his distance by focusing solely on the other side of the restaurant. Leave it to Sara to make a poor boy buckle at the knees without even realizing it. I popped a final fry into my mouth and grabbed my bag.

"One more for the road?" Sara asked with a laugh.

"Hey, we paid for it," I replied as I struggled to get the zipper up on my jacket. "That was fun. We should do it again soon."

"Yes, we should," Sara agreed. "I always forget how much I love this place."

"Mmm, shepherd's pie. I could eat it every single day."

"You're so weird, Leah."

"You love me anyway," I replied, and stuck my tongue out. "See you tomorrow?"

"I took tomorrow off. Mental health day, AKA I'm going to the spa with my mom. Early Christmas present," Sara told me.

"Very nice. That'll be fun. Tell her I said hello," I responded.

"I definitely will. She asks about you all the time."

"Your parents are so kind. All right, my love, I'm gonna head home. Text me tomorrow."

"Night, babe."

We parted ways and I walked home while Sara hailed a cab. Unless I had no choice, I'd always choose to walk through the park over riding in a cab. The smell of the winter air was my favorite, and it always reminded me of walking to town as a little girl. Snow on the horizon in any city always made me happy.

3

"UGH!" I GROANED, AND SMACKED MY ALARM CLOCK, PULLING THE covers back over my eyes and praying this was a dream. "It's too early for this."

I flung my blankets off and stepped out of my warm bed. Why had I agreed to breakfast? I ferociously rubbed the sleep from my eyes and made my way to the bathroom to shower and get ready. I usually loved meeting Josh for breakfast before work, but I just wasn't feeling it. I was starting to think that maybe Sara had been right about our relationship. At the same time, I was worried her feelings might be influencing mine. Whatever my feelings were, I needed to figure them out. This was my relationship, not hers.

The hot shower was exactly what I needed to help wake me up. I let my hair air dry while I got dressed and did my makeup. Luckily, I already had my outfit laid out, as it was the day of the biggest meeting of my life thus far. Once my hair was dry, I ran a curling iron through it quickly. Perks of having thick hair was that it curled quickly and lasted all day. I threw my pumps into my bag, slipped on my winter boots, and locked my apartment door. I was ready for coffee, and lots of it.

"Hey, Walter," I said as I hopped off the elevator.

"Well, good morning to you, young lady. Where are you off to this early?" he asked.

Walter was the sweetest man. I couldn't imagine having any other doorman to greet me every day. The way he knew, and genuinely cared about, each and every person who lived in this building was refreshing.

"Just off to a quick breakfast with Josh before we head to work," I answered, smiling back at him. It was nice having someone concerned about me.

"Well, you two love birds have fun. Stay warm out there," he said and held the door open for me.

As I stepped out onto the busy street, I noticed the hustle and bustle was at full force, even this early in the morning. After seven years, that was the one thing I still hadn't gotten used to about the city. Everything was just so fast.

I glanced at my watch and realized I didn't have time to walk this morning, so I had to take a cab. I didn't have to wait long, as one appeared right at the curb in front of me. *Hmm. A good omen?*

"Holly's, please," I told the driver as I put on my seatbelt and settled in for the drive.

———

THE CAB PULLED up to Holly's at six fifty-eight, and I could see Josh waiting for me at a booth and looking down at his watch. His eyes met mine when I walked through the door.

"Hey, babe," Josh said when I settled in across from him.

"Hey, Josh. Have you been here long?" I asked, already knowing the answer.

"About five minutes or so," he said coolly before sipping his coffee.

I noticed there was only one cup at the table, and asked, "You didn't think to get me a coffee?" The annoyance in my voice hung in the air.

"Sorry, I didn't know how late you were going to be," he said flatly. "You're never on time, so I didn't think it'd be a problem."

Stunned to silence, I wondered where the hell that came from. I took a deep breath and cleared my mind. It was just a cup of coffee. And he was right, I *was* always late to everything except work.

"Earth to Leah," Josh said and waved his hand in front of my face. "I'm sorry, but it's just a coffee. I can order you one now."

"Sorry, I was just…thinking about the meeting later," I lied. "A coffee would be great, thanks."

The waitress came over to the table as soon as Josh's hand went up. He ordered me a coffee, then pancakes with sausage for both of us. I wanted eggs, but whatever. I was too tired and annoyed to correct him, and there wasn't anything pancakes couldn't fix, so, why not?

"So, babe," he said. "I've been thinking about Christmas. What do you say we go to my parents' in the Hamptons and celebrate with them?"

"Actually, I kind of already have plans. Christmas Eve is a Saturday this year, and it happens to fall on the Saturday that my dad comes to see me. I can always meet you there on Sunday morning, though," I told him.

"Why don't you call him and ask him to come up on Friday instead? It's a short drive from Connecticut; I'm sure he won't mind. We can leave right after you have dinner with him and then we can spend Christmas Eve at the country club with my parents. There's a huge Christmas Eve gala, so pack a formal dress. It'll be great."

"Josh, it's Christmas Eve!" I exclaimed, disgusted by his offer. "I can't just switch it on him last minute and expect him to be okay with it. *I'm* not okay with it. Besides, he works Fridays, which means he wouldn't even get here until at least eight at night. I don't want to rush through my dinner with him and then send him driving back home that late."

"Babe, come on, he'll totally understand! You can both leave work early and meet somewhere for a quick dinner. You can even buy him a train ticket if he doesn't feel like driving late at night. If you pack everything beforehand, it'll be a breeze to get to the Hamptons by nine. And I really want to wake up on Christmas morning with you. Think about how romantic it will be to have our morning coffee on the balcony overlooking the Atlantic Ocean," he said, his doe eyes sparkling at me in pure manipulation.

"I'll think about it," I said, knowing I had no intentions of doing so. I'd never choose Josh over my father.

"Here are your pancakes, dears," the waitress said, cutting through the tension only I seemed to notice.

The pancakes smelled delicious. But I quickly learned I was wrong; there were some things pancakes couldn't fix, and a shitty, one-sided relationship was one of them. We ate in silence until the waitress came back over to refill our coffees. *At least the waitress thought of me.*

"What's up with you today?" he asked. "You're really on edge."

"Sorry, I guess I'm just nervous about my meeting with John. I really need this to go well."

"I understand," he said, all business as he looked at his watch. "I better get going if I want to get to the courthouse on time."

"I'll get breakfast today," I offered, and placed a twenty-dollar bill on the table before he could object. "You can leave the tip."

"Sounds good," he replied, reaching out his hand to help me out of the booth, sloppily tossing a ten-dollar bill on the table.

I waved thank you to the waitress as Josh rushed to the door. I quietly followed him out, not interested in any chitchat. We stood on the sidewalk looking at each other in silence for what felt like hours.

When Josh's Uber finally arrived, he asked, "Do you want to join me? The driver can drop you off on the way to the courthouse."

"Thank you, but I think I'm going to walk. I have a couple of hours before John arrives, so I think I'd like to get some fresh air. Good luck with the deposition," I said and kissed him goodbye on his cheek before quickly turning on my heels in the opposite direction of my job.

I glanced back at him and saw he was standing there holding the car door open. I could feel him staring at me as I walked away, so I waved and kept walking. You could cut the tension with a knife.

This couldn't keep going on. How had I fooled myself into thinking this was right for me? *I hate you, Sara.*

———

"GOOD MORNING, what can I get for you today?" a cheery voice boomed from the other side of the coffee cart.

"Morning! I'll have a large French vanilla latte with extra sugar, please," I said

"That'll be three-fifty," the vendor said.

I handed him a five-dollar bill and told him to keep the change. I took in all the sights I could on my walk into the office. I smiled at the group of kids lined up outside the ice rink, no doubt on a school field trip. I couldn't help but laugh when I saw all the young girls fixing their hair under their winter hats, probably hoping to look cute for the boys while the wind whipped their faces. I wondered if I was like that as a teenager.

A dog walker struggled with the leashes of five dogs. Every time he untangled one, two more would twist themselves up again. Businessmen and women were on their cell phones, teenagers hustled to get to school before the first bell, and nannies were dropping off their charges at preschool.

The hustle and bustle of the city excited me. It was the complete opposite of where I grew up, but I loved each location equally. Before I knew it, I was at the main lobby of my office building. I still had about an hour before John arrived, so I had plenty of time to prepare. Once I made it to my floor, I went straight to Sara's desk to fill her in on the morning's events.

"Spill it," Sara demanded before I could even get my coat off.

"I don't know what to do, Sara. I hate to admit you could be right, but it was not a good breakfast. I don't know if I've been blinded by his charm this whole time, or if I always knew what our relationship was and just didn't care." I paused, shaking my head sadly. "Lately, everything he says and does annoys me. And get this; he had the nerve to ask me to switch days for my visit with my dad so we could spend Christmas with his parents in the Hamptons," I spewed.

"You have got to be kidding me." Sara gawked. "How could he even think that was an acceptable request? He has to know how important your time with your dad is."

"I don't even know anymore, Sara. I wanted to end it right there in Holly's Diner, but I knew it would screw up both of our days. I have too much riding on this meeting to let myself fall apart now. I'll text him later this afternoon and tell him we need to talk. I'm sure he's feeling the same way, or at the very least, knows it's coming."

"Oof, girl. I wouldn't want to trade places with you! And I don't even mind being a bitch to someone who deserves it. You're on your own with this one, kid," Sara teased, grabbing a manila folder from on top of her desk. "I've got a meeting with Cameron. Shouldn't take long. If I don't see you before your meeting, good luck with John. You've got this!"

Sara strutted off to her meeting, and I sat down and got to work. After a few minutes, Casey buzzed my phone to let me know John and his team had arrived and were waiting for me. The moment of truth.

4

"WELL, I GUESS THAT ABOUT WRAPS THINGS UP! IT WAS A PLEASURE
doing business with you, John. I hope our paths cross again
soon," I said with a warm smile, my hand extended toward him to
shake on the completion of a long and fulfilling project. I had put
my blood, sweat, and tears into helping John create a marketing
plan for his Vermont ski lodge.

"I'm certain they will, Leah." John said. "Thank you again for
all your support and dedication over the past six months. I'll be
singing your praises for years to come." He picked his papers up
off the table and stacked them nicely before shoving them back
into his briefcase.

The mahogany and glass boardroom tables brought a level of
sophistication that could only be appreciated in a city as fine as
New York. The New York City skyline wrapped around the
entire eighteenth floor of World City Travel, New York's premier
travel agency. What a dream it was being able to enjoy this view
while helping others live their own dreams.

He walked out of the room with his burgundy briefcase
tucked under the crook of his arm. His small group of associates

followed closely, as if they feared they'd be stuck in the room once he closed the door.

And just like that, the meeting was over, and I was brought back to reality. I had been working on this project for months, and it was nice to finally see the fruits of my labor.

I looked over the large table and through the glass doors to the hallway that led to my cubicle. It wasn't a fancy workstation, by any means, but it paid the bills, my student loans, and then some. It also meant I was employed by the largest and most popular travel agency in all of New York City. One day, I would have that coveted corner office.

"You ready to head out to lunch, Leah?" Sara asked me, cutting my daydream short.

"Yeah, let me just get my things and we'll head out. I've got pizza on my mind!" I replied. "Shocking, I know!"

Blowing an auburn curl away from my eyes, I made my way to my desk to turn off my laptop and grab my purse from the bottom drawer. My deep-blue fitted peacoat and scarf dangled from the arm of the chair, and my snow boots were snuggly tucked under the desk, begging me to put them on.

———

WE HAILED a cab and zipped through the busy city streets, coming to a halt in front of my favorite pizza place. Coming here was like coming home, and although Sara always preferred sushi, it was my turn to choose. It was never a surprise since I always chose Giuseppe's. Sara knew not to even suggest anything else.

Giuseppe's Pizza was a staple in New York City, and according to the pictures on the back of the menu, not much of the restaurant had changed since its doors first opened in the sixties. As soon as I opened the door, I was transported to Italy. The restaurant's brick storefront matched the brick oven, and the interior walls made me feel like I was eating a slice of pizza on a stone sidewalk overlooking the canal in Venice. I paused for a brief moment to inhale the aroma of garlic, basil, and plum tomatoes. I couldn't wait to sink my teeth into a slice or two.

"Ahh, Leah! Always a pleasure seeing your beautiful smile! Come in, come in," Giuseppe called from behind the counter, as he slathered sauce on one of his famous pizzas. His accent was still as strong as ever. He waved us over to my favorite table and called out to his grandson to take our order. Giuseppe had a soft spot for me and treated me as one of his own. We met during my freshman year at NYU when I used to come here to study. He lost his daughter to cancer when she was in her thirties, leaving behind her son who he then raised. Giuseppe often told me, and anyone else who would listen, how I had helped to fill the void of loneliness.

"Hi, G," I said, looking back at him with a giant smile and soft eyes. I made my way over to the table with Sara and accepted the menu from Giuseppe's grandson, even though I already knew what I was going to get—two slices of his famous plum tomato pizza with extra pesto and a cup of pasta fagioli soup. Sara was just as predictable with her one slice of cheese and a side house salad.

"Are you excited about the Portugal project?" Sara asked, dipping her bread into olive oil. She lightly dabbed the corners of her mouth with her napkin before she took the daintiest of sips from her water.

"Excited? No. Nervous and anxious? Absolutely," I said, pausing before I continued. "This is even bigger than the Vermont project, and considering I've never been out of the tri-state area, I don't know how I'm even going to begin to plan this in a country thousands of miles away."

"Oh, don't worry about that at all. I've traveled all over the world. I can help you with the little details. It's sorta my thing," Sara told me, winking.

"I know and I'm grateful," I said, moving my hands to my lap so the waiter could put my pizza down.

"I love how fast they are here," Sara exclaimed, stabbing at her salad.

I giggled at how forceful she was with a piece of lettuce. But she was right. This was the best place to come to for a quick bite that also hit the spot. I wanted to talk to her again about how I was feeling regarding Josh, but I didn't want to start anything in a public place. I also wasn't ready to admit that things weren't as golden as I had been letting myself believe.

"Everything okay?" she asked, knowing something was up.

"Yeah, I'm just thinking. It's fine, though. What are you up to this weekend? I know you have something fun planned."

I picked at a piece of my pizza crust and shoved it into my mouth. Maybe if I kept my mouth full, I wouldn't have to answer any more questions. My plan worked and Sara started telling me this elaborate evening she had planned with some of her cousins. We finished lunch with just enough time to grab a latte and make it back to the office before the afternoon meetings would start.

"Good afternoon, ladies," Cameron said to us as he rounded the corner heading to the boardrooms. "I'll see you both in about twenty minutes, I presume?"

"Yes," we said in unison and hurried to our desks. Just as I was about to unlock my drawer, my cell phone flashed, indicating I had three missed calls and one new voicemail. I didn't know how I had missed them while we were out. My personal phone rarely had that many missed calls, so I knew something was up. I hit the notification for the voicemail and pressed play.

"Hi, pumpkin, it's Daddy. I know you're busy with your job, but please give me a call as soon as you can. I love you."

I couldn't remember the last time he left me a message, but his shaky voice had me stopping and staring blankly at Sara.

"Hey, Sara, I have to go return this call, but I'll see you in the meeting," I said, walking toward the empty boardroom across from the one Cameron just entered.

I sat in the corner furthest from the door so no one could see me, then called my dad back. I didn't know what to expect to come out of the other end of the phone, but I figured sitting down was probably a good choice.

My dad picked up on the first ring, and I jumped right into the call.

"Dad, what's going on? Is everything all right?"

"Oh, Leah. It's your mom," he said softly. "She was in a really bad wreck this morning, and... I'm so sorry, love. She didn't make it."

"What? Oh my gosh, Dad," I exclaimed, my body going numb. I was grateful I was sitting down.

"The other car crossed over the median and hit her head on," he said, his voice breaking. He paused, trying to compose himself. "The police are waiting for the witness reports to figure out what exactly happened. I didn't want to have you find out this way, but I thought you needed to know sooner rather than later."

"Dad, I'll be on the first train out tomorrow, okay? Don't worry."

"Ok, pumpkin." His voice wavered and I could tell he was fighting back tears. "I'll talk to you tonight. I love you."

"I love you too, Dad," I said and hung up the phone.

I sat there for a while—I didn't even know how long—looking out the window in a daze. What the hell was happening? First, the terrible breakfast with Josh, then the best moment of my career thus far, and now this. My day had been a rollercoaster of emotions, and I was so overwhelmed by them that I couldn't seem to make heads or tails of how to feel.

I walked quietly back to my desk, hoping not to draw any attention to myself. I slowly sat down in my chair, trying to comprehend the conversation I just had. My relationship with my mother could only be described as strained, and I hadn't spoken to her in over seven years. If this phone call came before our falling out, I would have lost my mind in that office. But my mother and I didn't have the typical mother-daughter relationship, and I wasn't sure how to handle whatever it was that I was feeling. Guilt? Confusion?

"You okay, girl?" Sara asked on her way to the meeting. "You look like someone died."

"Uh, yeah," I replied, not realizing that everyone was already either at the meeting or on their way. "Sorry about that. That was my Dad. He wants to know if I can come home for Christmas this year."

I sunk deeper into my chair and hoped I would disappear. Thoughts of my mother swirled through my mind and I was frozen. Sara placed her hand gently on my shoulder and looked me square in the eyes. This was one of the only times I wished she didn't know me as well as she did.

"Leah, honey, what's really going on?" Sara asked worriedly. "I get that you don't like to go home too often, but I've never seen you react to a message from your dad like that." She looked hard at me, showing me I couldn't get out of this conversation.

I stared at her for a moment before I opened my mouth and inhaled a deep breath. The news from my dad was real, even though I struggled to wrap my mind around it. My mom was really gone, and I never had the chance to reconcile with her. This wasn't the way things were supposed to happen.

"My mom died," I blurted out. "I don't know what happened, but I need to go home for the funeral and to see my dad." I silently pleaded with her to stop the conversation right then and there. Saying it out loud made it all feel too real.

"Oh my gosh, Leah!" Sara responded. Her face softened and tears gently filled her eyes. "When are you leaving? How long will you be gone? What do you need me to do? I'll handle Cameron. Don't you worry about that."

Cameron—the boss from hell. Well, that's not fair to say. He was a decent boss, but he wasn't typically okay with staff taking time off around holidays, bereavement purposes or not. The last time I took time off was to move from one apartment to the other. I only took one day off in the middle of the summer, and I had to make up for it by working the entire weekend after.

I shook my head and raised my shoulders. We stood in silence for a minute before one of the interns popped his head out and told us they were ready to start. Sara gave a quick nod and turned back to me, hugging me tightly. It was exactly what I needed.

"Thanks for being you, Sara. I really appreciate it."

"Yeah, well, what can I say? That's what I do." Sara smiled and winked.

"You go ahead and go to the meeting. I need to leave. I'm gonna walk around for a bit before going back to my apartment to pack," I told her.

"Walk around for a bit? It's twenty degrees out! You'll freeze that little behind off!"

I needed that, too.

"I'll be fine. I love the smell of snow on the horizon."

"Do you want me to tell Cameron you went home sick?" Sara offered.

"Yeah, thanks. Just let him know I'll shoot him an email later, and I'm sorry for leaving so suddenly. I love you." I hugged her again, not wanting to let go.

"Love you, too, girl! Call me when you're ready to talk more. And have a safe trip back to your dad. Give him my best."

I quickly gathered my things and left as fast as I could.

5

_____

"Hope you're staying nice and toasty," I said to Walter when I finally made it back to my building.

"Hangin' in there, little lady. Everything all right, though? You're home early today," he replied. *Man, he noticed everything.*

"I took a half-day. I'm heading out tomorrow to see my dad for Christmas, so I wanted to get a start on packing," I explained.

"Well, let me know if you need me to carry anything down for you. You know how to reach me." His smile warmed the foyer as he held the door open for me.

"You're the best, Walter. Thank you so much."

In true New York fashion, my apartment was tiny but cute. A small foyer opened up into the living room, where I had set the back left corner up as an office. My desk faced the balcony and overlooked a park. Whenever I worked from home, I loved to sit here and people watch.

A large flat screen TV hung above a gas fireplace, centered between two sconce lights. The couches were the lightest shade of brown I could find, and I added pops of yellow, orange, and green with the throw pillows and an afghan. An oval, tufted ottoman sat in the center of the room with a stack of books on top. Large paintings lined the walls, almost covering them floor to ceiling. Sara had picked them out. The right back corner of the living room was home to a quaint dining area, since the kitchen was too small to do anything but cook in.

A bedroom, bathroom, and small laundry area were to the left of the living room. Much like the living room, my bedroom had the same calm and serene feel that comforted me after a long day of work. An ivory and lavender quilt folded up at the end of the bed was the perfect touch to the light lavender curtains that lined the back wall of windows. A dresser sat across from my bed, and matching nightstands completed the set.

I dropped my keys into the wooden bowl that sat on the console table to the right of the front door. The bowl was a housewarming present from my dad, but it had my mother written all over it. I wondered if this would be my new norm; if everything would remind me of her.

I went into the kitchen and made myself a cappuccino. Much like pancakes, there wasn't much a hot cup of joe couldn't make better, so if I had to pack for my mother's funeral, I could at least enjoy a hot beverage while doing so.

Packing was the bane of my existence. How did I even pack for a trip when my plans included a wake, a funeral, and a Christmas tree? Not to mention that, regardless of the funeral, there was a Christmas Festival held every year, rain or shine. I could only imagine how the next week was going to play out.

"Okay, underwear, socks, jeans, black dress, shawl, and, oh!" I said out loud to myself, as I picked up a bright red peplum-style sweater and held it against my chest. *Mom would have loved this.*

"Into the suitcase you go," I said and shoved my suitcase aside, vowing to not get emotional. I had no idea how to feel.

My train wasn't set to leave until mid-morning the next day, so I decided to enjoy the last few hours of the night before I headed off to the station to go home. *Home.* What an odd title for a place you haven't been to in seven years. I couldn't help but wonder what was waiting for me back in Grace Valley.

I assumed the town hadn't changed all that much, but surely there were new families. Did the O'Connors still live next door? Was my parents' old, creaky porch swing still hanging, waiting to soothe me to sleep like it had on the most restless nights of my youth?

And Gnocchi, the old fur ball, was probably still purring all over the place; snuggled up on Dad, having completely forgotten about me. Serves me right for not bringing him to the city with me after college. He was the one I missed the most. Aside from dad, of course, but at least I was able to see him often.

And then there was Caleb, a ghost from my past. Even though I hadn't seen him in seven years, he was always there in the back of my mind. At this point, I wasn't sure any man would ever compare to him. It suddenly dawned on me that Josh never even stood a chance. Not with Caleb still haunting me.

My thoughts came to an abrupt halt when my phone rang. *Dad.* Surprised to find myself fighting back tears, I pressed the answer button on my phone. A single tear rolled down my cheek, but I quickly brushed it away. It was my father who needed me right now, not some distant memory.

"Hi, Daddy, how are you holding up?" I asked.

"I'll be better once you're home and in my arms again, pumpkin. I've missed you so much," he responded. The way his voice hung to every word let me know that he was trying desperately to appear more at ease than he really was. "Your message said your train arrives at one forty-five. I'll be there waiting for you."

After confirming all the travel arrangements, I reluctantly hung up. *Oh, Dad, you don't always have to be so strong.* I wished he would just allow himself some time to cry and let his feelings show. I feared my father was trying to be strong for me, and I knew I needed to make sure he didn't carry this burden alone.

I glanced over to a picture I kept of me and my parents from

42

the Fourth of July carnival in Grace Valley. My dad's arm was draped over my shoulder while my mom's head was tilted so it touched mine. We were always together like that, the three musketeers. It was taken the summer before my senior year of high school, when everything was still normal between us. The calm before the storm, as my father had always referred to the massive blowout that occurred just months later.

I picked up the photo and stared at it for a moment before placing it back on my dresser, face down. I wasn't in the right mind frame to look at it.

I was still unsure of the true details surrounding my mother's accident, and although our relationship had been strained, I couldn't help but feel the loss in the deepest part of my heart. It was as if I was being transported back in time to my childhood, and my love for my mother washed over me, breaking me.

I dropped my phone and fell to my knees, my legs like jelly, unable to carry the weight of my mother's death any longer. I let out a wail and the tears flowed unapologetically from my eyes. My sobs continued until a quiet rapping came from the front door. I sloppily wiped my hands and face with the corner of my neatly pressed comforter, leaving behind smudged mascara. I was going to have to clean that when I got back.

The knocking got louder as I slowly made my way to the door. I wasn't expecting anyone.

"Leah, are you in there? Open the door," Josh called worriedly, now banging on the door.

Shit... I dropped my head back and let out an audible sigh before I slowly and reluctantly opened the door.

"Josh," I said as my puffy eyes met his.

"Leah, where have you been? I've been calling and texting you all day. Did your meeting with John not go well? Why are you crying?"

He reached over the threshold to cup my face in his hands, and I jerked my shoulders back in an attempt to get away from him. How the fuck had I forgotten to call my boyfriend? Who even does that?

With my left arm, I motioned for him to come in, then closed the door behind him with my right. Turning toward him, I sighed. The last thing I needed was a lecture on communication. With all that was happening around me, I couldn't bear the thought of coming clean to him and having him want to accompany me back home. That was something I needed to do on my own, and I knew he wouldn't understand.

All stressors aside, Josh was a great guy; a powerful and young attorney who was on his way to becoming the youngest partner in his firm. This was something that originally connected the two of us, making our relationship feel like we were always striving toward something together. Unfortunately, I knew there was no romantic connection between us anymore, and we were just coexisting, if that.

"What the hell is going on, Leah?" Josh demanded.

The look in his eyes was sheer annoyance at this point, as he had completely passed the stage of concern. Just another reason why we weren't compatible. He couldn't even care more about me than himself.

"Sorry," I replied, trying to hold in my sorrow. "My, uh, my mom died." My voice cracked as I looked up at him, not moving from the entryway of my apartment.

"Oh my god, babe! What happened? Are you okay?" He voiced his concern overdramatically, almost as if he were trying too hard to be believable. "Why didn't you call me, Leah?"

And there it was, right on cue. The last thing I needed right now was to deal with Josh. I spent all morning thinking about how I was going to break up with him, but I just didn't know how to drop the axe. His insensitivity was enough to make me want to pull the trigger.

"I'm sorry, Josh. It all happened so quickly, and I just wanted to make sure I could get my stuff together and get back to Grace

Valley as fast as possible. My dad needs me right now. I wasn't even thinking about who I needed to contact."

"So you were just going to leave without telling me?" Josh questioned. "And I was supposed to, what, wait around for you? When were you going to tell me? This is ridiculous."

"Honestly, this was the last thing I expected to happen, and I don't even know how to comprehend it all." I paused, his reaction weighing on me. "Wait a minute. You're actually mad at me for grieving the death of my own mother and not calling you the minute I found out? No, Josh. This isn't ridiculous, you are!"

"Are you serious right now? I can't believe my girlfriend, the love of my life, is treating me this way," he yelled at me.

"Love of your life? Oh, please, Josh. Give it a rest already," I retorted. "The only love of your pathetic life is your stupid job. I'm not dealing with your bullshit. Get the hell out of my apartment!" I opened the door and tried my hardest to shove him into the hallway. *Fucking prick.*

When I tried to slam the door in his face, he stuck his foot in between the door and its frame. He wasn't about to let me go, not without a fight. I could see it in his eyes, but I was done playing this game.

He blinked a few times, seeming confused by my words, then went on as if I hadn't even spoken. "We just planned a wonderful Christmas trip this morning and in a matter of what, hours— minutes even—you decide I mean nothing to you?" he whined.

"Um, *you* planned. I listened and said I would think about it," I said curtly. "Guess what? I thought about it, and it's not gonna happen."

Josh stood in the hallway with his foot wedged in the door and stared at me. I couldn't tell what he was thinking this time. He looked lost and pissed at the same time.

"Maybe we can discuss this at a better time, don't you think? I need to finish packing and make sure I have everything in order before I catch the train tomorrow," I said, not sure why I even bothered to explain anything to him at all.

"Oh no," he said with that smug Cheshire cat look he used when he thought someone was trying to pull one over on him. "You always do this! You break news to me like it's no big deal. That's your mother and you wait until I show up unannounced to say something? Why do you always do this? You act like you don't care, you never show up on time, it's like you're in your own little world."

I had no idea where any of this was coming from. He had never spoken to me this way before, and up until now, I hadn't even known these things he spewed were ever even an issue. I rubbed my hands over my face and crossed my arms in front of my chest. With regret filling the room like helium in a balloon, I reached for Josh's hand and gently slid it off the doorknob. I slowly brought my tired eyes up from his expensive Cole Haan shoes, to his even more expensive Armani suit, and eventually landed on his equal parts sad, mad, and confused eyes.

"I think you should go," was all I could muster. My voice was soft and calm, but we both knew this was goodbye.

6

WAKING UP THE NEXT MORNING WAS A LOT HARDER THAN I HAD anticipated. I had about an hour before I needed to catch the train, so I quickly washed my breakfast dishes and double-checked to make sure I had everything. Suitcase? Check. Purse? Check. Cell phone? Crap. Where was my cell phone? Why did I always do this? I ran around the apartment looking for my cell phone, until I found it...in my hand. I scoffed and shook my head. Okay, it was definitely time to go.

I put on my boots, coat, and scarf and threw my bag over my shoulder. I locked the door and turned toward the elevator.

"Walter! What are you doing up here?" I smiled at Walter, who was waiting patiently at the elevator across the hall.

"Just thought you could use some company this morning," he told her.

"Sara called you, didn't she?"

"Guilty as charged," he said, taking my suitcase and leading me into the elevator. "She's a good friend, that girl. You're lucky to have her."

Boy, did I know it! We rode in silence to the lobby, and I tightly hugged Walter goodbye.

"Thanks, Walter. I'm lucky to have you, too."

Walter winked and watched me walk to the sidewalk before retreating back into the warmth of the building. He'd been doing that since the day I moved in.

It was far too cold for me to walk all the way to Grand Central Station, so I had no choice but to hail a cab. I was about to whistle when a cab stopped abruptly in front of me. Timing is everything.

"Grand Central," I told the cab driver, and he zipped through the busy streets, weaving in and out of cars like he was Mario Andretti. I held on to the door handle for dear life. I still wasn't used to traveling that close to other cars at such a high rate of speed.

I handed my Nascar driver the fare, grabbed my bags, and headed toward the station. I quickly purchased a ticket and made my way toward the platform. It was eerily quiet for a Saturday morning, and I wondered if this was a precursor to what was awaiting me in Grace Valley. The last place I wanted to be was stuck on a stuffy train when I could be curled up under my favorite blanket with a hot cup of coffee and a really good book. And yet, there I was, traveling to the same place I had been avoiding for years.

As I sat down in the seat furthest from the door, the stench of alcohol hit my nose, reminding me of how happy I was to have skipped over that stage in my life. I noticed the remnants of last night's party crowd still lingered on the train floor. I never understood how people could leave garbage on the floor. Beer cans, pizza crust, and napkins were strewn about.

I popped in my ear buds, ready to zone out to my favorite band and people watch. The strumming of the bass guitar almost lulled me to sleep, but of course, thoughts of my mother crept in, not allowing me the relaxing trip I had hoped for. Traveling home, I couldn't help but think of the story of how my parents met.

My mom, Lucia, was born in Italy and always dreamed of going to college in America. She wanted to become a teacher so she could be a bright light in someone's life, but her parents wanted her to have a more lucrative career. My mom was headstrong and resilient. She knew what she had to do regardless of how her parents felt. I was a lot like her in that aspect, and I liked that I shared those qualities with her.

My dad was a nineteen-year-old baggage handler at the airport and was working the day my mom arrived in Connecticut. My mom finished school in three years instead of four, and they were married the year after. My parents moved into a beautiful farmhouse in Grace Valley that had been in my dad's family for many years, and a year later, gave birth to me, the pride and joy of both of their lives. And as the story goes; the rest was history.

Oh, Mom. How had we ended up this way?

The train's sudden stop tore me from my thoughts, and I was grateful for the break. So was the skin on my thumb that I had been feverishly picking at. I still had a long way to go before I arrived back home, and I could only take so much before I had a nervous breakdown. I wanted to make sure I was strong for my father even though I was falling apart at the seams, but these memories were not helping. It was a shame the express didn't run to Grace Valley anymore. All of these stops along the way were annoying.

I looked down at the small speck of blood slowly coming to the surface of my finger and quickly wiped it away with a tissue before shoving the tissue into my sleeve. An annoying habit I had picked up from my mother. I better remember I put it there. I was getting tired of picking tissue pieces off my clothes and dryer vent.

My relationship with my mother hadn't always been on the outs. As a matter of fact, before the fight, we were so close that people sometimes confused us for sisters. I guess that was a perk of her having me at such a young age.

An older woman boarded the train and sat directly across from me. She was dressed like a high-level executive, with her black pencil skirt, cream floral blouse, and maroon cardigan. Draped over her arm was a maroon duster jacket that matched the cardigan and oversized handbag. I almost laughed out loud when she looked down because the woman had on the clunkiest rain boots that did not compliment her outfit at all.

"I know," the woman said to me. "I can see it written all over your face. *What* is this woman wearing?"

"Oh, no, I'm so sorry," I rushed out, embarrassed I couldn't keep my face quiet. "I didn't mean to offend you. It's been a rough couple of days."

"Care to talk about it? I'm a great listener," the woman offered.

"Thank you, but I'll be okay. Just a lot on my mind. I appreciate the offer, though."

The woman smiled at me and held out her hand, offering a caramel candy. My bottom lip started to quiver, and I immediately felt tears well up in my eyes. I was careful not to blink and let them fall. Of course, this kind woman would offer me my mom's favorite candy. I thanked her and quickly put my earbuds back in. I hoped the soothing sounds of Andrea Bocelli would keep me in a calmer state of mind.

I always listened to opera when I was sad because it brought me such joy. As a little girl, my mother would have it blasting throughout the house and we would dance in circles for hours together before my father came home. I would always sing the English verses even though I couldn't carry a tune to save my life. We had plans to see Bocelli in concert one day, something I'd still love to do.

I made a mental note to make sure I checked that off my bucket list. Maybe I could get Dad to come with me. *Ha ha, yeah right!* The chances of that were slim. Maybe if Andrea were actually John Lennon, but clearly, that wasn't possible.

It was apparent the memories of my mother weren't going to be leaving my mind any time soon, so I vowed then and there to allow myself to succumb to all of them. After all, I was my mother's daughter, and if there was one thing that Lucia left with me, it was her good-natured heart. Even though she had parted the Earth while we were on bad terms, that didn't mean I needed to be childish about my feelings. My mother wouldn't want me to hold my emotions inside.

I spent the remainder of the ride staring out the window watching the landscape move from trees to water to houses. I had forgotten how different it was outside of the city. I must have fallen asleep because I felt a tap on my shoulder, and when I looked up, the train was empty.

"Miss? This is the last stop," the conductor told me. The corners of his curled-up mustache brushed against his nostrils as he spoke.

"Thank you," I mustered before I gathered my belongings and headed down the train platform to the sitting area.

Since the train arrived almost twenty minutes earlier than expected, I knew I would have to wait for my father. He was a right-on-the-button type of man; never early and never, ever late. According to Josh, I hadn't inherited that trait. I smiled at a group of kids who stood with their parents and waited to board the train.

I walked over to the coffee bar and took a quick look at the menu. My eyes trailed over the column of different hot chocolates and teas. There were so many to choose from. Peppermint, chai, caramel. *Ooh, holiday blend cocoa?!* I pulled my wallet out of my bag and waited for the barista to take my order.

"Leah?" he asked when he finally turned around.

"Oh, hey, Matt! I didn't know you worked here," I said to an old acquaintance from high school.

"Wow, it's been ages! Yeah, I bought this place from the station after college. What can I get for you?"

"Oh, good for you!" I acknowledged his accomplishment. "There are so many options. The last time I was here, I think there was only decaf and regular coffee and tea! I'll just have a medium hot coffee with cream and sugar, please."

"Coming right up!" he said, grabbing an empty cup and filling it with my order. "So what brings you back to town?" He stopped abruptly. "Oh, I'm sorry, Leah. I can't believe I just said that." He handed me the coffee, his cheeks turning pink.

"It's okay, Matt. I came here knowing it would be a bitter-sweet reunion." I inhaled deeply and took a big gulp, savoring every bit of the earthy and nutty flavor. "But, hey, it was nice seeing you. I'm gonna go wait for my dad. Let's try to catch up soon, though."

Matt nodded, and I picked up my bag and threw it over my shoulder. I would have loved to stay and chat, but it wasn't the time or place. I clutched onto the steaming cup of coffee and started to make my way to the front of the train lobby to wait for my dad. Five minutes into this place, and I was already regretting not having come back sooner. I really missed all of the little things I had taken for granted.

I blew out a long breath of air and turned around, bumping right into the back of a man standing uncomfortably close to me, and spilling my coffee all over the floor and me. *Dammit!* I hurried to wipe off the coffee on my pants, then paused and looked up to apologize. My mouth gaped open, and I would have dropped my coffee if it weren't already all over the floor.

"Caleb?!" I gasped in shock.

7

SUMMER, SEVEN YEARS AGO

HEAT LIGHTNING CRACKED ACROSS THE SKY, ILLUMINATING THE little dirt path leading to the meadow. I could smell the freshly cut grass and was grateful I had put on my old, beat-up sneakers and not my brand new, white sandals. My mother would have been pissed if I ruined those. Lucia was already upset that I was leaving the state for college, so I could only imagine how she would react over grass stains.

As I got closer to the meadow, I could see Caleb's bike leaning against the side of Dooley Butler's horse barn. I still couldn't believe he was choosing this old farm over college, but I knew the closeness Caleb and Dooley shared wasn't something you came across every day. Dooley was one of Caleb's dad's best friends, and after he died, Dooley became a father figure to him. He took Caleb on fishing trips, gave him fatherly advice, and was around whenever he needed someone or something his mom couldn't give him.

"Caleb," I called breathlessly, tossing my bike to the ground when I finally reached the barn. "I didn't know it was supposed to rain tonight."

"It's not. At least, it wasn't supposed to," he responded, arms stretched out and ready for me to fall into them.

Caleb was taller than me by close to a foot. I had to stand on my tiptoes just to be able to wrap my arms around his neck. As he pulled me closer to him, his crystal-blue eyes sparkled in the moonlight, sending shivers down my spine. I inhaled his scent subconsciously, knowing it was all I would have to remember him by once I left.

"Come on," he said, leading me to the old, rusted pickup truck that sat at the edge of the property.

That old truck hadn't been driven or even moved in years and had become our spot to look at the stars. Ironically, it had broken down in this very spot after junior prom. Caleb kicked the wheel, and I laughed as the tailgate bounced open, its hinges creaking. An apple rolled, and Caleb reached around me and caught it before it fell to the ground.

"Using those cat-like reflexes again, I see." I giggled as I hopped onto the bed of the truck. I could see he had set something up from the ground but not all of the little details. Caleb had set up the most beautiful late-night picnic under the stars. A red, white, and blue checkered quilt was spread out across the bottom and throw pillows lined the back. I was sure he'd be getting into trouble for taking those from his mom's house.

There were two thermoses filled with hot chocolate and a tray of grapes, strawberries, and cheeses. Draped over the side of the truck were two large blankets I knew all too well. Wonderful memories of prom night started to creep back into my mind, but before I could fall too deeply into the past, Caleb appeared beside me, bringing me back to reality.

"Caleb, this is beautiful, but what is all this for?" I asked him, already assuming I knew the answer.

"Let's just enjoy," he said and gently pulled me down next to him.

He handed me a mug and opened a thermos. The steam from

the hot chocolate floated over to me, and I smiled as he poured. I wanted to remember this scent forever; the hot chocolate, the summer air, Caleb. As I brought the mug to my lips to savor the first sip, thunder boomed and we both jumped. Caleb fell back laughing and his hot chocolate spilled all over the quilt.

"Well, there goes that idea," he laughed.

"Guess I'll just have to drink yours then!"

"Caleb! That's not funny!" I exclaimed, scooting away from him. He was too quick for me and took my mug away, then wrapped his arms around me and kissed me softly on the nose.

"Come on, lie down with me. Let's check out this sky."

We laid cuddled up together in the back of the truck for what seemed to be an eternity. It wasn't until Caleb felt drops on his arm that he looked at me and asked if I was crying. Before he could even get the sentence out of his head, the heavens opened and rain began to pour all over us. We scrambled to get as much of our stuff as we could and ran to the barn, tripping over the hay bales as we finally got inside.

Caleb wiped the rain from my brow and gently tucked a loose strand of hair behind my right ear. I was wearing the small, heart-shaped stud earrings he had given me for graduation. I never took them off. I gently grabbed his hand and brought my gaze to meet his. With tears in my eyes, I swallowed deeply and kissed him. As I broke away from him, I knew his heart was breaking, and there was nothing that could be done to change that.

"Don't leave, Leah. Stay," Caleb pleaded. "You can work in your dad's store and go to the community college. Please. I can't lose you." He still had hold of my hands, as if holding onto me in this smelly old horse barn was going to keep me in Grace Valley.

"Caleb, don't do this. I can't stay and you know it. This is my dream. I can't just let it go," I replied, feeling my heart shatter into a million pieces. "I'm so sorry. I didn't want tonight to end this way."

"It's getting late," was all he could muster. I was afraid his tears were going to spill from his eyes and match the storm outside. "We should probably get home before this gets any worse. Do you want me to give you a ride home? I could borrow Dooley's car."

"It's okay. It's not that far, but thank you," I replied, kissing him on the cheek. "I do love you, Caleb."

Caleb shoved his hands into the pockets of his jeans, clutching his fists so tightly, I thought they were going to rip right off. He swallowed deeply and I hopped onto my bike and rode away. I turned around when I was almost out of his sight, and I saw him turn around and go back inside the barn. My dad told me months later that after I left, Caleb had sat on a hay bale, head in his hands, and sobbed.

And when Dooley Butler found him there crying, Caleb said the love of his life was gone, and he knew she wasn't coming back.

8

THIS COULDN'T BE HAPPENING. ONLY IN MY WORLD WOULD I BREAK UP with my boyfriend, head home for my mother's funeral, and literally bump into my high school boyfriend. And spill my coffee all over the place. And all over him. Oh my god, could he tell I was freaking out? Play it cool, Leah...

I grabbed a handful of paper napkins from the condiment counter to the left of me and bent down to blot at the coffee dripping down the front of my pants, even though I knew the stains had already begun to set in. Caleb picked up my wallet and the bag I had dropped and handed it over to me. He looked like he was going to throw up. I *felt* like I was going to throw up, but there was no way I grabbed enough napkins to wipe up both coffee and vomit.

"Leah, oh, wow! Umm, hi. How are... I was so sorry to hear about your mom," Caleb uttered. He stood there, nervously rubbing his hands together as he kept his eyes pointed down at his brown leather loafers.

Loafers? Wow, who had he become since high school? No more basketball sneakers, I'd guessed. He still looked exactly the

57

same, even down to the ever-so-slight cowlick just above his left ear. Well, minus the loafers.

"Yeah, thanks." I barely spoke, afraid of what else might come out of my mouth.

It'd been seven years and this was the way we were reconnecting?

"Uh, I should probably get going. My dad is going to be here any minute, and I'd rather not keep him waiting. You know he gets antsy." I bit my tongue, knowing I shouldn't have brought up anything that would allow him to think about us in the past. Or present, for that matter.

His face softened and he nodded. I hated how well I could still read him. "See you around, Leah," he mumbled, and I walked away, my heart in my throat, devastated. The same way I had seven years prior.

I wanted to turn around and look back at him, but I couldn't. Heartache filled my entire body. *How on earth could this still hurt so bad?*

I knew my dad wasn't going to get to the station for at least another ten minutes, but I rushed outside to wait for him anyway. A strong rush of cold air washed over me and I shuddered, tightening my jacket around my neck. I wasn't sure if it was the snow that started to flurry around me or the fact that I had just seen Caleb that caused the chill to travel up my spine. I really needed to get a grip. It'd been seven years.

I took a seat on one of the benches lined up outside of the station and prepared myself to wait for my dad. The door opened and another gust of wind blew, sending an old newspaper right into my face. Annoyed, I crumbled it up, tossed it in the garbage can, and went back to the bench.

I gasped when I saw Caleb come out of the station. I tried miserably to be inconspicuous while I gawked at him from the bench. He walked with a tall redhead who was wearing the highest stilettos I had ever seen. And I'd lived through seven years of New York Fashion Week. I never understood the point of wearing heels that high when you already almost reached the moon. Sara was a stiletto girl. She once pushed a taxi out of the snow in five-inch heels when it had slid off the road and gotten stuck in a snowbank on New Year's Eve.

Caleb had his hand placed gently on the small of the woman's back, leading her toward the parking lot. My heart sank, and I didn't quite know what to make of my new feelings. After all, I had been in a serious relationship less than twenty-four hours ago.

Just as I started to get into my head a little too much, my dad pulled up in front of the station. I smiled genuinely, grabbed my bags, and walked over to his car. Ever the gentleman, he rushed around to the passenger side to open the door for me. Being home wasn't just being in the physical place; it was being with the people who loved me most. After everything I did to my mom and the shit I put them through, my dad was still confidently in my corner, always lifting me up. I felt a sense of belonging when I was with him even though this wasn't really my home anymore.

"Oh, Dad," I said and hugged him deeply.

"I missed you, kiddo," he said, squeezing back. "Let's get you back to the house and all warmed up. We're supposed to get quite a bit of snow tonight, and I've got a pot of beef stew on the stove for you."

"That sounds wonderful, Dad. Thank you," I said as I got into the car.

I buckled my seatbelt and noticed my dad had a wedding picture of him and my mom tucked into the driver side visor. I smiled, happy that he still kept it there after all these years. It brought me so much comfort knowing that men like him still existed. Chivalry was important to my dad and it was something that he had always tried to instill in me when choosing a partner in life. He was beautifully devoted to my mother and he made sure to show her and the world that every single day.

We rode the next twelve minutes to the house in silence, and it was the most peaceful I had felt in ages. It amazed me how being back home with my father could make me feel like myself again. I mean, I felt like myself around Sara, but it was a different version. The calmness that my father exuded was not a trait I had gained. I had a fire in my soul just like my mother. I never appreciated it growing up, but as I got older, I learned just how valuable it was.

The gravel crunched under the tires as we made our way down the winding driveway. I stepped out and stared at my childhood home, suddenly unable to remember why I willingly left Grace Valley in the first place. It was the most beautiful house in town with its one-of-a-kind sage green siding and crisp white trim. I remembered when my mother dragged me to the local hardware store for paint. We stayed there for hours until the right shade was mixed and then we sat outside and watched my dad paint the entire house. It took forever, but we had so much fun.

It was a farmhouse by definition, but the only animal living there was Gnocchi, who I could see curled up in a ball on the swing hanging on the front porch.

"He's still kicking around," my dad said with a smile. "Even in the snow."

I loved that he always knew what I was thinking without me ever having to say a word. "I'll meet you inside," I told him, returning his smile. "I want to take it all in first."

He nodded in understanding. I looked around the yard briefly before I set my eyes back on the house. I closed them and breathed in the scent of winter before slowly walking up the side steps to the wraparound porch. New door. I never thought I'd see the day.

Gnocchi saw me and bounced off the swing. He instinctively rubbed against my legs and purred so loudly it made me giggle. I dropped my bag onto the swing and scooped him up. Our reunion was exactly what I needed, and I was so glad he hadn't forgotten about me. After a few minutes of kitty snuggles, I grabbed my bag and headed into the house.

The aroma of my dad's beef stew filled the air, and for a minute, I forgot why I was home. For a split second, I almost called out to my mom to let her know I was there. Even though I hadn't spoken to her, being here somehow changed how I viewed everything. My heart sank at the realization that I was never going to be able to do that again.

The house was exactly as I had remembered it, all the way down to the wallpaper adorned with laundry baskets, clothespins, and clothing in the mudroom. My mom was notorious for decorating like that, and I always loved those little touches. A picture of Gnocchi asleep in a laundry basket of clean sheets hung on the wall. I could see my father probably hadn't done a load since my mom's accident. I would need to remember to go back in there and wash everything after he went to bed.

"Just drop your things in the mudroom, sweetie. We have plenty of time to get you settled after lunch," Dad told me.

I put my boots on the mat and hung up my coat on the hook that had been put on the wall for me many years ago. I left my suitcase and laptop on the bench and went into the kitchen for lunch.

"Take a seat, pumpkin. I'll bring you a bowl. Did you want some crusty bread to go with it? People have been dropping food off like crazy, and I can't keep up with it all," my dad admitted. "I am so happy to have you home again."

"Sure, Dad. Thanks," I said and reached to grab the placemats and napkins to set the table.

I sat across from him in the chair I had sat in for my entire childhood. Just as I was about to put my spoon into the bowl of stew, something caught my eye. My mother's favorite sweater was draped over the chair to the right of me. The sight of it made my heart sink. How many times had I seen my mother wearing that sweater? Countless.

"You can have that if you want," Dad said quietly.

"The sweater?" I asked.

"I see you eyeing it. It's yours. She'd want you to have it," he replied. I smiled, thankful for his offer, and continued my lunch.

Gnocchi perched himself on the end of the table across from where my mom would have been seated had she been there. He was never allowed on the table before, so I tried unsuccessfully to shoo him off. My dad didn't seem to mind, though, and Gnocchi looked at me like he owned the place. I playfully rolled my eyes, happy to be sitting at the table with him.

"Hey, Dad. There's something I've been wanting to ask you, but I didn't think it was right to do over the phone."

His lips immediately drew into a line, and if you looked really closely, you could see the corners of his mouth ever-so-slightly curve into the beginning of a frown. He lifted his head and gently raised his eyebrows as if to say go on.

"Umm, so there's really no easy way to have this conversation, but what exactly happened to Mom? You just said she was in an accident and she didn't make it. Can you elaborate?"

"Oh, pumpkin..." He paused, placing his spoon gently in his bowl and looking me right in the eyes. "Well, she was on her way to see you."

His words had me choking on my stew.

"Excuse me, what?" I asked in between coughs. "Why would she be coming to see me? We hadn't spoken to each other in seven years. She hadn't even come to my graduation and she was coming into the city to see me? I find that hard to believe."

"She was. She couldn't take the distance between you two any longer and was afraid if she called, you wouldn't answer the phone. At least if she made it to your apartment and you wouldn't talk to her, she would have been able to see you in person and know she had tried."

"Wow. I'm... I don't know how to respond to that," I said.

"Now, isn't that a surprise," he teased.

"Very funny, Dad. So, what happened? Did the accident happen on the way to the city or on the way home? Was it the day you called? I'm sorry for making you go back over the events with me, but I think I have a right to know. Especially now that I know she was coming to see me."

"You know your mother liked to get an early start on everything. She woke up and got ready, had a quick bite to eat with me, and headed out. She was about forty-five minutes out of town when it happened. The witnesses said a deer darted out of the woods and the other driver swerved so he wouldn't hit it. He cut the wheel too hard, hit a patch of ice, and slammed into Mom's car head on. When the ambulance got there, she was already gone. There was nothing they could do to save her."

"Daddy, oh my gosh. I'm so sorry I wasn't here with you when you got that call," I said, tears forming in my eyes. "I can't believe this is happening." I reached across the table to hold his hand, and he squeezed back in acknowledgment.

"It hasn't really sunk in yet, and I'm not sure when it will," he said. "But I'm happy to know I have you here with me now. Even though I know you need to get back to the city and your job. I wouldn't be able to go through the funeral without you. I keep looking down the hall and expecting your mother to come walking out of the bedroom. Or see her grading papers at her desk in the den. I was supposed to go before her."

"Oh, Daddy, don't say that. You couldn't have known this would happen, and I can't bear the thought of losing you, too. I'm here for as long as you need me."

He squeezed my hand again, smiled softly, although still with sadness in his eyes, and stood up to clear his plate. Moments like these never needed to drag on. We both had always known when conversations had ended.

"Dad, I know I just got here, but do you mind if I go up to my room and get settled? I have a little bit of work to do, and I'd like to relax for a few," I told him, setting my dish into the farmhouse sink that was probably older than I was, but in better shape.

"Of course. Take your time. I'll be in the den reading the paper. I've got Mike in charge of the store for the next few weeks. I've started a bit on the funeral arrangements but not too much, so I'll probably work a bit more on that while you settle in, pumpkin."

I smiled, grabbing my things and heading upstairs to my old room.

9

I STOOD FROZEN AT MY DOOR, MY HAND LYING GENTLY ON THE doorknob. I never thought I'd be back in Grace Valley, let alone my old bedroom, so soon. So many years had passed since I had been here, and my heart wasn't ready. The girl who used to live here was not the same girl who was standing here now.

I sighed deeply and opened the door. It looked exactly the same as I had left it. Except there was no dust, which meant Mom had definitely been cleaning in there. As I looked around, I remembered how my mother used to pop out of the closet with a laundry basket trying to scare me. She never succeeded but I'll never forget her laugh every time she did it. I wished she had just called me before she decided to come to the city.

My room smelled like vanilla and lavender, the same as it always had. When I moved to the city, I had vowed to never have my home smell the way it had where I grew up. I wanted—no, I needed—to forget it all. How could I have been so stupid? All of that was for nothing. I'd have given anything to go back in time and change things.

I walked across the floor and lowered myself down onto the edge of my white, metal daybed, taking in my childhood room.

The bed sat underneath a large, long window that let in so much light in the afternoons, even on the dreariest of days. It always seemed to accentuate the white comforter, with its little pink rosebuds and green leaves. It was dainty and sweet, and not the least bit childish. The pillows were arranged along the back of the bed and appeared more like a couch.

I could remember the day we bought the bedding set as if it were yesterday. It was pouring outside and Dad dropped us off in front of the bedding store while he went to park the car. We, as usual, had forgotten umbrellas and were soaking wet despite being dropped off close to the door. Mom and I had laughed as we watched Dad run to the entrance, trying to dodge grocery carts being blown across the parking lot.

"Very funny, ladies! Next time, I'll make you run with me," he threatened, shaking his jacket at us and covering us with rainwater.

"It's just a little rain, Daddy," I said, shaking my jacket at him in retaliation.

I hooked my arm into my mom's and went inside. The three of us had walked around the store for hours looking at towels and dishes and toaster ovens. We had no need to be shopping, but sometimes it was fun to look. We were just about to leave the store when I spotted the comforter on the display bed.

"Mom! Please, can I have this? It's so pretty!" I jumped up and down in excitement and begged my mom to buy it for me.

"Paul? What do you think?" Mom asked Dad with a smile.

"I don't see why not. You sure you don't want to keep your My Little Pony sheets forever?" he teased.

"Positive!" I said with a laugh. I did love those pony sheets, though.

"You know what this means, though, don't you?" he asked. Mom and I both shook our heads in confusion. "You definitely need the matching pillows!"

As soon as the words were out of his mouth, I ducked so I

wouldn't get pelted by a pillow. Only my dad would start a pillow fight in the middle of a store. He lived by the "you break it, you buy it" rule, and since he was already buying these, he hadn't minded if anything happened to them. I could remember one of the associates laughing with us as she walked by, shaking her head.

"These are the times to remember," she told my parents. "They're only little once."

The rain had stopped by the time we were done shopping, and we all walked to the car together, each holding onto a bag. I jumped in every single puddle we passed, successfully splashing my dad with each strategic plop. By the time we got to the car, he was soaked from his mid-calf all the way down to his toes. My mom could barely breathe from laughing so hard, and I was full of love and content.

Those were the days.

My little pink teddy bear lay across the pillow closest to the head of the bed, practically begging to be picked up. Caleb had given it to me on our first Valentine's Day. I was fourteen. He was so proud of himself for getting me something that was sweet but not too cheesy. It was the first night we said I love you to each other. We were so young but that never mattered. It was real. We knew it. Everyone knew it.

I grabbed the bear and held it close, remembering the look on Caleb's face as he handed it to me, tied to the biggest box of chocolates I had ever seen. He was pale but blushing at the same time, and he looked like he was going to throw up. He really was the cutest.

I put the bear back in its spot on the bed and wiped a tear from my eye as I stood up. I walked over to my dresser and ran my fingers along the top. My jewelry box remained in the same spot it had since I got it for Christmas when I was thirteen. That was also the year I got my ears pierced and was gifted my mother's pearl earrings. What teenager needed pearls?

I brought my hand up to my face and rubbed a finger over my naked ear. I opened the bottom drawer of my jewelry box and felt around for the earrings. There they sat on top of the small note my mother had written for me when she gave them to me. *No grit, no pearl.* I lived my life by those words, now more than ever. My drive and determination had come from my mother. I closed the jewelry box and put the pearls on. I knew they wouldn't bring her back, but I felt closer to her with them on.

A replica of the picture I had flipped over in my apartment stared back at me from atop my dresser. Only this time, I left it up. I sucked in a long, deep breath and closed my eyes before I slowly blew the air back out.

Why had I spent so many years pretending my mother didn't exist? I would give anything to tell her I was sorry. I thought I was grown, making decisions like eliminating people from my life I thought were toxic. But now my immaturity was showing through, and I was paying for even more mistakes than I had thought I'd made.

I opened my tote bag, pulled out my laptop, and plugged the charger into the wall. Ugh, I did not want to turn it on. Lord only knew what kind of email Cameron had sent me.

As I waited for my MacBook to boot up, I unpacked the rest of my stuff. Luckily, I was the same size as I had been when I left, so I hadn't needed to pack too many outfits. No "freshman fifteen" here, thank you very much!

I opened my old closet and saw that my mother must have been in here because all my clothes were arranged for the winter season and not the end of the summer, as it had been before I left. *Oh, Mom. Couldn't help yourself, huh?* She was always one to be organized. Or, it was wishful thinking that her trip to visit me was going to bring me home. *Well, Mom, it worked.*

I hung up my dresses and blouses and shut the closet door quickly, as if leaving the door open would allow all of my old memories to come falling out.

I logged into my work email and scanned the messages for Cameron's name, finding nothing. Message after message from clients and my associates, but nothing from Cameron. That was weird. I went to my purse to grab my phone and noticed it wasn't there. I really hoped I hadn't left it on the train.

I was logging into my personal email when I heard a knock on the front door followed by my dad's footsteps shuffling along the wood floor. It was probably someone dropping off a casserole.

The door opened and I leaned back in my chair trying to listen to what the muffled voices were saying. I could have gotten up and gone downstairs to see for myself, but where was the fun in that? The door closed and I heard footsteps thumping up the back steps. I was so startled by the sound that I leaned too far back and the chair fell over, dumping me onto the floor.

"Knock, knock," came from the other side of the door. Before I could respond, my dad opened the door. "Missing this?" he asked, waving my phone. He stopped and looked at me quizzically as I scrambled to get off the floor.

"My phone! I was just looking for it. Thank you. Did I leave it downstairs?"

"Not quite. You didn't tell me you saw Caleb at the train station," he declared, raising an eyebrow.

"Uh, I saw Caleb at the train station," I said softly, biting the corner of my bottom lip.

"Yeah, I gathered that since he just came to my front door to drop off your phone."

"What?! He was here? How did he have my phone?" I quickly pushed my hair behind her ears and wiped the non-existent mascara from under my eyes.

"Well, apparently when you bumped into him, you must have dropped your phone and it fell into his bag. He went to get his student's papers to grade and saw the phone. Knew it was yours from the wallpaper picture of Gnocchi."

"Wow, this day keeps getting weirder." I laughed lightly. "Um, what else did he say?" I asked, hoping my father wouldn't be able to tell I was digging for more than I needed to know.

"He just wanted to reach out and offer his condolences. Your mother was like a second mother to him, you know. He came around here often after you left. We didn't tell you because we didn't want to upset you. It was really hard on your mom when he left for Tennessee, too," he told her.

"Tennessee? What are you talking about?" I asked, confused.

"Yep. Tennessee," he said with a wink before he walked out of my room and headed back to his paper downstairs.

"Wait, where are you going? Don't leave me hanging like this, Dad," I called out after him.

"It can wait," he replied.

Grading papers? I thought Caleb was going to be helping Dooley Butler on his farm. That's why he hadn't come to the city with me. I knew I shouldn't be mad, but it still hurt that I hadn't known what had been going on in Caleb's life while I was off living mine.

I shook my head and looked down to see many text message notifications on the screen of my cell phone. I really needed to sync my laptop with my phone. It was the twenty-first century, after all. I read through the messages from Sara, my assistant Casey, and Josh. But there was still no word from Cameron, so I decided to give the office a buzz. No one answered so I left a brief message. With a sigh, I got to work on the Portugal project.

If there was anything I was great at, it was deflecting from my current issue. My mother's death should have been a reason for me to slow down and think about things, but as usual, I drowned myself in my work. If I just worked a little bit longer and a little bit harder, maybe I could forget why I was home. Maybe I could get to the point in my career where anything that happened in my past was just a distant memory. *Yeah, right.* I'd never be able to forget this happened—or forgive myself.

I worked for a few more hours on the prep work for the resort in Portugal. Although I hadn't even been there, Sara told me so much about the country that I felt as if I'd visited many times. This project was different from the Vermont one for John because it was strictly a beach resort, and I had never worked on anything international or without snow.

When I had researched all I could, I retreated to my bed, crawled under the covers, and grabbed the remote. I knew there would be a marathon of cheesy Christmas movies on my favorite channel, so I settled in for a long night of guilty pleasure movie watching. I used to spend hours watching these movies with my mom.

Before I knew it, I was crying myself to sleep.

10

THE SUN BEAT DOWN ON ME, AND I BLINKED REPEATEDLY TRYING to remember where I was. I lifted the comforter off me and went to take a shower. Even my bathroom was the same as it had been seven years ago. I stared at myself in the mirror as I waited for the water to heat up.

How many times had I looked into this very mirror, yet it all seemed so foreign to me now? I blew out a long breath and got into the shower, letting the hot water drown out my thoughts.

Ten minutes later, I was downstairs pouring myself a cup of coffee from my dad's French press. It beat Starbucks any day of the week; I didn't care what anyone else thought.

"Morning, pumpkin. I trust you slept well?" Dad asked, kissing me on the forehead. "It sure is good to have you home."

"It was great, Daddy. Want me to make breakfast?"

"Already done. Blueberry pancakes and sausage. Your favorite," he responded, handing me two plates. "Why don't you go set the table, and I'll bring everything over. You want butter for your pancakes, too?"

I nodded and smiled at him. It took the death of my mother for me to come back home and spend time with my father. That was so messed up. I placed some napkins and forks on the table and sat down, waiting for my dad to sit before I started to eat.

"Dad, these are amazing. Is this the syrup you make from the trees out back? I can't believe you still have the time to do all this every single year."

"Mm-hmm." He took a big gulp of his coffee and wiped his mouth with a light blue fabric napkin. "I'll be making this syrup for as long as this old body lets me. It calms me."

"Then I'll be eating it for as long as this body lets me," I told him, shoving another big forkful of pancake into my mouth. "What's on the agenda for today, Dad? I do need to get a little bit of work done, but then I'm all yours. I thought maybe we could walk to town together and get lunch or something?"

"Well, there isn't too much planning needed for the funeral. Your mother had always told me over the years to not make a fuss over her services. But if you don't mind calling Becky down at The Flower Pot, I'd appreciate it. Maybe we can go to town another day? There are some things that aren't related to the funeral that I'd like to take care of."

"You got it, Dad. I understand," I said quietly.

"THANK you for calling The Flower Pot," said the voice on the other end of the phone. "This is Jackie. How may I help you today?"

"Oh, hey, Jackie. It's Leah Abernathy. Is your mom around?" I asked.

"Sure, just a second. I think she's with my dad right now, but I'll see if I can sneak her away for you. Hey, listen, I'm really sorry to hear about your mom. She was a really nice lady," Jackie added before she rushed off the phone and went in search of her mom.

I nervously chewed on the side of my thumbnail as I waited for Becky to pick up. Becky was my mom's best friend. I had known her my whole life and knew this conversation was not going to be easy.

"Leah!" Becky exclaimed. "I'm so happy to hear your voice. How are you holding up?"

"I'm okay," I lied. I was horrible, actually.

"Oh, honey, I can't imagine being in your shoes right now. What can I do?" Becky asked.

"My dad asked me to call you about the flowers for the funeral. I know lilies are the traditional funeral flower, but you know how much my mom loved yellow roses. I was thinking—well, hoping—you might be able to get some for the services. I know it's December and probably not the best time to be asking."

"Leah, you could ask me for hot pink sunflowers and I would make it happen. If you're okay with it, you can leave all the flowers to me, and I'll have it all set up for you the morning of the funeral. Do you know when her services will be yet?" she questioned.

Becky would have done anything for my mom and that meant continuing to do anything for me and my dad. She had the purest heart out of anyone I had ever met, and I was happy to know that if I couldn't have my mom, I at least had Becky to lean on.

"I'll call you back either this afternoon or tomorrow when I know more. My dad said we're going to wait a bit for the actual funeral. He hasn't mentioned it, but it wouldn't surprise me if he was trying to have it a little closer to the festival as sort of an honor to her. You know how much she loved Christmas and that festival."

"Okay, love. I'll speak with you soon. Give my love to your dad," Becky said, then hung up the phone before I had a chance to say goodbye.

I envied Becky's all-business demeanor, even in the face of a crisis. I grabbed my coat and purse and yelled back over my shoulder to let my dad know I was walking into town for a bit. I needed some fresh air, and what better way to get that than to take a brisk walk in the snow?

The walk to town was shorter than my morning commute to the office, but it seemed to take hours. I spent so much time taking in all my surroundings, as if I had never been here before. The giant pine trees that lined the sidewalk and the festively lit homes whose lights sparkled like sun in the snow brought back such happy memories, while simultaneously breaking my heart little by little. My head dropped in disappointment at the sight of a family taking their annual pictures with Santa in the gazebo on the green. What I wouldn't give to be able to do that again. I didn't even care that I was a grown adult.

The door to the bakery flew open, sending the sticky sweet scent from the cookie dough batter sailing through the air and directly into my nostrils. The line to Mrs. Kratz's bakery, The Kratz Outta the Bag, was almost around the corner, and I wasn't surprised one bit. The bakery was always busy, but the Christmas season tended to bring customers from all over the county hoping to get a box of her famous sugar cookies. Every year, my mom and I would bundle up in our coziest sweaters, hats, and mittens and walk from our farmhouse into town to grab a box of Mrs. Kratz's Kristmas Kookies!

Having Mrs. Kratz as a neighbor had always given us head-of-the-line perks, but that day, I walked up to the old bakery not knowing what to expect. I opened the door and my eyes were immediately drawn to the small porcelain Christmas tree with colored lights that I had gifted to Mrs. Kratz when I was a kid.

It was rare for a table to be free on the first day of the Christmas season, unless you came in early. But if you were lucky enough to snag one, you'd get to see Mr. Kratz drag in his big red bin containing all the Christmas ornaments. Sometimes, you'd even see him bringing in a small, freshly chopped tree to display in the storefront window. Each year, the tree was more beautiful and more extravagant, carefully decorated with ornaments handmade by the children in town. Mrs. Kratz always said, "Christmas isn't Christmas unless things are made with love."

"Good afternoon to my favorite little girl!" Mrs. Kratz called from over the counter to me. She wiped her hands on a towel and walked around to the side to hug me.

I wasn't prepared for the overwhelming feeling of regret I had for not coming back home sooner. Everyone seemed genuinely happy to see me, and I had left them all in the dust for my own personal gain.

"It's been ages, my sweet girl. How I have missed you!" she exclaimed, not letting me go. "Let me get a look at you."

Mrs. Kratz loosened her grip just enough to sneak a quick peek and then brought me back in for one more hug. This time, it was me who held on a little bit longer.

"Oh, Mrs. Kratz! I can't believe you still run this place! I was hoping I would get to see you while I'm home," I said with a smile reminiscent of my childhood days in this very spot. For the first time since I had come back home, I felt a strong happiness and not just the comfort of being at the house with my dad again.

"Ooh! My girl! Let me get you a coffee and some cookies and we will chat. Why don't you go take a seat over there in the corner like you used to? I'll have Bernie move the bins in just a second," she said and she disappeared into the back of the kitchen, her hair net sliding off on the left side of her head.

I laughed at the sight and took a seat as I smiled at the thought of being back in this old booth. It was the only booth in the whole place, and when I was little, Mrs. Kratz used to put a little reserved sign on it so my family could sit here to eat. *How could I have left this place?* It was becoming a recurring question in my mind.

I stood up when I saw Mr. Kratz come bouncing out of the kitchen. He scooped me up before I was even fully out of my seat. I laughed as we said hello. His scruffy beard smelled of cinnamon and pine, and I giggled, noticing how much about him had not changed.

"Sneaking some cookies again, I see," I teased him, hugging him back tightly.

"Oh, nothing gets past you," he bellowed, his rosy cheeks scrunched up into little balls, and his eyes smiled wider than an ocean. He still looked like Santa, and I wouldn't be surprised if he was.

"Let me get these things out of your way so you can catch up with the missus. I have to head out for a bit to help deliver some trees, but I'll catch you later, all right?" he stated and then kissed me on the top of my head and carried the bins into the back.

I gazed out of the window with my chin in my hand and a crooked smile on the corner of my mouth. I spent the last seven years in the city that never sleeps, and yet, not once did I have the feelings there that I had when I was here. This was home.

Mrs. Kratz approached, breaking me out of my trance and placing two cups of coffee and a plate of her famous cookies onto the table.

"I won't ask you how you're doing because I'm sure that's all you've been hearing since you got off that train. Why don't you tell me everything you've been up to in the big city? Your mom was always coming in here bragging about how successful you were," she told me.

I sat there in shock. My mom, who I hadn't spoken to since the day I left for college, was going around telling the people of Grace Valley how successful I had become?

Not wanting to bring any negativity to Mrs. Kratz, I smiled and told her all about my job and the most recent deal with John. But even while singing of my accolades, I felt pain at the thought of going back to my job and apartment. Being home was harder than I had expected, but for a completely different reason. Maybe my mother had been right after all. If only I'd learned that sooner.

11

I said my goodbyes to Mrs. Kratz and spent the rest of the morning wandering through town, remembering things I seemed to block out for so many years. The ice skating rink was being set up. I really needed to dust off my old skates at least once before I left. I didn't see anything other than the rink, and it was usually almost complete at this point. I wondered if the Christmas Festival was even happening this year. The only storefronts that were decorated for Christmas were the bakery and the flower shop.

Thinking of how Mrs. Kratz told me my mother used to praise me had me missing her more than I ever thought possible. I guess a part of me always thought we would be fine again one day. But *this* situation never crossed my mind. I sat down on a bench and just stared for a while, sipping my coffee and feeling thankful that Mrs. Kratz had put it into a to-go cup for me.

I closed my eyes, and memories of my childhood flooded my brain. For the first time in seven years, I was in no rush to shoo them away. Who knew when they would come back to me again? I hoped that if I thought about them long enough, they wouldn't leave this time. Maybe *I* wouldn't leave this time. Maybe I could work remotely and commute to the city once a week or every other week.

I stopped outside of the small post office where I used to leave my letters to Santa and smiled when I saw a little girl drop her letter into the mailbox. The last time I had sent a letter to Santa was the Christmas right before I turned ten. I could vividly remember what the letter looked like, from the holly leaves and Christmas tree, all the way down to the lopsided Rudolph I had drawn on the back of the envelope. It had been addressed to Mr. Santa Claus, The North Pole. I smiled at my childhood innocence, remembering what I had written and happy the mailman gave it back to my mom to save for me.

DEAR SANTA,

I know you get a lot of letters every day, from tons of kids out there just like me. This year, I only want one thing for Christmas, and that is a baby brother or sister. I'm almost ten and I think I'm old enough to be able to help my parents take care of him or her so they don't have to do it all by themselves. I really think I could be a great big sister! I hope you and Mrs. Claus have a great holiday.

SINCERELY,

Leah Abernathy, age nine (almost ten)

A SIBLING WAS the only gift I had ever asked for that I never received. Coincidentally, that was the year I stopped believing in Santa. I hadn't asked for much, and I knew my parents would never deprive me of anything. Okay, so maybe I was a bit of a brat at that age and hadn't realized it.

It wasn't until I was in high school that I had asked my mother why she never had any other children. She sat me down and calmly explained I was their miracle baby. They tried several times after I was born to have more children, but all of her pregnancies had failed.

"Don't you worry, my sweet girl," Mom had said. "I don't need anyone but you. I'm not missing anything in this life. You are my world."

I wiped a tear from my eye. *What had I done?* I wasted seven years being angry for something so stupid, and now I'd never get to tell her I was sorry. As I stood up and grabbed my purse, I saw Becky across the street, putting out a new sign in front of her flower shop.

"Becky," I called, waving my arm in the air and—*again*—almost spilling my coffee. I really needed to be more careful.

"Leah! Come on over here and give me a hug, girl," Becky called back, a huge smile forming on her face.

I ran across the street and hugged her tightly before following her into the shop. The bell chimed when the door closed behind me and it caused me to jump. I guess I was a little on edge. It was still early in the day, and The Flower Pot didn't usually get busy until closer to noon, so we had plenty of time to chat without interruption.

Straight ahead sat the register with boxes of chocolate artfully arranged on one end of the counter. On the opposite end was a small crystal vase with a single, red silk rose. Becky's husband had given it to her on their wedding day as a symbol of their love. "A silk rose never dies and neither will my love for you," he had told her that day.

Ugh, what a sap! I was still jealous, though.

I was their flower girl, and my mother was Becky's matron of honor. I always dreamed of having a wedding like Becky and Dooley's, but now I wasn't so sure. With Josh out of the picture and Caleb clearly involved with someone else, my romantic future didn't look so bright. I shouldn't be complaining, though. I did this to myself.

Behind the counter stood five refrigerators that held buckets of flowers ranging from singles to beautiful bouquets. To the left was the door to Becky's office where I used to spend hours coloring during the afternoons my mom had staff meetings or conferences. It was better than hanging out at my dad's grocery store. To the right of the refrigerators was the door to the back room where all the magic happened. And by magic, I mean pricking my fingers hundreds of times with the rose thorns. I rubbed them together remembering how badly it would hurt.

Rustic wooden shelving lined the walls along the right side of the shop. The rows were full of candles made by Jackie. I thought it was amazing that an eighteen-year-old already knew her passion and had the savvy business sense to put it to use at that young of an age. I noticed a new addition to the shop sitting next to the candles.

"Pottery?" I asked Becky, looking at the adorable clay pots and vases. They were all so beautiful.

"Your mom made those," she said softly with the slightest smile. "She took an adult education class at the community college and fell in love with it. She asked if we could sell them here, the profits going to a graduating senior in need of help with college tuition."

That didn't surprise me one bit. She always tried to brighten other people's day.

"Wow, that's incredible. I never knew she was so talented. Or, that she was ever interested in pottery to begin with. I feel so out of touch." I turned around to find a place to sit. And to hide the tears that were fighting to sneak out of my eyes.

Becky had created an adorable little sitting area—small but comfortable. Two metal tables, each with matching chairs that had flowers and leaves crawling up the legs, were perched in front of me. A little coffee bar was nuzzled into the corner with a single-serve coffee maker, a few mugs, and a variety of flavored coffee. There was a sign that readd, "Milk and creamer are in the left fridge. Help yourself!"

"Have a seat, love. Top off your coffee if you'd like." Becky pointed to the chairs. I shook my head as I settled into a chair. I'd had enough coffee already.

"Becky? I just left Mrs. Kratz and I'm not okay. I feel like I've ruined so much and now I'll never have the chance to fix it. And on top of all that, Josh and I broke up, my boss is ignoring my efforts to contact him, and I quite literally bumped into Caleb at the train station and then saw him walking out with a super-model redhead. Why did I even come back here?"

Having finished my rant, I burst into tears.

Becky reached her hand across the table to hold mine. We sat there in silence for a few minutes, knowing that each other's company was what we needed most in that moment.

"Leah, listen to me carefully. None of this is your fault. Things happen all the time that are beyond our control, and while you may not be able to understand it all right now, there will come a time when it all makes sense. I don't want to say everything happens for a reason, but there *is* a reason behind everything that happens. You're here because we need you here and because, quite simply, you need to be here," she told me. Becky had a way of being firm and maternal at the same time.

She reminded me so much of my mom. No wonder they were best friends.

I was about to respond to Becky when the door to The Flower Pot flew open, allowing a rush of cold air in. Shivering, I looked over my shoulder and saw the woman that was with Caleb the day before. Her fiery red hair hung in loose curls down her back. She was not dressed for the weather, so I assumed she wasn't from around here.

My jaw dropped and I almost stood up and ran out of the shop. This could not be happening.

"Hey, y'all," she said cheerily, a thick southern twang erupting from her mouth. "I need a fresh bouquet for the kitchen table. And a vase if you've got one."

Becky stood up and pursed her lips together, her eyes widening when she looked down at me. It was clear she hadn't seen this woman before, but judging from her reaction, she had just put two and two together on who she was. She furrowed her brows in confusion, but I didn't change the expression on my face. Then she walked over to the redhead and smiled politely.

"Hi, there! I'm Becky and I own The Flower Pot. I'd be happy to help you. Do you have a preference on which flowers you'd like for the bouquet?" she asked, leading her toward the options behind the counter.

I stared at her, judging. I couldn't understand what Caleb saw in her. Except for the fact that she was drop dead gorgeous with a perfect figure, perfect hair, and perfect skin. Okay, so I got why he was into her. But she was the complete opposite of me, with her long, lean legs and muscular upper body. Tennis player, probably.

"Anything really. I'm not picky. No roses, tulips, or lilies though. I just need to have fresh flowers near me, or I can't get any work done."

"Oh, what type of work do you do?" Becky asked her.

"I'm an interior designer," she said, flipping her hair over her shoulder. "Luckily, I can work remotely when I'm not in my office. I'm hoping this trip is short so I can get back to Tennessee. This weather isn't my cup of tea. Flowers make me feel like I'm back home working near my garden. It's much nicer there, you know. Home."

"How about one of my winter bouquets? They come with a vase, and I can put them in a box for you so they won't spill as you carry them. Or, I can have them delivered to you at no extra charge. Mind if I ask where you're staying? This is a small town so I probably know the location."

"That's perfect! Thank you." She giggled and took out her

wallet. She handed Becky a twenty-dollar bill and told her to keep the change. "I'm staying at the Patterson's house on Waverly. Are you familiar?"

Becky's eyes darted across the room and focused on mine like daggers. She was now one hundred percent certain who this woman was.

"Yes, I know them well. I will have them delivered by the end of business today."

"Wonderful," the red head exclaimed. "Have a wonderful day."

I couldn't help but stare the woman down as she turned and ferociously made her way out of the shop. Her perfectly-mani-cured hand slid across the bar on the door and that was when I saw it. The huge rock sparkled in the sunlight, and I had never wished more for a cloudy day.

"Becky, I gotta go," I said, rushing to the door. "I think I'm gonna be sick."

12

I GRABBED MY COAT AND PURSE AND SAID MY GOODBYES TO BECKY. I needed to get out of there—and fast. Luckily, I was able to blame my emotions on the death of my mother, which made it easier to conceal the feelings I still had for Caleb. I didn't know what to make of those.

I made my way down a short alley on the side of The Flower Pot which led to the other side of the meadow, eventually opening up to the main road. The complete opposite direction of my house.

Instead of thinking about Caleb, thoughts of my mother consumed me. I cried openly as I walked, remembering a time when I was a little girl. I woke up early one morning and crept into my parents' room. My dad had already left for the store to do month-end inventory, and when I crawled up into their bed, my mom smiled and wrapped her arms around me, pulling me in close. She smelled like vanilla and home.

"Good morning, peanut," Mom had said to me, gently tucking my hair behind my ear and kissing my nose.

I lived for mornings like those as a child. I'd kill for one of those moments now. Even though I didn't have any siblings, and always had my parents to myself, those calm and unrushed moments were few and far between. Someone always had something to do and somewhere to be, so we took full advantage when it happened.

We had spent all morning in bed eating pancakes, waffles, and strawberries; my most requested breakfast at that point in my young life. We watched hours of television, laughing and snuggling with each other. We hadn't even gotten out of bed until noon, when my dad had come home from the store for lunch. He laughed and hopped into bed with us, hanging out for a bit before taking our lunch order.

I wiped my tears away with the end of my scarf, trying to compose myself as I approached the school where my mother had taught. I scoffed at how different Grace Valley was from the city. There were more people employed in the travel agency where I worked than there were in the entire Grace Valley school system. In fact, the town was so small that there was only one school. Half of the building housed the students in kindergarten through grade six, and the other half held the seventh through twelfth graders.

I slowly walked through the parking lot, noticing that the playground had undergone quite the upgrade. There used to sit two swings, a seesaw, a slide, and monkey bars. Now, there was a massive climbing structure and two long rows of four swings each. Across from the playscape used to be a little field to run around in, but they must have knocked down a couple dozen trees because there was now a soccer field, basketball court, and a smaller open field.

"Leah, is that you?" I heard someone call.

I looked around the parking lot until my eyes landed on Mr. Palmer. I was shocked at how much he had changed. I wouldn't have even known it was him except for the fact that he was standing at his car, which was parked in the reserved spot for "Principal." His once skinny frame was now pudgy, and you could almost see his belt begging to be unbuckled. His once clean-shaven face now had a full beard including mustache. And his hair was balding at the crown. I made my way over to him, smiling but a bit nervous to see yet another familiar face.

"Hello, Principal Palmer. Yes, it's me. How are you?" I replied, unsure if being at the school during a vacation was permitted.

"Please, call me Bill. There's no need for formalities anymore," he said with a soft smile. "I am well, thank you. Marina and I have been thinking about you and Paul. We are beside ourselves with the news of your mom. She was one of a kind, as you know."

I closed my eyes briefly and nodded, letting out a shallow breath before I spoke. I wasn't ready for all the faces I would see that would be honoring my mother in such kind ways.

"Thank you so much. We're doing okay. As expected, I suppose. I'm not too sure it's all sunk in yet, you know? One minute she was here and then the next…" I couldn't get the rest of the sentence out.

Bill tossed his briefcase into the open passenger side of his car and held his arms out to me. Before I knew it, I fell into them and cried on his shoulder. I had known the Palmers since I was born, and although this was new territory for me, I oddly felt a safeness to his comfort. He held me until I was ready to come back to the world, and I was grateful.

"Marina is going to be meeting me here in about twenty minutes with lunch. Would you like to stay and have a bite to eat with us? We're going to be discussing the final arrangements for the festival. You're more than welcome to relax here if you'd like," he offered, and I kindly accepted, even though I wasn't sure I really wanted to.

I followed Bill into the school and down the long hallway to his office. I'd been here many times before but never to just sit and relax. It felt strange to be in the school again after graduating, especially while my mother was no longer there. He motioned for me to sit down at a little table in the back corner of his office and I obliged, looking out his window and into the school's courtyard. I smiled as I remembered taking my senior superlative pictures in that very courtyard years ago. Caleb and I had sat on the bench under the small tree, holding hands and smiling. We were voted Class Couple. *Ha... If only they could see us now.*

My smile quickly faded and I began to look around the office, admiring all of Principal Palmer's plaques and diplomas. Artwork that his kids drew for him when they were younger was framed and hung on his wall. A picture of him and Marina was sitting on his desk, turned ever-so-slightly. I wanted to stand up and straighten it, but I didn't. Just as I was about to ask him how his kids were, Marina walked through the door carrying to-go bags from Rosewater, a little hole in the wall Lebanese restaurant in the next town over.

"Leah Abernathy, my word! What a pleasure it is to see you here! I was so sorry to hear about your mom. Come give me a hug, sweetie," Marina said, coaxing me out of my seat.

Of course, I was delighted to see Marina. I had spent so many wonderful days over at her house playing with Janie, their youngest child and only daughter. Janie was four years younger than me but that had never bothered us. She was a cute kid and we had a lot of fun together. We always played school and took turns being the teacher. I wondered what she was up to these days.

"Hi, Mrs. Palmer. Thank you. It's good to see you, too."

"Well, will you be joining us for lunch, sweetie? There's plenty to go around. I always make sure to pick up extra when Billy and I get together for lunch." She winked and patted Bill's ever-growing belly.

"I would love to. Thank you," I replied, trying not to stare at Bill.

"Funny, Marina. Very funny." He laughed and pulled up a chair to sit at the table.

Marina laid out the containers of food, and she wasn't kidding when she said she bought extra. There was enough food to feed ten people. My mouth watered when I saw the kibbe pockets and lentil soup. Sure, New York City was home to the most amazing restaurants, but nothing could beat Rosewater's food. Especially the soup. I grabbed a plate and fork and began to dig into the ridiculous feast.

"So, Principal Palmer—I mean Bill—has told me you two are going to be discussing some things for the festival," I said between bites.

"We're planning on making a few announcements at the end of the festival so we need to collaborate on those, and we're also trying to decide who will light the tree. As you know, your mother won Teacher of the Year, so we were going to honor her there. Now that the plans have changed, we need to move things around a bit." She wiped the corner of her mouth with her napkin before gently placing it back on her lap.

"I see," I replied, sucking my bottom lip under my teeth. My fists were balled up under the table, and I was trying to remain calm. I was sure Marina didn't mean anything by it, but her words were like a thousand tiny daggers stabbing me over and over again. "If you don't mind, I'm just going to walk around and get some air."

"Oh, of course, honey," Marina quickly declared. "I'm sorry if I've upset you. I didn't mean—"

"I know," I told her, and walked out of the office, leaving my coat and purse on the chair. I knew Marina meant well; I just needed some air.

I walked through the secretary's office and into the main lobby of the building. I just stood there, taking it all in. It had been seven years, yet the school had not changed a bit.

If I went left, I'd end up at the lower school, the shared gym, and the lower school's cafeteria. If I went straight, I'd end up in the high school cafeteria. Right would take me down a long hallway into the main part of the school and all the high school classrooms. I went right.

I ran the tips of my fingers along a handmade bench that had been gifted to Principal Palmer by the class of two thousand and seven. I laughed when I remembered everyone getting questioned on the whereabouts of all the wooden hall passes.

The walk down the halls seemed much shorter than I remembered and eerily calming. Without the ruckus of students pushing and shoving to get to class on time, the stillness was soothing. Before I knew it, I was at my mother's classroom.

It was no surprise the room was organized in tip-top shape. The bookshelves were decorated with Christmas trinkets that had been gifted to her throughout the years from her many loving students. The ceiling was draped with Christmas lights that would flicker along with the music she would play during the students' breaks in class. She always had a way to make them feel special and relaxed.

I made my way over to my mother's desk and sighed. Mom's reading glasses were folded neatly and sat upon a stack of papers that were ready for distribution when winter break ended. The same picture I had in my bedroom of the three of us sat in a white, flowery frame right next to what looked like a more recent picture of her and my dad.

Your love story was always my favorite, Mom.

I gasped when I saw the last picture that stood alone on the other side of the desk. I didn't quite know what to make of it. My mom had the formal portrait of me from my NYU graduation. I looked at the girl staring back at me, wearing a deep purple graduation gown and black cap. In the bottom left hand corner was a selfie taken of my parents with the world's biggest grins on their faces as I was walking up to the podium to collect my diploma. They had been there? This day kept getting worse and worse.

I sat in my mother's chair and propped my elbows up on the desk, my head sinking into my hands once again. I couldn't believe I had pushed my mother out of my life, and yet there she was, still supporting me from afar. All these years that I refused to talk to her were so selfish.

In a flash of anger, I threw my arm across the desk and watched all of my mother's things fly to the floor. Her reading glasses cracked when they bounced off the floor, and I lost it. Crying had become the new norm and this time, I wasn't ashamed by it.

"Leah, honey? What happened?" I heard coming from the doorway.

Marina stood there with her mouth gaped open and her eyes as wide as saucers. I lifted my head and didn't bother to wipe my nose, which was running like a faucet at this point. I looked up at Marina and kept crying until my puffy eyes couldn't cry anymore.

"I'm sorry, Mrs. Palmer. I need to go home," I said and I rushed out of the classroom, not bothering to clean up the mess I had made.

I ran down the hall to the office to grab my things and left from the back entrance. I didn't stop running until I was safely on the front porch of my house. Gnocchi greeted me as if he had known exactly how I was feeling and I was eternally grateful.

13

_____

WHEN I FINALLY WALKED INTO MY HOUSE, IT WAS CLOSE TO dinnertime. My dad would probably be coming home soon from wherever he had ventured off to, and I knew he would need to eat dinner, so I decided to get it started. It was the least I could do. As I rummaged through the pantry trying to find something to make, my cell phone started buzzing in the back pocket of my jeans. It was the main line to my company.

"Hello?" I answered.

"Hey, girl, it's Sara. Is this an okay time to talk?"

"Hey, Sara. What's up?"

"Cameron asked me to connect you two. I don't know why he couldn't have Amy do it—or, I don't know, do it himself—but he wants to talk to you and it sounds urgent."

"Shit, okay. I hope he's not mad about me leaving early."

"Who the hell knows what actually goes through his mind except for how to make the most money while doing the least amount of work," Sara said and laughed. "I shouldn't be saying things like that on the work line. Who knows if it's being recorded? I'll put you through to him. Call me whenever you feel up to it, okay?"

"Sure. And Sara, thanks for everything. I really mean it."

"Anytime, my love. Anytime," she said and transferred the line.

I went to my room to take the call, figuring if I had to deal with this, I could at least be in the comforts of my own room.

"This is Cameron," came obnoxiously booming through the phone, and I had to pull it away from my ear.

"Cameron, this is Leah. Sara said you wanted to speak with me," I said, rolling my eyes and trying to conceal an audible sigh.

"Yes, I do. First, let me extend my deepest sympathies. I didn't receive any messages until this morning, and I apologize for not getting back to you sooner. I know I can be a bit harsh with time off, but please take all the time you need," Cameron said, shocking me.

I was absolutely not expecting that, and my expression of annoyance quickly faded into one of appreciation. I had worked for Cameron for many years and had never seen him show an inkling of the compassion and understanding that he was now.

"Thank you so much, Cameron. I really appreciate that," I said.

I pulled at the corner of my comforter and twisted the end of it with my fingers. I was nervous, although I couldn't pinpoint why. I knew I wouldn't be out of work any longer than was necessary, and Cameron had made it clear I could take all the time I needed. However, I knew I needed to get back to some level of normalcy. If I even know what that looked like anymore.

"I'm not sure if you're aware, but I lost my wife about five years ago to cancer. She struggled a lot while trying to have children and we later found out she had some cancerous cells that were slowly killing her. She succumbed to her illness, and I just haven't been the same since," he admitted. "If I am not mistaken, you came on board right after I returned after she passed."

"Oh, I'm so sorry to hear that. No, I was not aware, but thank you for being so understanding. I can't imagine I'll be out any more than a week. The funeral is in a few days and then I plan to be back to work the following Monday." Blowing out a huge breath, I waited for him to say more.

"Understood. You remind me a lot of her. I think that's why we work so well together. You are a breath of fresh air in our office, and I hope you know how appreciated you and your work ethic are," he told me.

I didn't know what to say other than thank you.

"Aside from that," Cameron continued, "the other reason I'm calling is because the Portugal project is becoming bigger than anticipated, and I want to offer you a more in-depth role. You would be heading the entire project while training Sara to take over the role that you similarly had with John's project. I know it seems like a lot, but you won't have to worry about any of that until mid-January, as I've been able to hold off on it for the time being. Also, this can all be done remotely. If you do feel that you need to spend more time with your family, or you just don't want to come into the office, you also have that option. I want to make sure you're happy and comfortable."

"Wow, Cameron, that all sounds amazing. Thank you so much. Can you have Karen draft up exactly what the job entails? I'd love to get a start on it while I'm here. I need to stay busy. I'm sure you understand what I mean."

"Of course. Do whatever you need to do," he said. "I just wanted to let you know that this position does come with a new title, as well as a significant pay increase. I'll make sure that's included with Karen's email. Your efforts are more than noticed and you should be rewarded. I'm proud of you, Leah."

I thought I was getting fired, and instead, got promoted. Who knew that Cameron had a soft side? I wonder if anyone else in the company knew about his wife. Surely Karen, his secretary, did.

"Have you told Sara about this yet?" I asked. "I know she's been working toward advancement as well."

"I spoke with her last week about her interest in other positions here, but I've yet to offer her this one. I could be jumping the gun, but I think we'll all find a happy medium. I plan to offer it to her when we hang up. I'm sure you two will have lots to catch up on after our chat," he said and I felt his warmth and smile through the phone.

"One more thing, Leah. And I may be overstepping here but hear me out. I know it seems impossible right now, but try to enjoy every minute of being back home with the ones who love you the most. Tomorrow is never promised, and you must go through life as if each day could be your last. Love the ones you're with and let them love you back."

"Thank you, Cameron. That was beautiful," I said before we hung up. I couldn't wait to call Sara back after dinner. I didn't know how I was able to be so happy and so sad at the same time, but I thought Mom would have wanted me to smile instead of cry.

I wiped a tear from my eye and tossed my phone onto the bed before I ran back downstairs and into the pantry. As I started rifling through the rows of pasta and rice, I struggled to find the right thing to make. Hmm...spaghetti and meatballs. Meatloaf with mashed potatoes. Chicken parmesan. And then my eyes landed on a box of garden herb crackers. I really hoped we had shrimp in the freezer!

I walked out into the mudroom to check if there were any shrimp in the chest freezer. My mother was notorious for stocking up on almost everything. She always feared we'd be living through some sort of global pandemic or zombie apocalypse and wouldn't have enough provisions to survive, even though my dad owned a grocery store. *Jackpot! Baked stuffed shrimp it was!*

Baked stuffed shrimp held so many memories in that small dish. My mom cooked it for my dad on their very first wedding anniversary and every single year since. She also made it for my birthday every year, at my request. We were never a family that dined out often. Usually, a brunch here and there or maybe lunch when we were out. There was the occasional visit to Tammy's diner, but that was mostly because she begged us to come taste test her latest creations.

It wasn't that we couldn't afford to dine out, my mom just preferred to cook, and we definitely preferred her cooking over a restaurant. One thing was certain, we always made sure to be home for family dinner, especially on Sundays. And even in college and at my NYC apartment, no matter what I had going on, I always made it home in time to make something for Sunday dinner. I usually ate alone, but the tradition never stopped.

"Mmm, it smells amazing in here!" my dad exclaimed. He threw his jacket into the mudroom, not even trying to hang it. "What have you been up to?"

"I thought you could use a nice meal. I wasn't sure what to make. I hope this is okay."

"Oh, pumpkin, it's perfect. She would have loved this." He looked down and cleared his throat, trying not to show any emotion. "Let me set the table while you plate those."

"Okay, Dad."

I grabbed the serving spoon and two plates and started piling the shrimp on. I handed them to him, carried the bowl of salad to the table, and sat down.

"I'm starving," I said, reaching for my fork. "I haven't had this in so long. I don't know why; it's the easiest thing to make."

"You know, we haven't had it since your birthday before you left for college," he admitted. "Your mom stopped making it when she thought you wouldn't be coming home."

It was like a punch to the gut. I was in between feeling sad and downright pissed that my mother never bothered to just pick up the phone and call me. Then again, I wasn't exactly mature enough to pick up the phone either. I probably would have seen the number and sent her to voicemail or ended up hanging up on her in the middle of the call. I still couldn't understand how it took my mother dying for me to be able to just grow the hell up and realize the mistakes I had made.

Regret tore through me like a Caribbean hurricane. I thought it was bad leaving Caleb, but that pain was a stubbed toe compared to this. I wasn't sure I had any tears left to cry, and at this point, I was just numb. I caused my mother's death and there was nothing I could ever do to change that.

"Hey, Dad?"

"Yeah, pumpkin?" he replied, shoving another forkful of shrimp into his mouth. "Mmm, this is so good."

"How come you never told me that Mom was at my NYU graduation?" I asked nervously.

He took a long swig of his water and cleared his throat. "How do you know about that?"

"I ended up at the school this afternoon and went to Mom's classroom. I saw the pictures on her desk."

Caught off guard, he didn't have time to fabricate some story to make me feel better, so he had no other choice but to tell me the truth. We both just sat there staring at one another, waiting for someone to say something.

"Dad?"

He cleared his throat and wiped his mouth with a cloth napkin before gently placing it back onto his lap. He clasped his hands and placed them on the table, looking straight into my eyes.

"How much do you want to know?" he asked me.

"Everything. And don't leave anything out."

14

MY DAD LET OUT A HUGE SIGH AND BEGAN TO FILL ME IN ON THE seven years I had missed. He didn't hold back, unafraid of hurting my feelings with what he was telling me. Like father, like daughter. After all, I was the one who had decided to leave and not be present in my own mother's life.

"When you were growing up, you definitely gave us a run for our money a few times, but nothing substantial and nothing that ever hurt us. But after you left for NYU, your mom struggled quite a bit. You leaving nearly killed her."

"But I didn't do anything! I went to college," I blurted out, my voice increasing in volume with each word.

"You asked me to tell you, Leah. Now let me finish," he commanded sternly.

"I'm sorry, Dad."

"She continued to go to work and teach and put on a brave face. Everyone in town would always ask about you and say how exciting it must be for you to be studying in the big city. It tore your mother apart, but she never let anyone know. Not even Becky. Each year, when they'd start decorating the town for Christmas, I thought your mom was going to have a nervous breakdown. You and I had our weekly phone calls, but you refusing to talk to her...it broke her heart."

My heart pounded at his words, and I sat at the dinner table feeling so embarrassed. This wasn't me, and it definitely wasn't the sum of our relationship. It was time I stopped asking myself how we got here and started to admit that I was the reason for our estrangement. I was to blame for everything. Not because I went to college, but because I refused to allow my mother into my life after I had left.

"We didn't set up the Christmas tree or decorate the house that year. Your mother didn't bake her sugar cookie snowflakes for the cookie booth at the festival. She just sat in her chair day after day, snuggled up in her sweater and reading until she went to bed. She did this every single night until she woke up on Christmas morning to an undecorated house. It was too much for her, I guess. She realized she had allowed it to consume her in the worst possible way. She was so distraught with not having you in her life, and for the first time since she set foot in America, she called her own mother."

"She called Nonna?!" I exclaimed in barely a whisper.

I had never met my grandmother and was genuinely shocked my mom would have called her. Truthfully, I didn't know much about my grandparents or my uncles. My mom never wanted to disclose any information about her upbringing. I only knew that my grandmother was selfish and wanted my mom to stay in Italy so she could meet and marry a successful man that would help improve the family name. Imagine a mother so self-absorbed that she wasn't willing to support her only daughter in following her dreams.

"Yep, she wanted to talk to her and see if they could somehow reconcile, or at the very least, have some closure. It had been twenty years since your mother left Italy. At that point, she felt it was now or never, and she had waited long enough. She was as stubborn as you, Leah. Maybe even more. I wonder where you get it from." He winked at me.

"So what happened?" I inquired.

"Well, it took your mother a while to find her because they had ended up moving out of their small village. As you may remember from your mother's stories, they didn't have a lot of money growing up. Once her brothers had settled themselves in financially, they bought your grandparents a plot of land and had a house built for them. When your mom was finally able to get a hold of them, your Nonna hung up on her. She later said she hadn't believed it was really her, and that a part of her just wasn't ready to confront the girl who had left her all those years ago."

"Oh, poor Mom," I said, embarrassed knowing my immature self would have hung up if my mom had called me, too. I was such an asshole.

"Well, your grandfather called your mom back instead, and they spoke for a very long time," he continued. "They didn't know she had become a teacher, or that we got married, or that we even had you. Your mom never reached out to anyone once she had arrived here, so no one even knew if she was still alive. I think that was her way of letting go of the past and allowing herself to live a life that *she* wanted."

"I tried to get her to contact them on many occasions, but you know how your mother was. As soon as she set her mind to something, there was no budging. She was her own person, that's for sure. You're so much like her, pumpkin. More than you could even know."

"What happened after Nonno called her back? Did she tell you what they talked about?"

"Well, eventually, your grandmother got on the phone and spoke with your mother. I stayed in the den while she sat here in the kitchen. I wanted to give her some space and privacy, but I also wanted to be close enough if she needed me. Of course, I couldn't understand anything because they were speaking in Italian, but when your mother hung up the phone and walked into the den, she was smiling and her face was covered in tears. I hadn't seen her smile like that since before you left. Your grandmother invited us all to Italy to visit. She wanted to meet us, and of course, wanted to reconcile with your mom in person."

"Did you go?" I asked.

"I didn't go. Your mother decided it was best for her to make the trip herself and then we would all go together the next time. It was a tough time with the store, so I didn't fight it. She ended up going the following spring for two weeks, and when she came back, she was planning on making a trip up to the city to see you and help you pack up to head back home for summer break," my dad told me.

"So why didn't she?" I questioned nervously.

I already knew the answer to that, though. I had decided to stay in the city for summer break and work instead. I was given an opportunity for a paid summer internship and the money from that coupled with my student loans was enough for me to rent my own apartment instead of a dorm room.

"When you told us you weren't coming back, your mother knew it was time to let you go. She figured if she gave you some space, you'd come back and everything would be normal again. But…you never came back."

He blinked a few times, seemingly trying to hold back the tears that had formed in his eyes. He walked over to the refrigerator and grabbed two beers. His walk back to the table was slow, but he twisted the tops off the beers and handed me one before taking a long drink from his. His eyes were red, but the tears were almost gone by the time he sat back down. He rubbed his thumb up and down the bottle, watching the condensation come and go.

"Dad? If you're not ready to tell me anymore, I understand," I offered. "I know this is hard, and I've been selfish enough already."

"It's okay, pumpkin. You asked and you deserve to know. Besides, memories are only good if we share them." He took another long sip of his beer. "Your mom was devastated when you didn't come back home, but after meeting with your grandmother, she vowed to not miss any of your important milestones, even if you didn't want her there. She came with me to every event that you invited me to. She sat next to me for everything and snuck off to the car when it was over. She was something else, your mom. You were her everything, and you crushed her by leaving the way that you did. But let me tell you something, kid. She never stopped loving and supporting you."

My dad's declaration made me break down right there at the kitchen table. I knew he wasn't saying any of this to hurt me, he just needed me to know. And in true Leah fashion, I wanted to run away from my problems, but I stumbled when I tried to get up from the table. The beer slid across the wooden table and crashed to the floor, smashing into a million pieces as it landed.

God, what the hell had I done? Who was I? I dropped to my knees and started picking up the pieces, careful not to cut myself, but it was becoming increasingly difficult to see through all of my tears. I felt my dad sit down next to me, taking the pieces out of my hands and gently placing them back on the floor. He pulled me close to him and held me in his arms like I was a little girl again.

"We all make mistakes, Leah. You had to learn to make these decisions on your own. Don't beat yourself up over it. Life lessons come to us in many different ways, and you don't get to choose which form they enter your world. Consider your mom's passing as the light that will lead you from now on. She was always there for you and now she'll always be right there with you. I love you so much."

I wiped the tears from my face with the back of my hand and smiled at my dad. The spilled beer had started to seep into my jeans, and there was definitely a piece of glass in my thumb. I stood up to grab a towel to start cleaning the mess, but my dad had me sit down and started cleaning it up for me.

"Stay right here a minute," he told me when the mess was finally cleaned up. Minutes later, he returned with a big box and set it on the table in between us.

"What's this?" I asked.

"You know your mother had to take pictures of anything and everything. These are some photo albums of the years you had spent apart. If she couldn't be with you physically, she could at least look at these pictures and feel as though you were here with her." His eyes filled with tears again.

I wondered how it was that this man didn't hate me. I tore his wife's heart out of her chest, still beating, and now I was responsible for her death. My selfishness meant he'd be without her for the rest of his life. If I were him, I wouldn't want to be around me.

He opened the book on the very top, and the first picture I saw was the same one from my graduation. I was taken aback when I saw how many pictures there were of me. My dad turned the book to face me, and I flipped through the pages, taking in each and every picture. I laughed when I saw the selfie of my parents outside of Gray's Papaya, New York's number one hot dog joint. Only my mother could be this happy eating a hot dog on the streets of New York City.

"Maybe we can eat there when you come to visit next," I suggested to my father.

"I'd like that," he replied, his cheeks plumping up as he smiled.

"These pictures are amazing. I knew she was a great photographer, but these are even better than I remember," I commented, pouring over the albums. "Wait, who is this little girl with me? I don't remember taking this picture."

He chuckled and took the picture out of my hands, thumbing over it. His left hand perched just under his chin made his face smush up, and I saw that his age had started to catch up to him.

"That's because it's not you. That is your mother and your grandmother. You are the spitting image of Giovanna."

"Giovanna? As in my middle name?"

"Mm-hmm. Your mother wasn't sure what the future held, but she wanted you to have something from her past that was strong and solid, and she knew that namesake was it."

"Wow, I wish I knew all of this before. I don't know what I would have done with the information, but it seems like there's so much more I'll never get to find out." My lip quivered and I held my tears in.

"Not necessarily. I've been in contact with your grandparents, and they're trying to come for the funeral. Your grandfather hasn't been well, but they're going to let me know. You are more than welcome to stay here if you want to spend some time with them and get the answers to all of your questions."

"Thanks, Dad. Let me clean up these dishes and head to bed. It's been a long day, and I just want to be alone."

I picked up the dishes off the table before he had a chance to argue with me. The dishwasher would have been the easier option, but I felt like letting the soapy water soothe me while I scrubbed the pots and pans. It had been a while since I did anything in this kitchen, and I began to think about how my life would be if I didn't end up going back to the city at all.

15

THE NEXT MORNING CAME MUCH FASTER THAN I HAD HOPED, AND the sound of voices bellowing up the stairs ripped me from my slumber. I reached for my phone to check the time. *Who the hell was here at seven in the morning?!*

I dragged myself out of bed and threw on some leggings and an old, beat-up hoodie. My favorite. I was so glad it was still here, shredded and all. I laughed as I pulled the hoodie over my head, my hand getting stuck in one of the many holes on the sleeve. The cuff was hanging on by a thread, but I would never get rid of it. My mother constantly told me to just throw it away.

"I'll buy you five new ones if you just chuck that one right now," she would say. But I couldn't let go of it. And now I never will.

The voices got louder as I walked closer to the kitchen, and I smiled when I saw Mr. and Mrs. O'Connor sitting at the table having coffee with Dad. So they did still live next door!

"Leah, how are you?" Mrs. O'Connor asked, getting up from the table to hug me. "I'm so happy to see you. It's been ages."

"Hi, Mr. and Mrs. O'Connor. It's so nice to see you. I wish it were under better circumstances, but I'm happy to be here, nonetheless. How's Casey doing? She must be getting ready to apply for colleges soon, no?" I asked, surprised I remembered that much after so long.

"Good memory! She's actually graduating early and is going to NYU. Pre-law. Maybe you can keep an eye on her while she's there," Mr. O'Connor piped up, winking at me.

"I'll be sure to leave my cell phone number with you before I leave. She is always welcome to call me if she needs anything."

I walked over to the counter and made myself a coffee. I had noticed some Italian sweet crème coffee creamer in the fridge the night before. I poured a generous amount into my mug and sat down at the table to join everyone. I had missed the closeness of Grace Valley. If anyone in my building knocked on my door at seven in the morning for coffee, I'd have to call the cops to have someone committed.

"Have you seen Caleb yet, Leah?" Mrs. O'Connor smirked. "I know you two were quite close, and I've seen him about in town a lot lately."

Just as I was about to answer, my cell phone buzzed loudly from the counter. *Oh, thank god.*

"Excuse me, I need to get this," I said, scooping up my phone and walking into the den.

A strange number I didn't recognize flashed across the screen, hanging up before I got a chance to answer. Maybe they'd leave a message. I decided I didn't want to make small talk anymore and went up to my room using the back stairs.

I wanted to dive into some work before I lost the energy to be productive, so as I waited for my MacBook to boot up, I went through my drawers and looked for something a little more presentable to wear. I laid my clothes on my bed and went back to my desk just in time to see a voicemail notification appear on my cell phone screen.

"Um, hi, Leah. It's me—Caleb. I got your number from Becky. I hope you don't mind. Listen, I was over at Joey's auto body shop, and he asked me to drop by some stuff he found in your mom's car. I wanted to give you a heads up before I stopped by. Wasn't sure if you wanted to see me or not. Anyway, I'm around all day, so just call me back or text me or whatever is easier for you. I guess I'll talk to you later. Take care."

What. The. Fuck?

I threw my phone onto the bed and got into the shower. I hoped the hot water would wash away my feelings and confusion. Why would he need to come here to deliver anything to me? He's engaged to another woman. Why couldn't Joey just bring it over himself? Why do I care so much?!

Soap suds gathered around my feet and slowly swirled down the drain. I stood in the shower and watched until the very last bubble disappeared. It was as if everything was just being washed away. If only certain parts of life were that easy.

When I got back into my room, Gnocchi was on my bed waiting to greet me. I was grateful to still have him in my life, even more so that he hadn't forgotten me. He looked up at me and purred when I sat next to him. His eyes connected with mine, and we just sat together for a while staring at the other. It was almost as if he were telling me everything was going to be all right. I wondered if he understood what was going on, and if he noticed that Mom wasn't here anymore.

He always knew how to make me feel better. I wasn't sure how I made it seven years without him by my side. I was definitely taking him back to New York with me.

Gnocchi's head popped up as if he could understand my thoughts, and he hopped off the bed and bounced down the stairs. *Don't start packing yet, boy.*

I had just finished getting ready when I heard the front door close. Finally, I could go back downstairs.

When I walked into the kitchen, I saw my dad holding onto the front of the sink, his shoulders hunched over and his head lowered toward his chest. He let out a big sigh, turned on the water, and started washing the coffee mugs. I stood in the doorway and watched him in silence. I wondered how many times he'd stood at that sink, washing the dishes from a meal Mom had cooked for us. A mug slipped from his hands and slammed against the porcelain sink, cracking down the side. I gasped as the weight he had been carrying for the past week fell to the ground, and he couldn't stop crying, clutching the sink as if to hold himself up.

"Daddy!" I called and ran to his side. "Daddy, it's okay. It's okay."

I'd never seen my dad cry before, and for someone as sensitive and loving as him, I wondered how he was able to keep his tears inside for so long. We somehow made our way to the floor and cried together, both of us finally understanding that my mom wasn't ever coming back.

"I need some air, Leah," my dad managed to say through heavy breaths. "I'm gonna take a walk alone."

"Okay, Daddy," I replied.

After about an hour, my dad returned. He looked like he hadn't slept in days. His eyes were red and swollen and his face was streaked with devastation.

"Dad, let me cook you some breakfast."

"Okay, pumpkin," he obliged. He took a seat at the table and grabbed the paper.

I opened the fridge and was surprised to find it fully stocked again. Yesterday, it was almost empty. Perks of owning a grocery store, I supposed. I gathered the ingredients for the eggs and hash and started cooking.

"Hey, Dad," I called, looking over my shoulder. "Runny or scrambled for the eggs?"

"Umm, runny," he answered.

I smiled, happy to be able to do this for him, and I hoped I was able to make it as great as my mom always had. I didn't know if he was thinking of her in that moment, but I wanted to at least bring some sense of normalcy to this house and help ease his pain a little bit.

Once I finished cooking, I tossed the pans into the sink and brought the plates over to my dad. I had to shoo Gnocchi off my seat so I could sit down, but I smiled at him and patted my lap, inviting him to come back. He looked at me with annoyance and went into the den instead. I rolled my eyes and started to eat.

"Yum, I haven't had this in so long," I announced. "I usually don't have time to cook breakfast in the mornings, so I just eat oatmeal quickly or grab something on the way to the office."

"I can't imagine you not cooking yourself breakfast," he replied, looking at me quizzically. "You woke up early every day senior year to cook for yourself even when your mother offered to make it for you."

"Yeah, well, I didn't want her to have to do that. Besides, I love cooking. I should try to cook more when I get back to the city."

My dad's eyes filled with sadness, and he went back to his breakfast. *Shit.* I should probably stop talking about going back. I didn't want to upset him any more than he already was.

"Do you need anything for the apartment?" he asked me. "I know you're simple, but there has to be something you can use. You could take one of your mothers cast iron pots if you'd like. We all know she has enough to pass around."

I smiled at the offer. My mom had a passion for cooking, and although she was simple like me, her kitchen never lacked the latest gadget or cookware. She could have ran a restaurant out of her own house if she had wanted to.

"Sure, Dad. Next time, though. I don't think I want to be carrying cast iron onto the train and through the city."

"Sounds like a plan, kiddo. Hey, sorry about the O'Connors. You know how nosy they are. They haven't changed a bit."

"Yeah, I could see that," I said, eating the last forkful of egg before clearing the table. "So, what else do we need to do for the funeral, Dad? I know it's difficult to talk about, but we need to figure it out."

"Yeah, I hear you. I spoke with the people over at the funeral home and the casket was delivered. Becky called and said the flowers are all set. She'll deliver and set them up, so we don't need to worry about anything. And Bill Palmer is having the high school choir come to the church to sing. So, I think that leaves food for after the funeral and her outfit," he told me, breathing in a huge sigh when he finished.

"Were you thinking of having the lunch catered?" I asked. "If so, you're a little behind schedule. Most places need more than three days to prepare."

"Well, I was thinking of calling Tammy, actually. I thought she might be able to put together a nice spread."

I'm sorry, what? Tammy, as in Caleb's mother? As in the woman I referred to as a second mother? AS IN CALEB'S MOTHER?!

"Um, did you want me to call her for you? I don't think I can do that, Dad. I haven't spoken to her since Caleb and I broke up," I stammered.

"No, I'll call her after lunch or I'll swing by there on my way to the post office. I have some stuff I want to drop into the donation bin they have set up outside," he said.

I finished up the dishes while my dad continued to read the paper. I still wanted to know about Caleb and this whole Tennessee business, but I knew it wasn't the time to bring it up.

"Dad, do you want to go pick out Mom's outfit now? The sooner we get that settled, the sooner we can relax with all of this," I offered, knowing it would probably be the hardest part, aside from the actual burial itself.

He nodded and folded the paper, setting it on the chair next to him. Mom's chair. He patted it and stood up slowly, taking in a few breaths before he pushed his chair in. He motioned for me to head down the hall to their bedroom and he slowly followed.

I sat on the bed, smoothing the holly leaf quilt with my hand. I still remembered the day my mother finished making it. It took her an entire year to complete it, but she had.

"Don't you laugh at me, Leah Abernathy," she had said to me, tickling my ribcage. "This will be yours one day."

Dad must have sensed me fading off into la-la land because he quickly walked to the closet and opened it, pushing the hangers one by one to find Mom's dresses. He stopped suddenly and turned to face me. Without saying a word, he pulled the dress off the hanger and held it out in front of him. I smiled and stood up, walking toward him. I took the dress from his hands and held it against my body.

"Mom's Christmas Show dress. I still can't believe she wore this every single year," I commented. "It's so damn hideous!"

We both laughed and I hung it back up.

"There's no way she is being buried in this thing, even though it should definitely be buried," I said, laughing too hard at my own joke. That was a trait I had inherited from my dad.

"I think you should keep it," he told me. "She'd want you to have it."

We spent the next half-hour looking through my mom's clothes and remembering so many wonderful things that had happened while she was wearing them.

"Listen, pumpkin, this is rough. I think it calls for some wine. I'm gonna go to the kitchen and grab a bottle and some glasses," he said.

"Uh, Dad? It's ten in the morning," I told him, a little shocked he was drinking so early in the day.

"Okay, so I'll bring in some mimosas, then. Orange juice or pink lemonade?"

"Pink lemonade," I answered. Mom's favorite.

Ten minutes later, he was back in the bedroom with a bottle of champagne, a gallon of pink lemonade, and two mason jars.

He plopped them onto the old trunk that sat at the foot of the bed and just looked at me.

"You okay, Dad?" I asked, my right eyebrow raised in confusion.

"You tell me," he replies, sliding my cell phone toward me. "Your phone was buzzing, so I thought I'd grab it and bring it up to you."

I picked it up and pressed the home button and the screen lit up. My eyes widened when I saw Caleb's name on the lock screen. My breathing became heavy, and I didn't know what to say. I looked back up at my dad, waiting for him to say something.

"Honey, why didn't you tell me you were talking to him again? Safe to assume things aren't going well with you and Josh?" he asked me.

"Caleb and I aren't talking again. As for Josh, we broke up the night before I left to come here. He stopped by my apartment after not hearing from me all day because I forgot to call him to tell him about the message you left me. So, yeah, things were not going well," I told him.

"Okay, well, that makes sense. Are you okay with that decision? He was a really nice young man, but you're the only one that can make those decisions for yourself."

"It was the right thing to do. I loved him—I still love him—but I'm not in love with him, as cliché as that sounds," I blurted out. "When he came over, he started arguing with me about how I should have told him, and that he was coming with me so he could be there for me. I told him I needed to be here for you, and that I wanted to do it alone. He couldn't accept that and it snowballed into this huge ordeal. Somewhere in the middle of the fight, I couldn't get Caleb out of my head. That's when I knew it wouldn't work out with Josh. Mostly because we weren't right for each other, but also because he's not Caleb. Sounds stupid, doesn't it?"

"No, pumpkin. It doesn't sound stupid. It sounds responsible. But you still haven't answered my question," he prodded. "Why didn't you tell me about Caleb?"

"There's nothing to tell. I quite literally bumped into him at the train station, as you know, and then he called to tell me that Joey asked him to drop a box of mom's stuff off to me. I missed the call, so he left a message. I haven't gotten back to him yet."

"I see. Well, what does the text say? I think you should give him a call back. You're obviously still harboring feelings for him, and he's reaching out to you so that must mean something," he said, trying to sound convincing.

Did Dad not know Caleb was engaged? Engaged to be MARRIED?!

"I'll text him back, but I don't think I need to see him. He's engaged and his fiancée is in town, and I don't need to be a part of all that," I said. "Which reminds me, what were you talking about before when you said Caleb was in Tennessee?"

"All right," he said and poured me a mimosa. "You might need this, so sit back down and I'll fill you in."

16

"You were probably too little to remember her, but Caleb's grandmother used to live with them before his dad died. She was living alone in Tennessee at the time, and Brad's siblings were still in college, so he invited her to live with him, Tammy, and Caleb. When Brad passed away, she wanted to go back to Tennessee to be with her other kids. So, she moved back home and lived alone in the same town as her daughter. About a year after you two graduated, she became ill. The doctors weren't sure what was going on, but she needed to have someone there to keep an eye on her. Tammy convinced Caleb that it would be good for him to get out of Grace Valley for a while, so he packed up his stuff and moved down there to be with her."

"I think I remember her. I have the faintest memory of snowman cookies," I said.

"Yes." Dad smiled. "She would bake sugar cookies for you and Caleb to decorate, and you always made yours into a snowman."

I sat on the floor of my parent's bedroom and picked the skin on my thumb. I wasn't going to have any skin left by the time I got back to the city. There was so much I had missed out on, and while most of the town was the same, I started to notice how much had changed while I was gone.

"Okay, so he went to take care of her and then what happened? He looked like he was back when I slammed into him in the train station," I said, annoyed with myself for pushing.

"It's nice to know the city hasn't changed your patience level, pumpkin," my dad teased.

I rolled my eyes and swatted at his knee. I took a big gulp of my mimosa and gestured to my dad to hand me the bottle of champagne to make another one. I lifted the lemonade bottle that was sitting next to me and poured my glass halfway before I handed it back to him. The circumstances sucked, but it really was a lot of fun being with my Dad.

"I don't really know the entire story, but I do know that when Caleb got there, his grandmother offered to pay for him to go to college down there. Apparently, he walked onto the basketball team and played there for three or four years. I'm not sure how many. Tammy said he didn't really talk about it too much because it was just filler between classes, when his grandmother was at her doctors' appointments."

"I'm not surprised." I smiled. "I always knew he was destined for bigger things than the community college he had planned on going to."

"Well, he did go to community college for a year before he moved down there. He transferred his sophomore year and was able to get his bachelor's and then master's in an accelerated program."

Overachiever. I rolled my eyes and my dad laughed at me.

"Don't be jealous, little girl. You were the one that pushed him to go to NYU with you, remember? You can't fault the kid for following his dreams after you tried to force yours on him."

That one stung a little, but he was right. He was always right.

"Fair enough. What did he get his degree in?"

"Secondary education. Social studies to be exact. He wanted to follow in his dad's footsteps," Dad told me.

"Oh, wow. And is his grandmother better now?"

"No, pumpkin. She died during the summer after his first year with her. She left him her house and enough money to finish school, so he did. And he's been teaching down there since he graduated," my dad explained.

"I met his fiancée," I told him, my eyes rolling to the back of my head. "She came into Becky's shop looking for flowers. Apparently, Tammy's house isn't good enough for her without fresh cut flowers all over the place."

"Yeah, I heard," he confessed. "About the flowers, I should say, not about you running into Brittany."

"Brittany is her name? Suits her," I muttered, my jealousy palpable. "She said she was an interior designer. Where would Caleb ever meet an interior designer?"

"I know they met on campus at the University of Tennessee, but I'm not entirely sure of the specifics. I'm sure he would tell you if you asked him." He winked, knowing this would get me going. Such an instigator.

"Ask him?! Are you crazy? I'm not going to ask my ex-boyfriend how he met his soon-to-be wife. That's insane. I don't really even care," I spewed.

"Mm-hmm, sure. Whatever you say, pumpkin." He smiled. "Another mimosa?"

"I'm all set, but thank you," I replied, and he took the remnants of our day-drinking back to the kitchen.

Still reeling from all of this new information, I grabbed my cell phone to text Caleb back. This was going to be good. I was four giant mimosas deep and sitting in a pile of my mother's old clothes.

Leah: Hi, Caleb! Yeah, today sounds great. Sorry I didn't get back to you sooner. I'm here, so just come whenever you want!

Almost immediately after I pressed send, three little dots

appeared. He was typing! I grabbed a blouse that was laying on the floor next to me and buried my head in it. PING!

Caleb: Sounds good. See you around five.

"Dad!" I called down the hall. "Can you come back in here, please?"

"What's up? Everything all right?" he asked, popping his head into the doorway.

"Well, your little mimosa idea gave me some liquid courage and I just texted Caleb back and told him to come on over whenever he wants."

"Oh. And how do you feel about that?" he questioned.

"How do I feel about that? Like I need another shower and three days to sleep off this regret. Why am I like this?"

He laughed and bent down to pick up the remaining clothes on the floor. He looked at me and gently grabbed my hand. "Leah, it's only Caleb. You know him. There's nothing to feel regretful for."

"He's isn't coming until five he said, so I'll putz around here for a bit and maybe clean a little before I head into town," I told him.

"Okay, pumpkin. Let me know when you're going, and I'll walk over with you. I want to talk to Mrs. Kratz about getting some cookies and desserts made for your mom's luncheon. Why don't you think about stopping by to see Tammy? It'll be good for the both of you," he suggested.

I nodded and finished putting away my mother's clothes and everything else that remained on my parent's bedroom floor. I felt comforted being home, but my anxiety about Caleb was at maximum capacity. I stood up and looked for Gnocchi. A snuggle from him would make this whole thing a lot less awkward.

When I finally found Gnocchi, he was curled up in a ball in my mother's yarn basket, snoring. I didn't want to wake him, but it made me wonder what my mother was knitting this week. It was the one trait from my mother I didn't get. Every time I tried to learn to knit, I stabbed myself more times than I could count and repeatedly tangled myself up. Me and knitting did not go hand in hand.

"Hey, Dad?" I called. "I'm gonna head into town. Did you still want to come with me or do you want me to ask Mrs. Kratz myself?"

"Give me five minutes to get myself together and we can head out. Could you make sure Gnocchi has food and water in his bowl?"

"Sure," I said and went to the pantry to fill his bowls. I noticed a new rug under his fancy cat bowls. There were little paw prints around the edging and it said, "King of the Pawlace." It had my mom written all over it. I filled the bowls and put the food back into the pantry closet. I put on my hat and gloves, slipped my feet into my boots, and wrapped myself up tightly in my jacket.

"Okay, pumpkin," my dad said as he walked into the mudroom where I was waiting. "Ready when you are."

"Uh, not wearing shoes or a jacket today?" I asked, laughing at my dad. He was standing there, staring at me with a scarf and slippers on.

He started to laugh and grabbed his jacket. He wiggled his upper body until it was on and put on his snow boots.

"I can't believe I almost walked out in my house shoes," he said, blushing.

"At least you remembered your underwear," I teased. "You did remember your underwear, didn't you?"

We both laughed and started our walk into town. I was nervous to go visit Tammy at the diner, but I knew it would be harder seeing her for the first time at the funeral. I kissed my dad on the cheek, and he disappeared into the bakery while I slowly made my way to Tammy's.

The diner was completely different than the last time I was there. It used to be an old hole-in-the-wall, but now it looked like someone plucked a small bistro right out of the heart of Paris. It was gorgeous. Instead of the booths that used to be there, the walls were lined with small two and four-person tables. There were candles and white linens on each table, and a wire menu holder that also doubled as the housing for the salt, pepper, and sugar. The walls were no longer a dingy shade of brown, but now held beautiful artwork of various flowers and gardens.

"Leah? Leah Abernathy?" Tammy sang from the kitchen, wiping her flour-covered hands on her apron. "My word! It's been ages."

I leaned into Tammy and hugged her as if no time had passed at all. She smelled of garlic and coffee. It was an odd but comforting combination.

"Tammy, it's so good to see you. I wanted to come and see you sooner, but it was hard making my rounds under these circumstances."

"Sweetie, you do not have to explain anything to me. I am just happy to see your beautiful face again. Come, have a seat. Can I get you anything to eat?" Tammy offered.

"I'll take a hot tea, thanks. I'm not very hungry," I said.

"Great! I'll be right back and we can sit and catch up. Oh, I'm so glad you came in," Tammy said and snuck around to the kitchen.

This was awkward and comfortable at the same time. Was this my new normal? I hoped I could get used to it.

About five minutes later, Tammy came out of the kitchen with two cups of tea and a basket of scones. Did this woman know me or what?

"Have one," Tammy said. "You're always in the mood for a scone, so don't try to tell me otherwise."

I laughed and took one out of the basket. I was pulling a piece off the end when the door chimed, and in walked the last person I wanted to see.

"Brittany, hello dear. What can I do for you?" Tammy asked, but she didn't get up.

Brittany sauntered over to the table like she owned the place and we were in her seat. She was dressed to the nines with not a hair out of place. I hated her for no reason other than she was with Caleb and I wasn't. It was immature and I had no business acting that way.

"I just came to pick up some lunch. Caleb is at home working on something, so I thought I'd surprise him. Is it ready?" Brittany asked. Her voice hung on every last word as if they were going to run away from her.

"Let me head to the kitchen and ask. I wasn't here when the order was placed. I didn't even know you were coming in," Tammy said.

"Where are my manners?" Brittany said, her hand extended out toward mine. "I'm Brittany, Caleb's fiancée."

"Pleased to meet you," I said, my mouth twisted into an uncomfortable smile. "Leah Abernathy."

Brittany ripped her hand away from mine and her eyes widened. "Leah? As in Caleb's Leah?"

"Well, I guess you could put it that way; although, I haven't been Caleb's anything in over seven years. Congratulations on your engagement," I said with a forced smile.

The door to the kitchen swung open, and the man behind the door called over to Tammy to let her know that Brittany's order was ready. Talk about saving the day. Tammy looked over apologetically at me, but I could tell it made her day to see her future daughter-in-law so uncomfortable.

"It was, um, nice to meet you, Leah. I'll see you back at the house, Tammy. Thanks for lunch," Brittany said confidently and unfazed, which made me hate her more.

As soon as the door closed, I looked Tammy dead in the eyes. "You are a mischief maker, Tammy Patterson."

Tammy shrugged her shoulders and smirked. "She will never be you."

17

"So, tell me all about life in The Big Apple. How's work? Your apartment? Are you seeing anyone?" Tammy prodded but I didn't mind. I loved her so much and appreciated her genuine interest in my life post-Caleb.

"Life is really great there," I gushed, ignoring her question about love. "My job is amazing. It's something I've always wanted, but honestly, never thought I could have. I just found out I'm being promoted, and it will bring on so many incredible opportunities. I can't imagine my life any other way."

"And love?" Tammy asked again. I knew better than to pull a fast one on her.

"I was seeing someone for about two years, but we ended it before I came back to Grace Valley. He's a good guy, but we aren't right for each other," I admitted. It felt good to tell the truth.

"Love is hard. It isn't always sunshine and rainbows. You'll know when you've met the one and then you won't need to question anything anymore," Tammy reassured me. "Your dad called earlier and left a message about food, but I can't find the note anywhere and my line cook doesn't remember what it said. Do you know what he needed?"

"We'd like to have a small luncheon after the funeral. Mom didn't want a fuss, but Dad feels it's important to have some people over to the house to celebrate her life. If you wouldn't mind catering it for us, we would be eternally grateful. I know it's last minute and that it's asking a lot, but we really think she would want it to come from you."

"Of course! I was planning on bringing something over anyway. What were you thinking in terms of trays? Finger foods? Sandwiches? Appetizer samplers?" Tammy asked.

"All of the above?" I laughed softly.

"Absolutely. I would do anything for you Abernathys. Absolutely anything."

The door chimed and in walked Dooley Butler. His goofy grin hadn't changed in all the years I'd known him. I knew that bumping into him would happen sooner or later given he was married to Becky and was my dad's best friend. I just hadn't thought it would be in the diner.

"Hey, Tam! Just came in to pick up some soup and sandwiches for Becky and Jackie. They're swamped over at The Flower Pot. How's your day?" he asked, not noticing I was sitting across from Tammy.

I slowly turned my head and smiled at Dooley. His eyes lit up like fireworks on the Fourth of July. He grabbed me and pulled me in for a massive bear hug, quite literally ripping me from my seat.

"My little Leah. How I have missed your face. How are you holding up, kid?" he asked, his face still smushed up against the top of my head.

"I'm okay. Sometimes I feel like I should be more upset, and I don't understand how I can be out catching up with everyone when my mother just died. Other times I feel like, if I had just called her, maybe she would still be here. But if I had called her, maybe I wouldn't be here right now and I don't know. Maybe I'm not okay."

My words came out all jumbled, and I struggled to say what I actually felt, which was *I'm the reason your best friend is dead.*

"Oh, Leah, no. This isn't your fault. There's no way to know that the same thing wouldn't have happened if she were driving somewhere else that morning," Dooley said, trying to reassure me.

"I know the weight grief bears on someone," Tammy said. "It's been almost twenty years since Brad passed, and it still feels like yesterday. It's okay to let yourself feel the pain, Leah. It's supposed to hurt. It's supposed to make you mad as hell and question everything you thought you knew. What it's not supposed to do is change you into someone you're not. Your mother knew how deeply you loved her. Don't let something silly ruin what little memories you have left of her."

I knew I could always rely on Tammy to be a mother to me, even if I wasn't romantically involved with her son anymore.

Dooley laughed and made an uncomfortable situation even weirder. That was the Dooley way, though. Tammy and I looked at him like he was crazy.

"Oh, sorry," he said. "I was just thinking about the time when Brad fell backward into horse manure."

"What?" I asked.

"I forgot about that day!" Tammy exclaimed. "I had to wash his jeans at least four times to get the smell out."

Dooley laughed so hard he almost fell over. It was nice to be able to have these moments in the middle of a crisis. I knew my friends back in the city loved me, but the kind of love I shared with everyone in Grace Valley was unparalleled.

"I need to know the story behind this," I demanded. "You can't say something like that and then just laugh it off."

"Brad and your dad came to the farm the day after my dad died to help me and my mom get the meadow set up for visitors after the funeral. Brad thought it might be easier to take a shortcut and run the horses back into the barn instead of tying them to the rope and walking them back up one by one. Your dad and I just let him do his thing because there was no convincing him otherwise. So, your dad was putting together the tents while I brought out all the chairs when we heard this god-awful scream.

"We ran down to the lower meadow where Brad and the horses were and saw he was lying on the ground, screaming. We panicked and thought he got kicked in the face by one of the horses. As we got closer to him, we saw he was flat on his back in a pile of horse shit!" Dooley laughed, out of breath.

"Oh gosh! I had never heard this story before," I told them.

"He walked home waddling because no one would let him sit in their cars," Dooley said.

"I hosed him down and made him strip down naked in the backyard before he could come into the house to shower," Tammy told me. "He smelled so terrible, I was afraid the neighbors were going to think we were crazy. Spraying a naked man with ice cold water in the middle of the lawn. I miss days like those."

The last memory I had of Brad was in the very meadow Dooley just spoke of, nearly twenty years ago.

Picnics in the meadow were a Sunday tradition. My family, Caleb's family, and Dooley Butler would all meet there after Sunday services. Our father had been meeting there since they were kids and they kept the tradition alive mostly to just have an excuse to get together. I really missed those days.

"Leah, sweetie? Are you okay?" Tammy asked me, gently rubbing the top of my hand.

"Yeah, sorry, I was just thinking. I think I'm gonna go home and rest up a bit. Caleb is stopping by this evening to drop something off. I don't know if he told you," I answered.

"Yes, he told me he saw you at the train station, too. Sounded like it was quite the eventful run in, no pun intended," Tammy teased me.

I had always felt so comfortable around Tammy. I never felt that way with Josh's parents, and I couldn't imagine it would have eventually turned into what I have with her, either. It was too late to turn back time, but I hoped I always remained close to her.

"That's one way of putting it," I said, my cheeks turning a couple shades of pink before they settled at bright red.

"Don't tell him I told you this, but he was very happy he saw you. Brittany, not so much. They got into a pretty heated argument when they got back to the house and he filled me in," Tammy said.

"Why did they argue? Nothing happened. I spilled my coffee on him, cleaned it up, and left as fast as I could."

"Oh, Leah. You'll never be able to escape his heart. You'll always be his one true love, regardless of if the two of you are together or with other people," Tammy said. "You know it, he knows it, and I know it. Brittany can feel it, too. That's why she was so upset. Instead of him just telling me he saw you, he went into detail and then started to reminisce about the day you left for college. I guess she couldn't handle it. She threatened to leave on the next train back to Nashville. It took me and him to convince her that it was the past, and that you weren't back here for good. I don't know why she even cares. She has her hooks in him, and he's going back with her after the festival anyway."

"You know I never meant to hurt him. I didn't want any of this. I just wanted to be able to explore and live a life I'd always dreamed of. I really thought he would follow me and we could do it all together," I told her.

"You don't have to explain anything to me, love," Tammy reassured me. "Hang on one second for me."

She came out a few minutes later with a to-go bag full of food.

"Take this home for you and your dad so you can have dinner. I know you both could use a night off, and this is my way of making sure you eat."

"Once a mother, always a mother. Thank you," I said.

"I love you like my own, Leah Abernathy. Don't you ever forget that."

I smiled and took the bag from Tammy. Of course, I'd never forget that. I fought back tears as I walked back home. I almost felt as if I were grieving two mothers at the same time.

18

DAD WASN'T HOME WHEN I GOT THERE, SO I PUT THE FOOD IN THE refrigerator and wrote him a little note that I stuck to the freezer with a cat magnet. I went upstairs to shower and change my clothes. I wanted to look and smell good for Caleb. How many times had I showered since I got here? My skin was going to melt off. And why was I getting dolled up for him? I was terrible.

I settled on leggings, an old Christmas sweater, and my fuzzy slipper boots. I dried my hair and put lotion on my face, but only applied a touch of mascara. I didn't want to overdo it. After all, I wasn't the makeup wearing type, and Caleb preferred a fresh face anyway. Wonder how he dealt with his fiancée painting her face every day.

I still had forty-five minutes before he would get there, so I decided to call Sara to catch up. Once again, I picked at the skin on my thumb while I waited for Sara to pick up. This nervous habit was becoming an annoying one.

"Hey, Leah! How ya feeling?" Sara boomed from the other end of the line. "I'm so happy to hear your voice."

"I'm doing okay. It's hard but that's expected. I'm actually calling because I need to tell you some stuff," I told her.

"Okay, everything all right?" she asked.

"I broke up with Josh before I left to come here, and when my train arrived back home, I spilled my coffee all over my ex-boyfriend and then I met his fiancée in a flower shop and she's horrific, and he's coming over in like forty-five minutes to drop something off that the mechanic found in my mom's car, and I think I'm still in love with him." I stopped to catch my breath.

"Wait, what? That was a lot. Start from the beginning and slow it down," Sara replied. "It hasn't even been a week and all of this is going on?"

"Girl, I don't even know what's going on anymore. After we went to the pub that night, I couldn't stop thinking about everything that was wrong with my relationship with Josh. When I left the office the day my dad called about my mom, I went home and didn't even bother to call him. He came over when he couldn't get ahold of me and that's when I told him," I admitted.

"What the hell is wrong with you? How do you forget to tell your boyfriend of two years? Jesus. What did he say?"

"Well, he said he didn't even know I had a mother because he didn't remember me ever speaking about her," I cried. "I'm the worst person in the world."

"No, you're not. You just can't help being so damn stubborn," Sara said.

"We got into a huge argument. The entire time, all I could think about was Caleb and how he would never have treated me that way. Then I asked him to leave and went and cried myself to sleep," I told her, embarrassed at the response I expected to come next.

Sara was the kind of friend that everyone needed in their corner. She was loving and loyal but would always tell you like it was, whether you liked it or not. Sometimes she was careful with her wording, and other times, she didn't bother to censor her mouth. Either way, she never let me down. I had never met anyone like her aside from Caleb, although his words were always carefully thought out. I knew that Sara would always be a part of my life, even when I was being a bit much—like right now.

"Shit, Leah. I mean, I'm not mad you ended it with him. You deserve more than you were getting, but you could have done it a little nicer. But keep going. You dumped your coffee over Caleb and then met his fiancée? You live a weird life, dude."

"I wasn't paying attention at the train station, and I turned around quickly and bumped into him. I was mortified and went outside to wait for my dad, and I saw Caleb walk out with some chick. Fast forward to where I saw her again in a flower shop with the world's biggest ice skating rink on her finger," I said.

"Ugh! I'm sorry. Did she know who you were?"

"She didn't in the flower shop, but she found out when I was sitting with Caleb's mom at the diner having tea. His mom introduced us and let me tell you, it was horrific. I wanted to crawl into a hole and die, but also, I wanted to punch her in the throat," I said.

"Oh, I would pay top dollar to see that," Sara responded. "What's she like?"

"Tall, lean, and redheaded."

"So, totally not you, then. What did she say when she found out she was talking to *the* Leah Abernathy, former love of her man's life?"

I filled her in on the past week, probably going into more detail than necessary but I missed my best friend.

"That's hysterical. But I'm confused. He's going to your house tonight? Why again?" Sara asked.

"I guess the mechanic found something in my mom's car and he offered to bring it over. I'm not sure what it is, and I definitely regret saying yes to having Caleb drop it off. At the same time, I really want to see him," I admitted. "That makes me a bad person, doesn't it? He's engaged to someone else, and I'm home for my mother's funeral and all I can think of is him."

"You are not a bad person, Leah. Not at all. You're allowed to have feelings, regardless of what they are. You absolutely cannot act on them, though. That's not okay to Caleb or his fiancée. And that's not who you are."

I wiped a tear from my eye and smiled. My best friend always knew the right thing to say. Just as I was getting ready to thank her for being the world's greatest friend, a loud knock came from the front door.

"Crap, he's here. I have to go. How do I look?" I asked.

"How the hell should I know? I can't see you," Sara joked. "But in all seriousness, you're fine. Go answer the door before he leaves. I love you. Call me later."

"Ahhh! Love you, too. Bye."

19

I THREW THE PHONE ON MY BED AND RAN DOWN THE STAIRS TO THE front door. I paused before I opened it and wondered if I should turn around and go back upstairs instead. That would only make matters worse, and I knew I was bound to run into him throughout the week. It was now or never. He was just dropping off a box. I really needed to stop being so weird.

When I opened the door, I almost fainted. Caleb stood on the other side of the threshold looking better than I ever could have imagined. For starters, he didn't have on loafers. Instead, he was wearing pristine work boots, dark denim jeans, and an ever-green-colored peacoat. His scarf was loosely draped over his shoulders but wasn't tied at his neck. His hair was a bit longer than he used to wear it, so it hung closer to his eyes. But it was perfect.

"Um, are you going to let me in? It's a little cold out here," he asked.

"Oh, I'm so sorry. Yes, please. Come on in," I said and blushed. "Do you want anything to drink?"

"Sure. What've you got?" he responded.

My cheeks burned at the thought of him staying long enough

to have a drink with me. I knew if I offered him anything alcoholic, I would lose all inhibitions and morals and that would not be good for either of us.

"Water, tea, coffee? I could put a pot on quickly if you want," I offered, knowing he could never say no to a hot cup of freshly brewed coffee, even if that meant staying long enough to drink it.

"I'd love a cup of coffee. Thank you," he said.

I could feel his eyes on me as I moved throughout the kitchen. It was comforting and uncomfortable at the same time. Neither one of us said anything until the coffee was finished and we sat across from each other at the kitchen table. I handed him the milk and sugar bowl and took a deep breath.

"You said in your message that you have something for me," I blurted out. My aloofness surprised me.

"Oh, right. Yes, there was a box found in your mom's car. It hasn't been opened, but I thought you might like to have it. Whatever it is," Caleb said.

He tapped his thumbs on the side of his mug before taking a big gulp of the coffee. Good. He was nervous, too. It was amazing how much you could remember about someone you hadn't seen in so long.

"Where is the box?" I asked.

"It's in my car still. I can go out and get it now if you want," he said as he stood up.

He came all the way over here and just left the box in the car? Did that mean he wanted to see me? I internally chastised myself for my thoughts. He wasn't available anymore. I had my chance and I blew it.

"Sure, thanks. I'm interested to see what it is."

Once he was outside, I let out a big breath, recognizing my shaky nerves. I had known him since I was born, and yet, I felt as though this was our first meeting. I couldn't help but wonder what would have become of us had I stayed in Grace Valley and not broken up with him. I didn't want to step on any toes, but I was determined to find out.

When Caleb made his way back into the house, he said, "Here it is," and handed it to me with shaking hands. "I hope you know how special your mom was to me."

"I know," I replied through tears. "She would hate who I've become."

"Don't say that. She loved you and was so proud of you. She told me everything you've been up to. She was sad that you wouldn't talk to her anymore, but she never stopped loving you. Not even for a day. I think knowing you were living out your dream made her happy."

"Oh, Caleb. I feel like this is all I've been saying since I've gotten home, but what have I done? I've been shutting people out of my life for so long," I admitted. "I'll never get to see her again. Her last memory of me is watching me leave her and never even saying goodbye."

"You have to stop beating yourself up over this. There's no way her last memory of you was your disagreement. If anything, she always hoped you would come home one day, but she told me once that her love for you ran so deep that she was willing to let you go just to keep you happy," he told me, and reached across the table to hold my hands. "I know what she meant because I felt that way, too."

I felt my blood racing through my veins the second his skin touched mine. From the look on his face and the way he nervously licked his lips, I knew he felt it, too. I quickly pulled my hands away from his and brushed my hair out of my face. My breathing was quick and uneven, and I stood up to avoid having to look at him any longer.

"I'm sorry," he said. "I didn't mean to."

"No, it's okay. This is all just too much for me. Everything from the past seven years is all falling apart in my lap, and I don't know how to handle it."

"I don't remember much about when my dad passed away, but I know I don't remember my mom *handling* anything," Caleb said and stood so he was right in front of me again. "She was a mess. Sure, she was strong for me, but she leaned on Becky and your mom a lot. There were times where Dooley would come and pick me up just so I was taken care of. Some days I would wake up and she would still be on my dad's recliner crying from the night before. Not once did my opinion of her change. Grief is hard and we all handle it differently. Some choose to let it consume them, and others use it as fuel to become the best possible version of themselves. Don't let her death do anything other than keep you living your dreams. She would want you to keep moving forward."

I stood there and cried while he comforted me. It felt so wrong to be in the arms of another woman's man, but it felt right that it was his arms I was in.

"Caleb?"

"Yeah?"

"I'm so sorry about how things ended," I said.

"Leah, that's water under the bridge. It's been so long now that it's not even important. Right now is about you and your mom," Caleb said as he stroked the side of my face. I should have moved away but I relished in his closeness.

"Please. I have to get this out. I shouldn't have left the way I did and I'm sorry. I wanted so much to get out of here and become something bigger, and I didn't really care who I hurt in the process. I never meant for it to end that way. I think a part of me thought I could control the situation and force you to come with me. But you didn't budge and I don't blame you," I admitted.

"I need to come clean about something. The first few months that you were gone were the hardest for me. I was at community college and I was doing well, but it was the only thing I was doing. If I wasn't in class or doing homework, I was helping your dad at the store or grading papers for your mom. I barely even spent time with my own mother for fear I would break down. About a year after you left, your mom convinced me I could either get over it or do something about my pain, and I hopped on the train and went to New York," he told me.

My heart raced and I felt like I was going to vomit. What the hell was happening? Caleb took a deep breath and sat down cross-legged in the middle of the kitchen floor. He patted the space in front of him in hopes I would sit down with him. I remained standing.

"Leah, I applied to NYU and was set to transfer there. I wanted to surprise you. I even had room and board and a job to start," Caleb said.

"What?" I asked, shaking my head slightly. "I don't understand."

"When I got to the campus, I walked around for a while before I was supposed to go to admissions and collect all my information. It was warm out that day, so I grabbed a bottle of water and sat down on one of the benches. I was so nervous you wouldn't want me to be there. Anyway, just when I was gathering up my bags, I saw you walking out of the admissions office, arm in arm with another guy. You looked so happy with him, and I couldn't bear the thought of losing you a second time. So, I turned around, threw my papers in the trash, and got right back on the train to come home," he admitted.

I sat with him, quietly trying to figure out who he saw me with. I was almost always with Sara or alone. But then it hit me.

"Caleb, I never dated anyone until I was out of college," I told him. "The guy you saw me with was Josiah. I was a volunteer with a program that helped students with disabilities for a semester, and he was one of the people I worked with."

"Are you kidding me?" he asked in disbelief.

"No, I'm serious. I knew I wanted to do something that would help the world somehow, and when my friend Sara told me about this program, I signed up immediately," I said.

"Shit. So it looks like we both fucked up then," he said and laughed.

"And it's too late now," I said.

"What do you mean? I'm here, aren't I?"

"Caleb," I said and went back to my seat at the kitchen table. "You're engaged. I met Brittany. Lovely, by the way." I hope he couldn't see me rolling my eyes.

"That doesn't mean we can't be friends," he offered.

"Friends? Caleb, I'm sorry but that's just not possible for me. I don't mean to sound immature, but that's not something I can do."

"Why not? We have so much history, Leah. We've moved on, but that doesn't mean we can't been in each other's lives."

"I made a mistake, but you were always it for me. I wasn't important enough for you to follow through on. You swore you would never leave Grace Valley, but you did. And you're marrying someone else," I exclaimed.

"What the hell, Leah?" he asked, confusion streaked across his face.

Things had suddenly taken a turn for the worse. I told myself not to do it. I couldn't lose my shit on this man, but I knew it was coming.

"How could you do this to me?" I screamed at him, my knuckles white as I clutched onto my coffee mug so tightly I was afraid it was going to shatter in my hands.

"Me? *You* did this, Leah. You left me, remember?" Caleb retaliated. "You were the one who just had to go all fancy and couldn't bear the thought of staying behind to see where life took us. It's not my fault you felt the need to go to the city."

"I went to college, Caleb. College! I didn't go off to some southern state and marry some chick on a whim!" I spit the words in his face like venom. "And I asked you to come with me. I wanted to stay together and you didn't. You were too stubborn and thickheaded for that. It was all or nothing for you."

"We're not married, Leah. We're engaged. And it could have been you if you stayed. So cut the melodramatic bullshit."

"It could have been me?!" I shouted back. "We were seventeen years old! Who gets married at seventeen? You begged me not to go because you would never leave Grace Valley and then less than a year later, you move to Tennessee, go to college, graduate, and get engaged! How do you expect me to act?"

"Get the hell out of here with that crap, Leah! You left," Caleb yelled back at me. He didn't seem the least bit concerned with hurting my feelings. "You honestly thought I was going to wither away all alone for the rest of my life in hopes that maybe someday you'd return and realize what you left behind? I'm sorry, but life had other plans for me, and if you can't handle that, I don't know what to tell you."

"It's not that I can't handle it, Caleb," I said. "It's just a lot to take in and it hurts. You don't owe me anything. I'm sorry, I know I shouldn't have said anything. You can go."

I felt as though I had been transported back to our last summer together, and I turned and walked away from him and into the mudroom. I closed the door behind me and jumped up onto the small chest freezer. Nothing could keep my tears from falling. I kept staring at the checkered tile floor until I heard the front door gently close. He was gone again. Forever this time. Somehow, this pain hurt more than our actual breakup had all those years prior.

What a mess I'd made. Maybe I should have just stayed in the city.

20

I COULDN'T BRING MYSELF TO GET UP RIGHT AWAY, SO I STAYED IN the mudroom with Gnocchi.

"Sorry you had to see that, little man," I said, leaning down to pet Gnocchi's head. "I'm glad you're still here with me."

I couldn't stop thinking about Caleb and Brittany. I'd never be the type to break up a relationship, but that didn't stop me from wishing they would call off the wedding. But it didn't matter. I was going back to the city in a few days, and my life would resume as normal. It was time to stop moping. I was stronger than that.

I hopped off the freezer and scooped Gnocchi up. The mudroom was heated, but the spoiled little cat that he was deserved to be curled up on a pillow by the fireplace. Once he was settled and cozy, I got my mother's sweater to put on. After my conversation with Caleb and hearing about how much she had missed me, I needed to feel connected to her. I sat down at the kitchen table and stared at the box, rubbing my eyes until all of my mascara had transferred to my fingertips.

I wondered what could have possibly been in there. I wasn't sure if I should open it or wait for my dad to come home. Whatever it was could have been his. Or it could have been nothing at all and I was making it out to be something, like I always did for absolutely no reason.

The box was beautiful. I knew my mom had a similar one that held onto all of the cards she had received over the years from her birthday, Mother's Day, Christmas, etc.

This one looked like it was designed specifically for me. It was covered with vintage stamps from all across the globe. Everywhere I had mentioned I'd wanted to travel and then some. In bold newspaper block on the front, it said, "Wherever you go, go with all your heart." I smoothed my hands over the top of the box for a few minutes while I looked at all of the stamps and wondered what was inside.

When I finally mustered up enough courage to open the box, I saw a stack of envelopes, each with a different date. I moved them around to see what was underneath, and I saw a little package of Mrs. Kratz's sugar cookies, which were my absolute favorite, and a small clay heart. I picked up the heart and twirled it around in my fingers. There were two small hearts and a dotted line in between them. NYC was written in small letters at the heart on the left and CT was next to the small heart on the right.

I slammed the lid closed and started to pace around the kitchen. I was so confused as to what all of this was, but I was too afraid to open it back up. Instead of continuing to explore the box, I did what I always did when I was under stress. I made a giant pot of coffee and started to think about what to cook for dinner even though Tammy sent a full meal for us. Coffee and cooking were two of my top three stress relievers, reading being the third. No way could I concentrate on a book right now. I needed food.

But what could I make that didn't remind me of my mom?

I grabbed one of the old cookbooks my mom kept in the cabinet above the fridge and started to flip through the pages. Of course, this wouldn't keep my mind off my mom or Caleb, but at least it would fill my belly, and that's what I needed in order to keep going. Before I knew it, I had reached the end of the cookbook and had not a single recipe in mind. I put the book back and opened the fridge, hoping for some inspiration. I decided on a pesto and tomato grilled cheese. At least I could whip up a quick batch of pesto from scratch, which would make me feel accomplished, and I'd still have room for dinner from Tammy.

The front door slammed shut, which told me that either Caleb had come back to sweep me off my feet or my dad was home. When I heard the loud thud of work boots hit the mudroom floor, I knew it was the latter.

"Hey, Dad," I called out to him. "Are you hungry? I made grilled cheese sandwiches."

"That sounds great, pumpkin. I'd love one. There's some tomato soup in the fridge if you want to warm that up, too. I made it last night after you went to bed. I couldn't get my mind to stop racing so, you know, I cooked but didn't eat!" he said and laughed.

The two of us had so much in common, and it was nice to be able to share this level of grief with each other so we didn't fall apart. I looked up to my father in so many ways, but his absolute strength in situations like the loss of his wife was admirable.

"Dad?" I asked.

"Yeah?" he answered and walked to the cabinet to get the dishes.

"Did you know about this box that Mom had with her in the car?"

He stopped mid-walk to the kitchen table and looked at me. I couldn't read his expression, but I knew he didn't want to talk about it. He would because I was his whole world, but he definitely didn't want to. I felt bad for asking and continuing to bring my mother up, but I was afraid to look deeper into the box on my own. God only knew what I might discover.

"Leah, your mother and I never kept anything from each other. Ever. Even when we were upset with one another for something, we were always honest and open. Relationships without trust and understanding will never amount to anything. You know that. So, yes, I knew about the box. Have you opened it yet?" His tone was full of annoyance, and I knew I was pushing when I should leave him be.

"Yes. I closed it after I saw the clay heart, though. I still can't believe she was taking up pottery as a hobby," I said as I plated the food for us to eat.

"Maybe after you've eaten, you'll want to take another look. It's okay to be afraid of what you might find, but don't wait too long. You don't want to lose sight of what's important," he advised me.

What was he trying to say? He was being so cryptic.

"Yeah, maybe you're right. How was your day?" I asked, changing the subject.

"It was all right. I was able to get the cookie order set up, and Mr. Kratz will deliver them before we leave for the church. I went over to Dooley's for a bit after lunch to help him out with some stuff in the barn. He told me he saw you at Tammy's."

"Yeah, he's not the only one I saw," I said with a disgusted look smeared across my face.

"Uh-oh. Do I even want to know?" he asked.

"I was having a nice cup of tea with Tammy. We were reminiscing about old times and catching up in general, and Caleb's fiancée came in to pick up lunch. It was fine until I told her my name and she freaked out. I mean, she was *not* happy. I saw Tammy gloating on the inside. What the hell does Caleb see in her?"

"Pumpkin, you need to use this trip home as a cleansing period because you have way too much in that heart and mind of yours. If you're feeling this way, you owe it to yourself to find closure," he told me in that 'I'm your father, so I'm always right' sort of way.

"Dad, what am I supposed to do? Go up to him and say, 'Hey, Buddy, I'm still in love with you! You shouldn't marry Brittany because I'm your soulmate, and I never should have left you all those years ago?' I'm not a homewrecker," I said.

There was a glisten in his eyes as he listened to me finally admit what had happened was my fault. I knew he didn't like to see me in pain, but in order to move forward, I had to come to terms with my mistakes. I didn't want to hear it, even though he was right.

"Well, if you say it like that, then yes, you'll look like a home-wrecker," he stated.

"So then you see my dilemma?"

"There is no dilemma but there are poor conversation skills, and that's what's happening here. Just be honest with him without involving anyone but the two of you. Listen, Leah, I've known Caleb since the day he was born. He was a good kid and is an even better man. He deserves to have closure just as much as you do. If you don't feel comfortable telling him how you feel in person, you can always write him a letter," he suggested. "Just be aware that you may not get the response you're hoping for."

"Yeah, I guess. I don't know what to say. I didn't expect to have any of these feelings. I had pushed them aside for so long and they hadn't crept back in until last week. It's almost as if the universe knew what was going to happen and forced this all on me at once."

"Dramatic, but plausible," he teased me.

I smirked at him then got up to clear the table. "Do you mind doing the dishes tonight? I want to open the box alone in my room."

"I thought you'd never ask," Dad said, hugging me tight. I'd never outgrow the feeling of being his baby girl.

Once I was upstairs in my room, I pulled out the sweater I

had tucked underneath my pillow. When I was a little girl, I would hide things under there that I wanted close to me but didn't want anyone to know about. My parents always knew but they hadn't told me until I was much older. They said that they felt it was important for me to have some things all to myself. I stripped out of the sweatshirt I was wearing and put on my mother's sweater. I sat cross-legged on my bed and pulled the box in front of me. I could do this. I had already been through the worst. Dad was right. Closure was necessary and this was my closure with my mom.

I opened the box a second time, and this time, I smiled. I was genuinely interested in seeing what those envelopes held and what else was in the box. I pulled out the envelopes and sat them next to me on the bed. I rifled through the rest of the box while I snacked on the cookies from Mrs. Kratz. *Wouldn't want those to get stale.* Underneath the letters and pottery were loose pictures and what appeared to be tickets and other keepsakes.

Each picture had a date on the back, and when I turned them over, I saw that my mother was at every single one of my events. She had managed to take a selfie with my dad everywhere I had a function. And I was always in the background somewhere. This must have been her way of celebrating with me.

There was a ticket to my graduation from NYU, every train ticket stub from the trips that she had secretly taken to the city with my dad, and even a ticket to the ceremony where I was awarded for being a part of the program for the disabled students. I tried to maintain my composure and reached over to pick up the stack of envelopes. I gently pulled the string and opened them one by one. Some of them were birthday cards from over the years and some were letters that my mom had written to me.

I rubbed the top of one of the letters which was in a different envelope than the rest. I noticed it was dated from the night before the accident and that there were some smudge marks, which I assumed were my mom's tears that had met the ink. My heart raced as I smoothed out the letter and started to read through teary eyes.

My Dearest Leah,

There are not enough words in the English language to describe the level of pain I feel while missing you. You are my miracle, my absolute joy, and my greatest accomplishment. I want you to know how much I love you. I am writing you this letter in the event you refuse to see me because I need you to hear some things.

First, the way we left things when you went off to college was terrible, and I blame myself for that. When I left Italy, my mother was so angry with me. I no longer fit into the picture she had created for her perfect family, and she didn't know what to do. She didn't understand that I wanted to create a life for myself. I fear you may think I was doing the same to you, but I was just so afraid I wouldn't be able to protect you if you moved away. I quickly learned you were far more intuitive than I was at your age, and you would be just fine.

Second, I accompanied your father on almost all of his trips to see you. I chose to keep in the shadows and watch you accept all of your awards for fear that my presence would ruin your day. I regret not telling you this sooner.

Third, I am so unbelievably proud of the woman you have become. You continue to amaze me daily, and I will continue to shower you with my love from afar if you choose to still keep this distance between us. Happiness and safety are what parents wish the most for their children, and I can see you've excelled at providing yourself with both.

Lastly, I have reconnected with your grandparents, and I want you to have their contact information if you so desire. I think it's important for you to know them, and I hope you do reach out.

Leah, I love you more than I have ever loved anything on this planet. I love you so much that I am opening my arms and letting you go to continue to live your life. I will be here if and when you are ready to return, but I won't push you. You are the pot of gold at the end of every rainbow, my dear. Don't you ever forget that.

Loving you always, Mom

I SAT ON MY BED, frozen. I didn't cry. I didn't breathe. I didn't move. I was numb from the inside out. I was the definition of the worst human being to ever roam the Earth.

I didn't deserve you, Mom. And you deserved so much better than what I gave you.

21

I RUBBED MY EYES AND LOOKED AT THE CLOCK. SIX FORTY-TWO a.m. How long had I slept? I didn't even remember putting my pajamas on or brushing my teeth last night. I looked over at the mess littering my desk and remembered trying to write the eulogy. After I had cleaned up the letters and gifts in the box, I brought it over to my desk and tried to pen the most thoughtful and personal letter to my mother. It was the least I could do after the shit I pulled over the past seven years.

I groaned, rolled over, and covered myself back up with the comforter. I couldn't bear the thought of getting up just yet, and I knew I had time before my dad would call me down for breakfast. Well, if he hadn't gone to the grocery store, that was. Who knew how he felt that morning. After an hour of tossing and turning, I got up and got myself ready for the day. I made my way downstairs and noticed the eerie silence of the house. There was usually some sort of noise, but today, nothing.

I looked for a note from my dad or the paper that would be half-opened on the kitchen table if he had brought it in, which he usually did. The house looked barely lived in and I was confused. Then I noticed that my dad's boots and jacket were missing from the mudroom, and I peeked outside to see if he was out there. I gasped when I saw him sitting on the railing of the porch talking to…Josh. *What the hell?* I quickly grabbed my coat and boots and threw them on before I went outside to see them.

"Josh? What are you doing here?" I spat out in the most accusatory tone I could produce.

"Hi, Leah. I'm sorry to surprise you like this, but you weren't answering my calls or texts," he answered, his tone completely differed from mine.

"So you took it upon yourself to just come to my house unannounced?" I yelled.

"Now, Leah, you mind your manners and hear this man out. He traveled a long way to be here for you," my dad said as he glared at me. "I'll be inside putting on a pot of coffee if you need me."

He rubbed Josh's shoulder reassuringly and that made me cringe. *Whose side are you on, Dad?* He closed the door and I turned back to face Josh.

"Well, you are the last face I thought I would see in Grace Valley, and I have seen a lot of those this week already. What are you really doing here, Josh?"

"I tried to call you to apologize. Multiple times. The calls were always sent to voicemail. After a few days, I just stopped calling altogether. I wasn't sure if you blocked me or not, and I wasn't about to make myself look even more like a fool," he told me, his eyes fixated on the ground instead of on me.

"I would never block you, Josh. I was just angry and emotional, and I didn't want to talk to you. To anyone, really," I explained. "But why would you have even continued to call? I thought I made it perfectly clear where I stood with this relationship."

"Because you were right. We're not meant for each other," Josh admitted. "And I really just wanted to be there for you while you're going through everything. As a friend."

"Really?" I responded, doubt flying out of my mouth.

"Yes, Leah. Really. I think we both know that the only reason we were able to last as long as we did was because we had a firm base of friendship under us. I was angry you didn't want to confide in me about your mom, but I understand why and I'm truly sorry."

"I appreciate that, but for future reference, Josh, when someone is going through something, you don't get to be jealous and tell them how they should have handled their grief. I understand it was a tough position for you to be in, not in control and all," I said calmly, "but it was my mother who passed away. Someone who I hadn't spoken to in years. And you came in guns blazing trying to make me feel worse than I already had."

"I know, babe—I mean, Leah," he started. "Sorry, old habit. That's why I came here today, though. I really do just want to be there for you."

"Josh, I didn't ask Sara to come to Grace Valley with me because this was something I needed to do alone." I explained."Well, I thought I needed to do this alone. It is nice that you're here."

"Your dad filled me in on everything. Don't be upset with him. I think he was trying to make it easier on you and take away some of the guilt he thinks you've been carrying this week. I wish you would have opened up and told me more about your family and the life you left behind, but I truly get why you didn't."

"Thank you, Josh." I looked him right in his eyes to let him know I meant it. "Now, let's get you inside and out of this cold! It's freezing. Did you walk here?"

"Yeah, but I'm used to that. You're worth it."

"Josh, you just said—" I began before he cut me off.

"Geez, Leah. Have some confidence in me! Not everything needs to have an underlying meaning."

"You're right. Old habits," I teased him back. "Coffee? My dad grinds his own blend for Christmas and it's amazing."

"Oh, absolutely." He smiled at me.

Josh followed me into the cozy farmhouse and dropped his boots and coat off in the mudroom. Dad had already carried his luggage up to the guest room. He'd always said that no friend of the Abernathy family should stay in the bed and breakfast in town; they should stay with us.

I reached up and grabbed two mugs from the cabinet and started to pour the coffee my dad made for us while we chatted outside. The smell of the nutmeg and ginger traveled from the mugs to our nostrils, and we both inhaled deeply before taking a big gulp at the exact same time. We laughed and followed my dad into the den.

"Oh, wow. This is amazing, Mr. Abernathy," Josh said as he took a seat next to my dad.

"Call me Paul. And thank you. Leah created this blend accidentally when she was around nine years old and dumped random spices into the French press. It took Lucia two weeks to figure out what was in it until, one day, Leah came into the kitchen and handed her the bottle of spices she had used. We laughed for hours. What other nine-year-old kid creates the world's best holiday coffee blend?" He laughed as he remembered the sweet moment. "My Leah, that's who."

"You never told me that story, Dad," I said as I sat across from him on the floor, my back soaking in the heat from the fire. "I don't even remember that."

"Some things are better left as memories, pumpkin."

We spent hours in the den chatting and drinking multiple pots of coffee in front of the fire. My dad told us stories of when he first met my mom, I told Josh about my childhood, and Josh told us about his homelife. It was nice sharing and learning and being able to all love our lives despite the differences.

Before we knew it, it was lunch time and we were all starving. My dad suggested we head into town and grab a bite to eat at Tammy's Diner; show Josh what a real small-town meal was like.

Internally, I was against it, afraid we might run into Brittany again. Or worse, Caleb. I didn't think I could handle either of them at that moment. We collected our jackets and boots and set off down the snowy path that led to the main street in town.

"Wow!" Josh exclaimed, taking in the sight around him.

The main strip of town was lit up and decorated for Christmas. There were wreaths wrapped in twinkly lights set on each street lamp, a large red bow hanging from each one. Every storefront was decorated with a different theme, and it almost looked like Christmas had exploded in the middle of the road. At the center of the town green, we could see little kids ice skating on a makeshift rink and a tall Christmas tree right in the center.

"Yeah," I said and grabbed onto his arm. "Welcome to Grace Valley!"

"Is this how it looks every year? It's somehow more amazing than Christmas in the city." Josh stood and stared at the small-town life bustling around him.

"Yup! There's a huge Christmas Festival every year and we have contests for the best sugar cookies, gingerbread houses, decorated storefronts, and even the ugliest Christmas sweater. My mom actually created that one when she wore what she thought was the most beautiful Christmas sweater and her best friends teased her. And every year since then, the sweaters have had their own contest," I told him.

"That sounds amazing. And so much fun."

"Oh, that's not all," I said. "There's a snowman building contest, stocking decorating, finding Rudolf's nose—that one's for the kids—hot chocolate making contest, and so much more. We really go all out. And the proceeds from everything goes to the children's hospital in Hartford. My mom's idea."

Josh smiled and snickered.

"What?" I asked him.

"Nothing. I just thought that I knew everything about you, and I actually barely know anything. It all makes sense now that

I'm able to put it all together. But if you had asked me if I saw you partaking in any of this, I would have bet my life that you wouldn't have."

"Well, welcome to the good life, my friend. This is the best place you could be." I opened the door to Tammy's Diner and motioned for him to follow me.

"Hey, Dale," my dad said to the guy behind the counter. "We'll seat ourselves today, thanks. Is Tammy here?"

"Hey, Paul. No, she's off today. Out doing something with Caleb. I'm not sure if she'll stop in or not," Dale told him.

My dad nodded and grabbed three menus. He sat alone, across from me and Josh. It was weird sharing the same side of the booth with him, but it was nice for me to be looking at my dad instead of Josh. As he handed us our menus, I noticed him glance outside and mutter, "Hmm, I thought he was with Tammy," under his breath.

"Did you say something, Dad?" I asked.

I followed his gaze to see Caleb standing across the street, looking directly into the window at me. As soon as our eyes connected, he took off.

Josh interrupted our secret chat. "So, what's good here?"

"Everything," we answered simultaneously.

Ten minutes later, the table was covered with pancakes, waffles, bacon, sausage, and eggs. We devoured our food as if it were the last time we would be eating. I laughed inwardly at the site of Josh going to town on his meal. I'd never seen him eat like that. He wiped his mouth and placed his napkin back onto his lap.

"That," he said, "was amazing."

"Tammy is the best. And even when she isn't back there cooking, she hires the best line cooks out there," my dad told him. "When we were younger, we used to have game night at her house. Brad, her husband, would make the weirdest drinks imaginable, and she would always manage to always make a delicious snack to complement his concoctions. Man, I miss those days."

"Why don't you have game night anymore?" Josh asked innocently.

"Brad unexpectedly passed away when Leah and Caleb were little. We haven't had a game night since," Paul replied shortly.

"I'm sorry," Josh said, looking at his hands. "I didn't know. Who's Caleb?"

"No worries. They were good times. I just miss him, that's all," he smiled softly.

"Oh, Caleb is Tammy and Brad's son. We played together a lot when we were younger," I said before my dad could answer him. I never told Josh about Caleb specifically, just that I had a boyfriend in high school. I did not need to rehash that again.

"So, Josh, how long are you planning on staying in town? Leah tells me you're a busy lawyer, so I imagine you must have to run out of here soon," Dad said, picking up on my interjection.

"I am busy, indeed. Lucky for me, I just made partner and negotiated some time off. I won't need to return to the office until after the new year. However, that means I probably won't see the light of day for a while," he chuckled.

"Partner? Congratulations, Josh! Why didn't you tell me?" I asked. "Oh, wait. Never mind."

"No, it's okay. I get it. I just found out a couple of days ago, and I wanted to give you your time. This trip is about you, not me," Josh said, making me blush.

My dad smiled at me, and I knew he was thinking about how cute it was that his little girl was paying so much attention to our new guest. I shot him a quick *not happening* glance to let him know it wasn't romantic excitement.

"I always knew you were destined for great things, Josh. All that hard work, those long nights and early mornings, the terrible office coffee." I laughed.

"Well, if this is the definition of a great friendship then sign me up," my dad teased us. It made me a tad uncomfortable, but what else was new. "Josh, I'm happy that my baby girl has a friend like you in her corner. I hope you'll continue to keep an eye on her in that big city."

"Of course, Mr. Aber—uh, Paul."

I suddenly wished my mom could have met him. He might not have been the one, but he was a good man. My mom would have liked him.

22

HOW WAS IT THE MORNING OF THE FUNERAL ALREADY? HOW WAS I about to go bury my mother? How could I stand up in front of all those people and give a speech about the woman I had unintentionally gotten killed?

I spent the majority of the morning sulking in my childhood bedroom, a multitude of scenarios playing over and over in my mind. Innumerable what-ifs clouded my already foggy brain. Somehow, I was able to do my hair and makeup and look somewhat decent, but I couldn't bring myself to get dressed. Everything I had packed and everything that remained in my closet didn't seem good enough for my mom or that day.

"Pumpkin? You okay in there?" came from the other side of my door. "We need to leave in less than an hour, and you still haven't been downstairs for breakfast or coffee."

"You can come in, Dad. I'm just sitting in here thinking," I called back to him from my bed. My long hair cascaded in waves down my back, just like my mother always wore hers, and I didn't know if he would be happy or sad at the sight. When he opened the door, his eyes glistened with a combination of happy and sad tears.

"Oh, Leah. You look just like her. A spitting image," he said. "Is that your dress?"

I looked at the black A-Line dress and back up at my father. I burst into tears and feverishly blotted at my eyes to not mess up the mascara I just applied.

"It was supposed to be but it's not right. I just can't find anything that's right for this. For her. She needs the best and I just don't have it," I cried.

"I'll be right back," he said and walked out of my room.

A few minutes later, my dad's feet thumped up the back stairs. He stopped and took a deep breath before he walked back into my room. He was holding a beautiful, black silk dress with a matching shawl.

"Leah, this is the dress your mother wore to Brad's funeral. She told me after his mass that she wanted to be buried in it, but I convinced her it was far too beautiful to remain underground. I told her she should save it for you to wear someday for a job interview or a holiday party," he told me, holding the dress out for me to take.

I looked at him, puzzled, not understanding how a dress that someone wore to a funeral would ever be appropriate for a holiday party, but then he handed me the shawl and I lightly fingered the pattern. At first glance, I only saw a little silver shimmer, but when I looked closer, I saw that the silver strands of string were actually intricate snowflakes. Leave it to Mom to wear a snowflake shawl to a spring funeral. I giggled and my dad smiled.

"You should wear this. She would be honored and it just might help you feel closer to her. You have her pearls still?" he asked.

"I do."

"Well then. There you go. I'll leave you to it and see you in the kitchen? You don't need to eat a lot, but you should really put a little something in your stomach before we go. Josh is in the den with Gnocchi. It's quite the sight to see."

I smiled and closed the door after my dad went back downstairs. I held the dress in front of me and smoothed it out, feeling the delicate touches of lace that scattered the fabric. *You can do this. It's just a dress.* I hung my bathrobe on the back of the door and stepped into the dress, careful not to snag the fabric. As soon as I zipped the back, I felt my mother's presence. In a matter of seconds, I felt like my old self again, and I knew things were going to be okay. I put her pearl earrings on and looked into the mirror.

Wow, Mom. I really do look like you.

I grabbed the eulogy from my desk before I picked up the shawl and my shoes and went downstairs to the kitchen. I popped a mini blueberry muffin into my mouth, grabbed a few more, and went to the den to sit with Josh and Gnocchi.

"Hey, guys," I said as I sat down next to Josh on the loveseat.

Josh looked up at me and scooted over to give me some room. Gnocchi reluctantly hopped off and plopped himself in front of the fire.

"Good morning," Josh said. "Are you ready to do this?"

"Not even a single bit, but I'll do it," I replied.

The back door opened and in walked Tammy, Becky, and several members of both their staffs. Vases upon vases of flowers were placed throughout the lower level of the farmhouse. Trays of food were brought in and put in the oven or the fridge. I stood up to help but Becky shooed me away.

"No way, little one," Becky said. "You sit and enjoy some quiet time over there. We'll take it from here."

I sunk back into the loveseat and smiled. *Little one.* I hadn't heard that in years. A sense of calm and warmth swept over me, and I felt at ease once again. Josh must have picked up on it because he slid closer to me and put his arm around my shoulders.

"You're gonna do great," he said, beads of sweat appearing on his upper lip. "She would be so proud of you."

"Just friends, Josh?" I asked and swatted his arm away.

A deep, throaty laugh came out of him and caused the staff in the kitchen to stop and stare.

"Yes, Leah. Geez."

Dad walked into the room holding his tie out. "Who wants to tie this for me?" he asked, his shoulders shrugged in defeat.

"Oh, Daddy. Will you ever learn to tie that thing?"

"Probably not. Once more for old times' sake?"

"Come here," I directed him. "I hope you don't need to wear a tie anywhere once I go back to the city. It's an awfully long train ride for me to come and help you with it."

"Ha ha, very funny. You know I hate these things anyway. I'll take a nice polo shirt over a tie any day."

I patted my father's chest and rested my palms on his shoulders. *You wear your pain so well, Dad. No one would ever know what you're about to do.*

"All right, goofball. Let's get this show on the road," I said. "Is there anything we need to get done before we leave?"

"No," Tammy shouted from the kitchen. "There most certainly is not."

We all laughed. Tammy and Becky were machines and the house was almost all set up for the luncheon. I wonder how bad it would be if I just skipped this thing and stayed home and ate everything.

"Is it bad that I could eat all of this myself?" Josh whispered to me.

My head whipped toward him. "I was just thinking the same thing."

The way Josh smiled at me led me to believe that he might not have been completely honest with me about this whole *friends* thing. But I had told him how I felt, so at least he was aware.

Luckily for everyone, my dad walked into the room right in the middle of the awkwardness.

"All right, looks like it's time to go. We need to meet with Father James before the service begins," he told us through tired eyes. "Leah, you have everything you need?"

"I do, Dad," I said and grabbed ahold of his arm. "Ready when you are."

"Oh, pumpkin. I will never be ready." He tried to smile but tears filled his eyes.

I wasn't happy to see him so sad, but I was glad he was finally able to let his guard down and allow his emotions to come through. Tammy and Becky both stopped and hugged us tight.

Josh got everyone's coats and shoes and told Becky to call his cell phone if they needed anything, promising he would come right back to help. Romantic gesture or not, I was so glad he was here.

THE THREE OF us stood outside of the small church and stared at the entryway doors. The cold air whipped our faces, but they remained as frozen as the temperature. Josh didn't understand why, I'm sure, but he stood with us, nonetheless. My mom loved the winter season most of all and always said that the smell of snow alone could warm the coldest days. I inhaled the scent of the impending snow and let go of my father's hand.

"I'm ready to go in now," I declared and walked up the stairs. "You coming?"

I was anything but fearless, but I knew if I didn't go in at that very moment, I would run as fast as I could in the opposite direction and never look back. Rows and rows of poinsettias greeted us. Josh hung around the back of the church while my dad and I slowly made our way down the aisle to where the priest was standing.

"Paul. Leah. Let me offer my deepest sympathies," Father James said as he held out his hands to us. "Lucia was a valued member of this church and our community, and she will be terribly missed."

"Thank you. I appreciate that," my dad said solemnly. "May I see her before services start? I'd like to be the first to say goodbye."

"Of course. Follow me," Father James said, leading the way. "I'll give you a few minutes. If you need me, I'll be right over there."

I turned my head to follow where Father James was pointing. He sat down carefully next to the small Christmas display, and it reminded me of my childhood singing here in the choir. I don't know how they hadn't kicked me out. I suck at singing.

I looked back over to my father kneeling in front of the casket. His elbows rested on the edge, and his hands were clasped together, pressed against his forehead.

"My sweetheart. I'm not sure how I'm going to go on without you. I miss you so much," he whispered to my mom. "Our girl is back home. I don't know for how much longer but she's here. She came back for you. She's a wreck about what happened. Please help her heal."

My hands rushed to my mouth as I tried to cover my sobs, listening to my father say his final goodbyes to my mom. I quickly took a pencil from the pew and scribbled more notes onto my already polished eulogy. If I was going to give the damn speech, then I was gonna do it right. I let my father finish and went to sit down, waiting for the services to start.

I'll save my goodbye for last, Mom.

Friends and relatives started to gather in the church, and my dad rushed to sit next to me. He put his arm around me and pulled me close. It was comforting and I felt safe in his arms. It wasn't where I wanted to be, but for the first time in over seven years, I was with both of my parents at the same time and we all knew it. I kept my eyes focused on my mother's beautiful face as she laid peacefully in her casket.

"I like that your mother knew how she wanted to have this. Brief, unconventional, and full of love; much like her life," my dad said.

Music began playing as the guests took their seats. Father James stood up to begin the service, and a fast silence spread across the room. He briefly spoke of his relationship with my mom and our family and thanked us for being a part of the church for all of these years. I smiled remembering my childhood and my mother's love of the church and togetherness.

"Tammy Patterson would like to share a short story about Lucia," Father James said, motioning for her to come up to the podium.

Tammy walked confidently to the podium and adjusted the microphone. She winked at me when we made eye contact and took a brief minute to look down at her notes. I was surprised it was her making a speech and not Becky, but I was happy either way. After taking in a deep breath, she began her story.

"Good morning. I met Lucia almost thirty years ago in this very building. Paul had brought her here to meet Father James and to become a member of our parish. I thought he was crazy when he told us he had only met her the week before." Tammy laughed and looked at Paul.

"Little did we all know, he knew what he felt, and she was the one. Anyway, she was standing right over by that window." She pointed to the stained glass that glistened brightly from the way the sun bounced off the snowbank outside. "In her thick accent, she said to me, 'I've never seen windows so beautiful before. And I'm from Italy!' I laughed and she asked if I would take a picture with her to remember the moment by. She always had her camera in her hands, capturing every moment she could. Tonight, when the sun goes down and the stars come out, look for the brightest one. That's Lucia, taking a picture to remember today by. Thank you."

Tammy kissed my mother's hand and gently touched the side of her coffin. "I will forever be here for your girl. I promise you that."

She paused by me and my dad and placed her hand gently on my shoulder while she locked eyes with Paul. He closed his and nodded in silent agreement. I looked up at her, my eyes pleading with her to say this was all a dream.

She leaned down and whispered in my ear, "You will always be the daughter I never had, and I will love you like my own for the rest of my days."

I swallowed deeply and my bottom lip began to quiver. "I love you, too," I replied, barely audible.

"Thank you, Tammy. That was beautiful," Father James said, taking us all out of our moment. "Leah, if you're ready."

This was not a dream.

23

ALL EYES WERE ON ME AS I RELUCTANTLY APPROACHED THE PODIUM to celebrate my mother. I opened my paper and smoothed it out across the stand, looking out at the crowd. Small towns usually meant you recognized every face in the crowd, but there were so many people I had never seen before. I noticed an older couple in the back of the church and wondered if they were my grandparents. I straightened my back and prepared myself for quite possibly the biggest speech I was ever going to make. *I hope I'll make you proud, Mom.*

"Good morning, everyone. Let me just start by thanking all of you for being here today, and for being here for the last twenty-five-plus years for our family. Grace Valley is more than a home, and I thank you all from the bottom of my heart. When my father asked me to give the eulogy today, I must admit I wasn't sure I'd be able to do it. I didn't think I was the right person to honor my mother and that maybe he should be the one to do so. After sleeping on it, I realized if I'm ever blessed enough to have a child, I would want them to honor me. So here I am.

"The relationship between a mother and child is like none other. And for me, the bond between a mother and a daughter is the strongest bond there is. You can go through hell and back and still come out on the other side full of so much love and support for each other. I was recently reminded that no matter what happens, my mother will always be there rooting me on, even from afar. And even when I'm unaware.

"My mother was an extraordinary woman who lived life to the fullest and loved with every fiber of her being. Anyone who met her immediately felt the love radiate off her. She was kind, caring, funny, an amazing cook, and the most positive ray of light I have ever met. She had this way of turning any unfavorable situation into a learning experience that left me with a megawatt smile on my face. Every single time! I remember once in elementary school, there was a going away party I wasn't invited to by someone I had thought was a good friend of mine. I came home and cried to my mother about it, and instead of dwelling on why I wasn't invited, she threw me an ice cream party—in the bathtub! We were covered in ice cream, chocolate sauce, and nuts. When Dad came home and saw us, I thought he was going to fall over from laughing. That will always be one of my favorite memories.

"As most of you know, my mother came to America from Italy almost thirty years ago. You'd never know it by the perfect way she spoke English. She fought for what she believed in and knew her future was here; although, I'm fairly certain she hadn't known exactly what her future entailed when she was that young. My mom came to America to become a teacher. She had big plans to teach in an inner city and help some of those kids get out of the homes and trouble that would inevitably find them. Even though she ended up teaching here instead, she would take me to the city one weekend every month to volunteer and tutor some of those less fortunate students. I think a part of why I wanted to go to NYU for college was because the city had taken up such a large part of my heart from all of those special moments with her.

"Meeting my dad on the tarmac at the airport the second she set foot on American soil changed her entire plan, but she always told me it was the best decision she had ever made. She told me, 'The minute you meet your soulmate, your entire being feels it. You're unable to describe it, but it's a force so strong that no matter what tries to get in the way, you will always be pulled back to each other. Soulmates are magnets and true love is a force that cannot be broken.' I can honestly say I watched my parents' love grow and never waver, and I'm blessed to have learned to fight for what I believe in and work hard to keep my relationships going strong."

I looked up at the crowd and locked eyes with Caleb. I quickly looked around for Brittany but I didn't see her. My heart began to beat at an uncomfortable speed, and I needed to finish my speech before I broke apart.

"Thank you, Mom. Thank you for giving this entire town a happier feel. Thank you for loving Dad so deeply that I know he will be okay after this. And thank you for teaching me what unconditional love is. I promise to spend the rest of my life trying to fill the shoes that you have left for me." I paused and looked over to the casket. "I love you more."

I smiled at the crowd as I made my way over to my mom's casket. "I'll be back to say goodbye," I whispered before heading back to sit with my dad.

"Pumpkin, that was beautiful. She would have been so proud of you," he told me, his eyes now full of tears.

We sat in silence together until Father James was finished with the service. It was beautiful and everything that represented who my mother was. I hoped when my time came, people remembered me the way they remembered my mother. I watched everyone pay their respects then gathered with them at the back of the church to thank them for coming.

Josh played the role of the gentleman suitor and kept his hand securely on the small of my back. I was so emotionally raw that I initially didn't even realize he was doing it. Either that or I just didn't seem to care, but I honestly couldn't tell you which was true in that moment. Every so often, my dad glanced over and saw Josh's protectiveness, and although he never said anything, I knew he trusted my judgement.

I also noticed Caleb standing over by his mother, and I watched as his eyes glanced over to Josh and then to Josh's hand. He was too busy being fixated on Josh to notice I caught on to what he was doing. He leaned into Tammy and whispered something in her ear. I looked over at Josh hoping to get him to stop touching me without actually brushing him off in the middle of the church. When I turned back to Caleb, he was gone. Tammy was the last one to pay her respects, and I was glad she had waited until everyone else had left.

"Caleb and Brittany left to go tie up some loose ends with her job. They should be at your house later," Tammy said as if she could read my mind. "Becky and I set everything up so you can both enjoy your company and not worry about a thing. I also have staff coming in afterward to wrap up all of the food for you and clean the kitchen. And I don't want to hear a peep about it, Paul Abernathy. Let us do this for you."

"Yes, ma'am," my dad said. "We really appreciate this, Tam. It means a lot."

"Why don't you guys head on over to the house and I'll catch up with you. I'd like to spend a few more minutes here with Mom alone," I told them.

"You sure?" my dad asked. "We can wait for you."

"I'm sure. I could use a little alone time and fresh air. Thank you, though," I said and kissed him on the cheek.

"She's been like this since she was a little girl," I heard my dad say to Josh as they walked out the side door. "A walk in the cold air did something for her and her mother. I, on the other hand, prefer to be warm when I think."

I smiled and walked back down the aisle to the direction of

my mother's casket. Father James hadn't closed it yet, so I knew I had some time with her before he needed to. The actual burial wasn't until the day after, but it would be closed by then and just us. I knelt down and stared at her. She looked so peaceful and beautiful and alive, almost like she was sleeping. I stared hard, hoping to catch a glimpse of her chest rise and fall. But I knew that wasn't possible. I knew I wasn't going to wake up from this nightmare because it was actually our new reality.

"Mom, I don't know how many times I can say I'm sorry before I'll stop feeling guilty for leaving you the way I did. If I knew then what I know now, things would have turned out so differently. I know you wanted me to be happy and I let myself believe it was easier to push you away. But I'm here now. I'm present and I'm home. I promise to come back more often and take care of Dad. And Mom? I am with you always," I said, touching my pearl earrings.

I took an envelope out of my jacket pocket and slipped it into my mother's hands. "I love you so much," I said.

"I didn't think you would still be here," came a voice behind me.

I froze before I slowly turned around.

"Caleb, what are you doing here?" I asked.

"I didn't get to pay my respects before Brittany needed to get something done for work. I wanted to make sure I saw your mom before...you know."

"That was kind of you. Thank you for coming," I replied. I couldn't believe how not awkward this encounter was. "I should get back to the house now."

"Do you want a ride? The car is just outside. Brittany is with me, of course, but you're more than welcome."

"That's all right, but thanks. I think I prefer to walk," I said. There was no way I was getting into a car and going anywhere with her. I wasn't even sure if I would have said yes if he were alone.

"Are you sure? We really don't mind. And it's pretty cold out."

"Yeah, I'm sure. I should get going. My dad and Josh are waiting for me," I said quickly, knowing what Caleb thought about me and Josh but not caring. "Thanks again for coming and for the offer. I'll see you guys at the house."

Once again, I turned around and walked away from him. Leaving uncomfortable situations like this was beginning to happen far too often and that needed to change.

24

"Leah, are you ready? I'm just about done here," my dad called upstairs. I could just picture him taking a big swig of his coffee while looking at his watch.

"Yeah, I'll be right down. Can you put some coffee in a to-go cup for me, please?"

"You got it," he replied. I could hear him talking to Josh. "We won't be gone too long. An hour and a half, tops. Help yourself to anything in the kitchen. There's more coffee in the pantry, and there's more wood right outside in the woodshed if you need to throw another log onto the fire. You shouldn't have to, but just in case."

"Thanks, Paul. I appreciate it. Are you sure you don't want me to come?" Josh asked.

"That's kind of you, Josh, but Lucia made me promise that the burial was only to be me, Leah, and Father James, or whoever the priest was at the time of her passing. She was a stubborn woman, and I don't need her raising hell because I didn't follow her wishes."

"Fair enough, sir."

I bounded down the stairs and grabbed my coffee from my dad. "Thanks, Dad. I'm ready now."

"You look cute, pumpkin," he said. "I'm glad you're wearing her sweater today."

I put my coat on and wrapped my scarf loosely around my neck. I held my coffee tightly between my hands and inhaled the sweet aroma. "I wanted to feel close to her when we let her go."

"Understandable. Shall we?"

"Be back soon, Josh. Text me if you need anything from town," I called out as I shut the door and followed my dad to the cemetery.

"Dad?" I asked after ten minutes of walking silently.

"Yes?"

"This is really the last time we'll see her," I said. "Well, you know what I mean."

"No, pumpkin, it's not. She will forever be all around you, and when you feel like you can't see her anymore, close your eyes and you'll feel her. She is in everything that you are and everything that you do. She never left you when she was on this Earth and she most certainly won't start now."

He held onto my hand and we walked into the cemetery to meet Father James. The sun was beating down, almost blinding me with the reflection off the snow, and it felt surprisingly warm for a December day in New England. It was almost as if my mom were smiling at us and letting us know she was with us.

The minutes ticked by, and as the casket was lowered into the ground and the men began to cover it with dirt, I felt a sense of calm envelop my body. I hugged my dad tight and we watched until my mom's casket was completely underground.

"Thank you for coming home, pumpkin. I know how hard this was for you."

"Oh, Dad. I'm so sorry I made you think I wouldn't want to. I promise to come home much more often."

"I know you will," he said. "Now, let's get back home before we freeze and Josh burns the house down."

"Good idea. My coffee is getting cold, and I want to rest a bit before the festival tonight. Is it bad that I'm looking forward to it? I mean, after the funeral and all?"

"Not at all. Your mother would have wanted you to continue going about your business as normal. You know that. You can't stop living your life because of the guilt you feel for something out of your control," he told me.

"Yeah, I know," I replied. "Josh is pretty excited about it too, and it'll be fun to show him a bit of the town."

"What's up with you two, anyway?" he asked, raising his eyebrows.

"Nothing. It's done. He's here as a friend. And even if he wants more, I made it clear I don't have any romantic feelings toward him anymore. Besides, it wouldn't be fair to be with someone just for the sake of not being alone."

"What about Caleb?" he pried, as he usually did in times like these.

"What about him? He's engaged," I exclaimed, horrified at what my father was insinuating. "And he is definitely over me."

"If you say so."

***

"HEY, JOSH. WE'RE BACK," I called, slamming the door behind me and tossing my snow-covered boots into the mudroom.

"Leah, look," my dad whispered.

Josh was asleep on the couch in the den, snuggled up with Gnocchi. That was a sight to see. I pulled my phone out of my back pocket and quickly snapped a few pictures of the two lovebirds. I texted it to Sara immediately, then I giggled as I showed my dad the pictures.

"What's so funny?" Josh asked groggily, wiping drool from the corner of his mouth.

"Oh, nothing," I answered. "Did you enjoy your nap?"

"It's too cozy in here. How can you get anything done in this house? I've slept more here than I usually do in a whole week in the city."

"Good," my dad said. "Then all of the work I've put into this house has paid off. You should always build a life you don't have to run from and a home you don't need to vacation away from. That's what makes it so special here."

I smiled at my dad and the way he spoke of this house. Not for the first time, I wondered if I could stay. I didn't have to go back to the city right away. Maybe I could convince Cameron to let me do my work remotely and teleconnect for any meetings. It would be nice to spend more time with Dad. I'd have to bring it up to him after the festival.

"Are you still excited about tonight?" I asked Josh, pushing his legs over on the couch so I could sit down.

He lifted himself up onto his elbows and awkwardly got himself into a sitting position. "Definitely. I really want to taste that hot chocolate you were telling me about."

"It's outta this world, son," my dad chimed in. "You're never gonna want to leave Grace Valley after you've tried it."

"Ain't that the truth?" I giggled. "It starts at seven, so we have plenty of time before we need to leave. How about I put a pot of soup on the stove and then we can watch a movie?"

"Sounds good," Josh said. "Paul, your house, your choice."

"Me?" Paul asked. "I choose Home Alone. The first one. We watched that so much when Leah was a kid that we broke the VCR. Thank goodness DVDs came out quickly after."

"Oh my gosh." I laughed out loud, walking into the kitchen to start the soup. "I completely forgot about that! We should make that a new Christmas Eve tradition."

I could easily see into the den from the kitchen, and I watched as my dad smiled, a look of content spreading across his face.

"Does this mean you'll be coming home every Christmas, now?" he asked.

"Absolutely," I said, returning his smile. "I wouldn't miss it for the world."

I guess you made it to the other side, Mom. You've done your job and we're all okay over here.

My dad looked to Josh, who was still standing in the kitchen doorway. "So, Josh, do you have any family holiday traditions?"

"No, we're pretty simple. My parents usually have their decorator come to the house two weeks before Christmas to get everything set up. And then we have Christmas Eve dinner at the club."

"The club?" Dad asked.

"Yes, my parents are members of the Maidstone Club in East Hampton. We've been going there for as long as I can remember."

"Oh," he said. "Well, that sounds fun."

"Yes, it's nice. The food is wonderful."

"Do you have any special family traditions you share on Christmas?" Dad asked.

"We generally wake up and have brunch and then open gifts and carry on with our day as usual. Mom usually does some work for her charity, and Dad is always busy working on something political. You know how it is," Josh said.

"Is the soup almost ready, pumpkin?" my dad asked me.

"Yep, I just need to get it in the mugs. Can you grab some napkins and spoons?" I asked right back. "Hey, Josh, do you mind setting up the TV trays in the den? They're right behind the big chair, against the wall. And throw another log on the fire while you're in there, would you?"

"No prob," Josh called from the den.

We ate our soup in silence with the exception of our own laughter during the movie. I sat on the big couch with my dad while Josh and Gnocchi were on the loveseat. Josh had always hated cats, so it was quite the sight to see the two of them snuggling up so close.

"All right, kids," my dad said at the end of the movie. "It's six-thirty. Do you want to clean up and head to the festival?"

"Yes," Josh answered. "I can't wait to see what this is all about."

We bundled up and walked to the town green.

25

GRACE VALLEY'S TOWN GREEN LOOKED AS IF IT WERE PLUCKED right out of a Hallmark Christmas movie. It was amazing how much more had been added overnight. The stars twinkling in the dark night sky created an almost simulated atmosphere. A sea of red floated up and down the sidewalks as most of the little kids were dressed in their Santa sweatshirts, almost ready for the Children's Christmas Concert to begin in the gazebo.

On the right side of the green, the stations were almost finished being set up. Buckets of props were being carried over to the snowman building station. I could see by the items in one bucket that my dad had donated some of his old shirts. Tables were being brought in for stocking decorating, and I laughed at the thought of the last stocking that I decorated.

"What's got you laughing, Leah?" Josh asked.

"I was just thinking of the festival before I left for college. I entered the stocking decorating contest but instead of decorating a Christmas stocking, I brought an old pair of my mom's stockings and decorated those instead. Everyone thought it was so funny, except for Bill Palmer's mother. She was pissed that she had decorated hers so fancy and 'a bratty little jokester' had beat her," I said, doubling over with laughter.

"Quite the prankster, were you?" he replied. "What did you win?"

"You know, I can't even remember. I do know that I donated it back to the children's hospital, but I can't for the life of me remember what it was."

Station after station made me happy and sad all at the same time. I couldn't stop asking myself why I had ever left. There were familiar faces at every turn, and everyone seemed so happy to have me back. Josh looked around us with wide eyes, as if he were a child noticing the magic of Christmas for the first time. He bent down to pick up a giant fake snowball that had rolled off the gazebo.

"Thanks, mister," a young boy said, as he plucked the snowball out of Josh's hands and ran back up the steps to put it back into place.

"Cute kid," Josh said. "Seeing all this small town has to offer, I feel like I missed so much growing up. I can see why you love it so much."

"Yeah, that and the people," I said, noticing some movement coming from the next station over.

"Hey, Leah," Tammy called, her head popping up from behind the hot cocoa station. She had melted chocolate smeared across her cheek and mini marshmallows stuck in her hair.

"Tammy, what is going on?" I laughed. "You look like you jumped into a vat of chocolate. Not that it would be a bad thing."

"I'm trying to help set up for the hot cocoa contest and I tripped over the basket and... You know what, never mind! How are you, honey? Are you enjoying the festival?"

I nodded over to Josh, who was making his way over to me. "We just got here. My dad is putzing around here somewhere. Are you judging the contest this year?"

"No, I actually joined it. Trying my hand on a new cocoa take.

I'd tell you but then you would know which one was mine." She winked, her eyes lighting up as bright as the night sky.

Josh stood uncomfortably close to me during my conversation with Tammy. His hand quickly met the small of my back just as Caleb and Brittany rounded the corner to the hot cocoa booth.

"Hey, Mom," Caleb said to Tammy and kissed her on the cheek.

"Hi, honey. I was just telling sweet Leah and her friend that I was competing in this year's hot cocoa contest," Tammy said, rubbing Caleb's arm.

Caleb looked over to Leah and Josh and extended a hand out. "Caleb," he said, shaking Josh's hand.

"Nice to meet you, Caleb. I'm Josh, Leah's," he started as I slyly elbowed him in the ribs, "friend from New York."

"Welcome to Grace Valley, Josh. I hope you enjoy your time here in our little town," he replied. "Leah, pleasure."

I smiled uncomfortably and nodded. Was there a hole somewhere I could crawl into? Brittany was staring at me, as usual, and I couldn't stand being there any longer.

Tammy must have seen the pain creeping across my face because she quickly reached out and pulled me closer to her. "Leah, sweetheart, there's something of your mother's I've been holding onto that I think she would want you to have. Do you mind stopping by my house tomorrow morning?"

"Of course," I answered. *Just please make sure Caleb is nowhere to be found.*

Bill Palmer came over from the other side of the tent and smiled at me and Caleb. "Well, isn't this a nice surprise seeing the two of you together again in Grace Valley."

"Hi, Bill. What's up?" Tammy asked.

"We need a third judge for the contest. Marina is out. She had to help the kids get ready for the concert. One of the parents couldn't make it so she offered. Do you know of anyone who would be interested?"

"I could do it," Brittany offered.

Everyone turned and looked at her and an unhidden look of disgust spread across Tammy's face. She quickly recovered and smiled at all of us.

"What about you, Josh?" Tammy asked him instead of responding to Brittany. "Would you be interested? You'll definitely get the full Grace Valley Christmas Festival experience."

"I just said I would do it," Brittany snapped.

"Oh, I know, dear. But I think it would be fun for Josh. And I know how much you try to stay away from sugar."

I don't know how I had any strength left inside of me, but I held my laughter in. I couldn't believe the way Tammy was talking to her son's future wife. It was incredible.

"Okay, so it's settled then," Bill said. "Josh, we'll see you in about forty-five minutes. Thanks a bunch. Leah, Caleb, so nice to see you both again."

"Wonderful to see you, too, Bill," I said.

"Likewise," Caleb chimed in.

"Oh, and Caleb, please do stop by my office before you go back to Tennessee. There's something I would like to pick your brain about," Bill said.

"Will do."

Brittany rolled her eyes and hooked her arm tightly onto Caleb's. If looks could kill, I would drop dead right there on the sidewalk.

"Come on, Caleb," she whined. "I want to get some cookies before they're all gone."

Caleb followed suit, but not before leaning over to kiss his mother on her cheek. "Good luck, Mom. I'll try to head back this way in time for the judging."

"Caleb," Brittany whined again, glaring at Tammy. "I said let's go."

What a bitch. No man could ever keep me from spending time with my father.

Somehow, Brittany's ring seemed to sparkle even more from the reflection off the snow than it had the day she was leaving The Flower Pot. I shivered and Josh put his arm around me, pulling me close to keep me warm. I quickly pulled away and turned to face him, noticing that Caleb was watching as he walked away.

"Josh," I said sternly, as if I were a mother scolding my child. "We talked about this. Just friends, remember?"

Embarrassed, Josh nodded and turned to the street. "Would you want to check out some more stations?" he asked.

"Sure. Tammy, I'll see you in a bit. Good luck!"

As soon as we were out of Tammy's ear range, I let loose. "What the hell was that, Josh?"

"What? You looked cold. I was only trying to keep you warm. You've made it perfectly clear that we're over," he responded quietly.

"Bullshit," I snapped but then calmed down when I saw the kids in the gazebo were staring. "But I appreciate the gesture."

"Anytime, toots," he teased and winked at me. "Why don't you take me to another station so I can get a feel for this Grace Valley lifestyle you all rave about."

I smiled and grabbed his arm. "Okay, but no more tricks."

I took in a deep breath and smiled. My mother would have loved this. I wondered how much of this was her idea in the first place. I nodded to Josh and we made our way through the crowded sidewalk to the snowman building contest. I leaned down and swiftly grabbed a handful of snow and threw it in Josh's face.

"Ah, what the—" he yelled, wiping the snow from his face. "Oh, you are so on!"

Josh grabbed as much snow as his hands could hold and made a beeline for me. He threw the snow at my head just as I ducked, and he thankfully missed me completely.

"Oh, Joshua, when will you learn not to mess with the master?" I gloated and bent down to collect more snow.

As soon as I turned to get up, a snowball hit me square in the back, causing me to pop up in shock. My eyes widened and I charged at him, knocking him to the ground and throwing snow all over his face. We laughed so hard until I couldn't hold my weight anymore, and I collapsed into his arms. We laid there staring at each other. I was comfortable in his arms, but I felt nothing.

CALEB

I DIDN'T MEAN to stare but I couldn't help it. It was heartbreaking to see her with another man, but there was nothing I could do about it. I saw Josh notice me out of the corner of his eye. He leaned closer to Leah and then planted a huge kiss right on her lips. I knew they were together, but it still caused my jaw to drop.

"What's so interesting?" Brittany said, blocking my sightline.

She turned around and saw Josh kissing Leah in the snow and her face dropped, but not for the same reason as mine. She whipped back around and jabbed her finger in my face.

"Is this a joke?" she asked. "As if it's not bad enough that you dragged me to this nothing town to go to your ex-girlfriend's mom's funeral, but now you're watching her kiss her new boyfriend with your fiancée two feet away?"

Brittany's nostrils flared and her lips pursed, and I snapped out of it and grabbed her hand.

"Come with me," I demanded.

I walked down the sidewalk trying my best to be inconspicuous, but Brittany continued to wear her snotty, too-good-for-Grace-Valley expression, and it made it hard not to think that everyone had noticed. We stopped right on the other side of the gazebo and I turned to face her, grabbing both of her hands in mine.

"Britt, I haven't seen her in over seven years. I'm sorry if it looked like anything other than me standing there noticing someone. Leah and I are over. We've been over for quite some time. You know this."

"Well, it sure didn't look that way to me," she snapped back.

"I understand and I'm sorry," I said, kissing her hands. "Can we please forget it and continue with the festival? We'll be back in Tennessee before you know it."

"Fine," she agreed. "But I'm still not happy about this."

Brittany and I followed the path going in the opposite direction of Leah and Josh. When Brittany was busy reapplying her lipstick, I snuck a glance back and saw Josh helping Leah up and wiping the snow off her jacket. They were laughing and looked so in love.

In that moment, I knew I was marrying the wrong girl. I looked down at my feet, not sure what to do.

"Ready," Brittany told me, making a kissy face.

I took her hand and we headed down toward the ugly sweater contest booth.

LEAH

My eyes widened and I slapped Josh so hard it could have been heard across the state of Connecticut. I was seriously losing my patience with him.

"What the fuck was that, Josh? We just got through talking about this. Why the hell would you do that?" I said, pushing off him and sitting in the snow.

"I'm sorry, I couldn't help myself. I saw an opportunity in the moment and I took it. I thought maybe you'd changed your mind and you felt the same way," he said. "Did you really have to slap me?"

"You're lucky that's all I did, Josh. I can't believe you thought I would be okay with that. Maybe you should just go back to the city and I'll see you around," I said and walked away.

"Leah, wait. Stop," Josh said. "I really am sorry. Full disclosure? I saw your ex standing across the way, and I wanted to make him jealous. I could see how hard it's been for you being here and, I don't know, I wanted to make him feel that way, too."

"Josh…" I said quietly. "That's very sweet in a really twisted way, but you have to stop doing this. You keep telling me you're trying to help me or it felt right in the moment. I keep telling you it's over. You don't have to leave, but please be honest with me. Why did you come here?"

Embarrassment swept across Josh's face, and I knew the answer to my question before he even opened his mouth. Why else would a newly-broken-up-with man travel to a small, country town in Connecticut? Surely, not to attend the funeral of someone he hadn't known.

"I promise you, I really did only have the purest of intentions when I decided to come here. I knew you were hurting based on the way we ended things, and I wanted to be able to be there for you," he told me. "But, as soon as I got here and sat outside with your dad, I knew I wasn't going to be okay with everything. I really just want to be with you."

"I respect your honesty, Josh, but I told you I couldn't do this and that I really needed this time for myself," I responded. "This was also one of the main reasons I had to end things with you. You're always only in it for yourself. I loved you so much, but I love myself more. I understand if you want to leave. I can have someone collect your things from the house if you want."

"If you really want me to leave, then I will. But who is going to judge the hot cocoa contest?" he teased.

"Oh, gosh," I said, swatting his arm. "You can stay, but for Pete's sake, stop making moves on me. It's never going to happen."

We smiled at each other and continued our walk throughout the festival. The smell from the sugar cookie station wafted down the sidewalk, and I watched as every child and adult who walked by stopped to sneak a peek.

"Want to decorate some cookies?" I asked him. "They're all homemade and donated by Mrs. Kratz. We don't have to join the contest, but it'll be fun to decorate."

"I don't have an artsy bone in my body, but I love me some sugar cookies," he said. "I'm game. Let's go."

It was such a shame I didn't have romantic feelings for him; he was quite the catch. But I hoped he'd find his forever one day.

"What are you thinking about?" Josh asked me.

"Oh, nothing," I replied. "Just happy to be on the same page. And surrounded by cookies."

Josh laughed and started to decorate his cookie. He chose a Christmas tree but it ended up looking more like it had gotten struck by lightning. I must have inherited some of my mother's artistic genes because I ended up decorating my snowflake cookie so beautifully. I chose white icing and used a silver edible marker to create the dainty lines on each small corner of the flake. Then I dusted the top with shiny silver glitter and the cookie sparkled in the light.

"Well, excuse me, Cake Boss!" Josh teased me. "Looks like someone might have a new career path."

I giggled and looked at my cookie. I wanted to eat it and frame it all at the same time. "I haven't done this in years. It felt good to decorate again. But this is just a hobby. I couldn't do it for a living. Although, my mom used to tell me that once you turn your hobby into your work, it's like not working at all because you're doing what you love."

"Your mom sounds like she was a wise and sweet woman. You must be a lot like her," Josh said. "I'm sorry I never got the chance to meet her."

I smiled and packaged up my cookie. I grabbed a few cookie kits to bring back to the city and paid the woman who was running the station. It was almost time for the hot cocoa contest.

"You ready to pick the best cocoa, Josh?" I asked. "This is Grace Valley so you'd better choose wisely."

26

THE WALK TO THE HOT COCOA STATION WAS SHORT BUT WE TOOK our time. The kids who weren't doing their final rehearsal for the concert were busy seeing who could find Rudolph's nose first. Marina Palmer set up a scavenger hunt and the children had to make it through fifteen clues. Once they made it to the second to last clue, they had to close their eyes and pin the nose on the reindeer to reveal the final clue. Judging by the ever-present excitement in their eyes, they were only about halfway through the hunt. Most of the kids were over it by the time they neared the end. They just wanted to win and head home at that point.

Josh looked over to me and nudged my arm. "Hey, I know it's over and done with, but I really am so sorry about before. I don't know what got into me."

"I know," I replied, sliding my arm through his. "It's an adjustment. We were together for a while. I get it."

"You're the best," he said.

"Yeah, I know," I teased and rested my head on his shoulder.

We reached the contest just in time for the judging to begin. Ironically, the winner of the contest would receive a two-hundred-dollar gift certificate to Tammy's Diner. I wondered what she would do with it if she won. Josh took his place next to the other four judges and rubbed his hands together.

"Now, this is what I call hometown fun," he exclaimed, and the crowd erupted in laughter.

I stood with the crowd and watched as all the judges tasted the hot cocoa. It reminded me of the time in high school when I decided to judge the chili cook off. What a mess that was! Mr. Kratz entered and he put habanero peppers instead of jalapeño peppers. My mouth had been on fire for days! I'd die if someone up there made Mexican hot chocolate. Josh would wet himself. He couldn't even chew cinnamon gum, let alone drink spicy hot chocolate.

I watched to see if I could tell which entry was Tammy's. Tammy was so giddy that I honestly thought every batch was hers. I was about to try to find a seat when I felt a rough tap on my shoulder.

"Oh, hello," I said when I turned around.

"Listen, I know this is your *town* and all," Brittany spat, emphasizing town while rolling her eyes, "but I'm going to need you to leave Caleb alone."

"Excuse me, what?" I asked, laughing. "I've barely spoken to him since I arrived. I'm not sure where you're going with this."

"I've seen the way he's been looking at you, and I've noticed you always seem to be around."

"This is a small town and there aren't many places to go. You're bound to bump into everyone at some point during the day," I replied, trying not to laugh at her.

"You need to leave him alone or else," Brittany warned.

I smirked and nodded. "Or else what, Brittany? You're going to kick my ass? Please. We all know Caleb and I are long over. Before my mother's passing, we hadn't spoken in over seven years. Now run along and go back to your fiancé and leave me be."

I watched as Brittany scoffed and quickly found her way back over to Caleb who had witnessed the entire altercation. She muttered something to herself and kissed him on the cheek as soon as she reached him. Then she nuzzled up next to him. I was glad I was close enough to hear everything.

"Thanks for bringing me here. It really is magical," she said, brushing the hair out of her eyes. "I can't wait to create more magic with you when we finally get back home to Tennessee."

"Brittany, what did you just say to Leah?" Caleb asked, brushing her off him.

"Nothing. I was just saying hello and that I was sorry to hear about her mother, that's all," Brittany lied.

"I don't buy it. I've known Leah my entire life and I've known you for well over four years. I know the both of you like the backs of my hands," he said, his face showing every annoyance of his mood. "Neither one of you would have acted that way if the conversation you just explained had actually happened. So, what did you say?"

"Ugh, fine. I just told her she'd better stay away from you," Brittany admitted.

"Are you kidding me?" he asked, his anger rising with every word he uttered. "Why would you say something like that to her? Her mother just died and that's what you thought would be a good conversation starter?"

"I don't like the way you look at her, Caleb. And I don't like the fact that she has the ability to take you away from me."

"Brittany! No one is taking anyone away from anyone else. You have to stop this. Jealousy doesn't look good on anyone."

"I'm sorry. I won't talk to her again," she agreed, reaching for his hand.

Caleb pulled his hand away from Brittany. Immediately, we made eye contact and my heart began to race. It was one thing to eavesdrop; it was another to stare. I pulled my eyes from his and looked at Josh who was happily sipping away at the hot cocoa. I had never been more confused about anything in my entire life. I had a great guy who loved me that I didn't want, and the one guy that I had never stopped loving was engaged to be married to the worst woman in the history of women. And there had been a lot of questionable women in this world.

Bill Palmer broke me out of my unnecessary trance. "Ladies and gentlemen, our judges have chosen a winner!"

A round of applause and cheering interrupted his speech. He smiled and motioned for the crowd to quiet down. Josh stood up and handed him the envelope with the winner's name, and he shook it in the air for all to see.

"And the winner of this year's Grace Valley hot cocoa contest is," he started, drumming on the podium, "first time entrant, Tammy Patterson! Congratulations, Tammy! You have won a two-hundred-dollar gift certificate to…your own restaurant!"

Get out! You couldn't even make this stuff up.

"Oh my word! I won?" Tammy asked, tearing up as Bill handed her the gift certificate.

"Yes, ma'am, you sure did," Bill replied. "The judges were unanimous. Would you like to say anything?"

"Thank you, judges! This was so much fun! I would like to donate my winning certificate to the children's hospital, as well as add three hundred dollars to that total. I know times can be tough, and sometimes, you just can't eat any more of that hospital food," she told the crowd.

"Tammy, you are one heck of a gal," Bill said. "Round of applause for Tammy Patterson."

Tammy did a little curtsy and handed Bill back her gift certificate. He smiled and put it in his pocket and headed off to another station. I waved to Josh and he came over to where I was standing.

"Now that was a lot of fun," he said. "But I don't know if I can drink hot chocolate again for a while."

He put his arm around me and we walked to the gazebo to

wait for the concert to start. I didn't want to admit it, but it was nice having a friend to share this with.

CALEB

"Congratulations, Mom. I'm so proud of you," I said, helping my mom gather up her things. "I know Dad would have been, too."

"Sweetheart. Thank you," she replied, kissing me on the cheek. "It was his recipe that I used. I just added a touch of my own thing."

"I miss him," I said solemnly. "I wonder what life would be like if he were still here. During Lucia's services, all I kept thinking about was how Leah must be feeling. When I lost Dad as a little boy, I thought my life was over. But I was able to consume my time with all sorts of activities and, of course, spending a lot of it with her. She's got to go back to the city knowing she'll never get to see her mother again. I can't even imagine."

"My sweet boy. You have always had the heart of an angel. Your father is so proud of you. I just know he is," she said.

"Mom, I want to talk to you. Will you let me help you bring this back to the diner?"

"Of course, sweetheart. Is everything all right?" she asked.

"Yeah, I just need to get your take on some things. Let me go tell Brittany and I'll be right back to help you pack up the rest of this."

"Sure thing," Tammy replied.

I smiled at my mother and turned around to find Brittany glaring at Leah as she talked to Josh. She wasn't hiding the fact that she felt threatened. She also wasn't doing what she promised, which was to back off and leave Leah alone. I took a deep breath and walked over to her.

Anticipating Brittany's reaction, I said, "Britt, I'm gonna help my mom bring the rest of this stuff back to the diner so she doesn't have to carry it all herself. Do you want to come or do you want to stay out here a bit longer?"

"Ugh, really, Caleb? Now you're going to leave me here all alone for who knows how long?" she answered in a snotty tone. "No, of course I don't want to walk all the way to the diner, so I guess I'll just hang out over by the gazebo with the kids until the concert starts. Are you at least going to be back by then?"

"I'm sorry, I know this isn't fair to you. I'll be back in twenty minutes tops," I said and then kissed her on the forehead before going back to my mom.

I glanced back at Brittany before ducking back into the tent and noticed she went right back to burning a hole through Leah. Leah didn't seem to notice, and if she did, she didn't seem to care. I smiled at her and continued to help my mom.

"All right, my love. We're done here. Are you ready to tell me what you wanted to talk about? Brittany isn't pregnant, is she? Please tell me she's not," Mom said.

"What? No. Wait, why would that be a bad thing?" I responded.

"Honey, I love you more than all of the stars in the sky and all of the droplets of water in the ocean, but I do not like that girl. And I can't stand the fact that you're going to marry her. I know it's none of my business, and I promise to always love and support your decisions no matter what, but if I could choose your future wife, it would definitely not be Brittany," she admitted. She shrugged her shoulders and tilted her head as a half-ass apology.

"Well, then. You just started the conversation I was about to have with you. I had a feeling you weren't her biggest fan, but I didn't realize this was the level of detest you felt for her," I said.

We stood and looked at each other for a moment, a sad smile on both our faces. I grabbed my mom and pulled her in tight for a giant bear hug.

"You're the best mother anyone could ever have. I don't know what I would do without you," I said, kissing her on the cheek. "Now, what am I going to do about this mess I've made?"

"Honey, if you truly love her and want to be with her, then do so. I'm not going anywhere and you have my blessing. But if you don't want to be with her, you have to let her go. It isn't fair to her to string her along," she advised. "Just be careful because her stuff is still at our house."

"Mom," I laughed, "you're bad. She would never do anything like that, but I'm pretty sure her bags are packed. She threatened going back on the last train tonight about five times today."

My mom's mouth and eyes opened wide. "You have got to be kidding me. What is she, twelve? Caleb, honey, I think you already know the answer to this problem."

"Yeah, you're right. Let's head back to the festival. I want to see the kids sing, and I think I want to decorate a gingerbread house. I haven't done that in ages."

27

CALEB

THE WALK BACK TO THE FESTIVAL WAS COMFORTING. THE SNOW glistened against the full moon. The children laughed and ran through it, probably happy they were getting to stay out past their bedtimes. Many couples strolled hand in hand, stopping to take in all the decorated storefronts.

"Mrs. Kratz won again this year," my mom told me. "I'm beginning to think the contest is rigged."

"She probably bribed the judges with her sugar cookies."

"Oh, I wouldn't put it past her," she said. "Hey, there's Brittany. Good luck with whatever you decide to do."

"Thanks, Mom. I love you," I said.

"Love you too, kiddo," she replied and kissed my hands, squeezing tightly. "And remember, this is your life. Choose wisely."

I winked at my mom and walked over to the gazebo to find Brittany. The show was about to start, and all the children were carefully taking their places in the center, appearing to be on the verge of intense laughter. On the other side of the green, Leah and Josh stood talking. I couldn't stop finding them, no matter where I went or what I did. Was that a sign or an omen?

"There you are! Took you long enough. I thought you went back to Tennessee without me," Brittany attempted to be funny through her overly rude demeanor. "I picked this spot because there's no way you have any view of Leah over here."

"Brittany, be quiet and be respectful of the kids, please. They've worked so hard on this. At least just pretend you give a damn about someone other than yourself." Word vomit spewed from my mouth and Brittany looked stunned. I didn't care.

She kept her mouth shut and watched the kids perform, but unbeknownst to her, I could still see Leah, and Leah was definitely watching us. My height advantage was working in my favor this evening because I could see clearly over the top rail. Leah was watching us through the balusters, and I don't think she knew we saw her.

She looked happy, peaceful. It was a nice sight to take in after all the seriousness that had taken place over the last few days. I watched her as she twirled her hair between her thumb, pointer, and middle finger. It was something she'd done since she was a young girl, a tell that she was thinking about something important, and I wanted to know what it was.

"They're quite the bunch, aren't they?" a voice came from behind me, causing me to jump.

"Hey, Paul," I said, extending a hand to shake Paul's hand. "How are you tonight?"

"Good, thanks. Love watching these kids every year. Reminds me of when you guys were little," Paul said. "Do you know we still have Leah's red sweatshirts? Lucia bought a red bin and stacked them in there. I don't know what in the world she'll ever do with fifteen red sweatshirts that don't even fit anymore, but you gotta love the sentiment."

"Hey now! Don't make fun," my mom chimed in, sneaking in from the side. "Lucia and I bought those bins together. I have one in the attic with all of Caleb's, too."

"You ladies were too much," Paul howled with laughter. "Way

too much! Caleb, you and Brittany need to have kids and move back to Grace Valley so you can pass yours along."

"Yeah, right," Brittany mumbled under her breath. "That'll be the day."

"What did you say, dear?" my mom asked.

"Oh, nothing," Brittany said, a fake smile stretched across her face. "I was just thinking out loud."

My mom and Paul exchanged glances and began to talk about something that had happened earlier in the day, so I took this opportunity to talk to Brittany.

"Walk with me," I said, extending my hand to her.

"Why? You just told me to acknowledge these kids and now you want me to leave?" she asked, raising her eyebrows and placing her hands on her hips.

"Just walk with me."

"Fine, but then can we go? It's freezing and I'm ready to take a hot bath and go to sleep," she whined.

"I never realized just how much you complain until you came to Grace Valley. What's so wrong with spending a little quality time with my family during the holidays?" I asked her.

"I didn't mean it like that. I just miss the warm weather and my own bed. You know I like to be around what I know," she said, batting her eyelashes. Her charm didn't work that time

I looked at her, wondering if all couples went through rough patches like these, or if our troubles were non-negotiable. I knew what I had with Leah was different because we were so young, but I couldn't help but look at Brittany and wish I was having an entirely different conversation with an entirely different girl.

"Brittany, I know you don't like to be out of your own delusional bubble. You put yourself before everyone every chance you get. When my grandmother died, you asked if I could sell her house to get you a bigger ring," I countered.

"Oh, please. I was only kidding." She laughed, using her thumb to roll her ring around on her finger. "Why are you acting like this? It's because of her, isn't it? You're still in love with her. I knew it!"

This wasn't happening the way I had played it out in my mind, but it *was* happening. I wasn't sure what to do or say, and before I knew it, I was doing what I had known I should be doing for a while.

"As a matter of fact, Brittany, I am. But I know she's happy with some other guy. That's fine because I would never try to take her away from anyone, and I'm so sorry, but I can't hide the fact that you and I just don't work."

Brittany took a step back. Her nostrils started to flare and her knuckles turned white as she fisted her hands. "You're damn right we don't work, Caleb. Because I'll never be her. Look at her! Plain Jane over there. Little miss simple. I have more class and sophistication than she could ever hope to have. You're making a big mistake, Caleb Patterson. A big mistake!"

"I'm gonna need to ask you for that ring back, Britt. I'm so sorry. I never intended for this to happen," I told her, not wanting this to drag on any longer than it already had. "I really did love you."

"Oh, save it for someone who actually gives a damn! You're so full of shit, Caleb," Brittany yelled, throwing the ring at me. "Do you know how many men are lined up waiting for me back home?"

"Oh, good, so you won't be lonely then," I snapped back. I knew it was immature and uncalled for but it felt good.

I watched the ring bounce off my chest and bury itself in the snow at my feet. I looked down to see the spot it landed and looked back up at Brittany.

"I can take you to the train station first thing in the morning. I'll stay at Dooley's house tonight so you don't have to see me," I offered.

"Nope. My bags are already packed and the last train leaves at nine-thirty tonight so I'm leaving now," she yelled. "Don't look me up when you get back, either."

I watched her walk away and then bent down to pick up the ring, wiping off the snow and carefully placed it in my pocket. I looked over to the gazebo before I wandered around more and saw Leah and Josh walk past Brittany, who was storming off the green.

"Have a good night, Brittany," Leah called out genuinely.

"Oh, shut up," Brittany replied before disappearing into the night.

"Somebody's not in a good mood," Josh said, holding out a hand to Leah. "I had a wonderful time with you, Ms. Abernathy. What do you say we call it a night and go watch a movie by the fire? I think there's a cat that's really going to miss me when I leave tomorrow."

Leah smiled so wide it almost reached her eyes. She kissed Josh on the cheek and leaned in for a hug. "Thank you for every-thing. I couldn't have made it through all this without you."

I stood frozen as I watched them walk back to Leah's house arm in arm. In a split second, I had lost both of the women I had loved. I looked at my watch and saw I had a half-hour before Brittany would be out of Grace Valley for good, so I made my way over to the gingerbread house station and got to work.

By the time I was done, I could finally go home and go to bed and—hopefully—forget about this day completely.

LEAH

"OKAY, RED OR WHITE?" I asked Josh as I stood on my toes trying to reach the wine above the fridge. I never understood why my parents kept it there when we had a bar set up on the other side of the den.

"Red," he replied. "What movie should we watch? I'm thinking a Christmas comedy."

"Yeah, I'm down for that. Let me get the wine glasses and I'll be right in," I replied. "Did you want something to eat? I'm kind of hungry and we have all the food left over from the funeral."

"I could eat," he said and laughed. We both knew that meant he was starving, too.

"Okay, why don't you come grab the wine from me and set the movie up, and I'll grab a couple of plates and some food."

"Sounds good. What movie?" he asked me.

"You pick." I knew if I chose, it would be something he wouldn't be in the mood for.

Josh sat on the couch with Gnocchi, and I sprawled out on the loveseat in my mom's sweater, snuggled up under one of the many blankets she had crocheted over the years. Every so often, I would glance over at him, watching him pet Gnocchi and laugh at the movie.

"Refill?" he asked, holding the bottle of wine up for me to see.

"Yes, please," I said, leaning over the arm of the loveseat so he wouldn't have to reach too far.

"This has been really nice, Leah. Thank you for letting me be a part of your family for a few days. I know it wasn't easy for you."

I smiled and curled back under the blanket, swirling my wine around in the glass. I simply nodded before taking a sip.

"As much as I thought I wanted to be alone, I appreciate you coming here," I said in return. "You know, Josh, I really loved our time together as a couple, but I think I like our friendship even better. As weird as that sounds."

"No, I hear you. I didn't want to admit it because I always thought we would end up old and gray together, but I agree. We have a lot of fun together."

The back door opened and a gust of wind tore through the den, causing us both to shiver. "Dad? Is that you?" I called out.

"Well, it isn't Santa Claus," my dad replied. "What are you two up to?"

"Just watching a movie and having some wine. Care to join us?" Josh asked him.

"Sure, let me grab some more wine," he said, sneaking off to the pantry and coming back with another bottle.

"Hey! Where did you get that?" I asked, confused.

"The pantry. On the wine rack. Where else would it be?"

Josh started to laugh and looked to the fridge.

"Leah, you climbed up there for wine? That's the overflow," my dad said, equally as humored as Josh at my apparent brain fart.

"I left when I was seventeen. How was I supposed to know this?"

"You guys are funny together. My parents are a bit, well, uptight," Josh said. "They think they know how to have fun, but it's pretty stiff. They definitely don't know how to take a joke. I love them, of course, but I wish they would ease up a bit."

My dad smiled at him and patted him on the back. "I'm sure they love you just the same, though."

"No doubt about that," Josh said, smiling back. "I think I'm gonna call it a night. I'll see you both in the morning."

"See you in the morning," my dad said.

"Good night, Josh," I said. "And thank you again."

He smiled and walked to the guest room, disappearing down the hall.

"Sit with me," my dad said, pointing to the kitchen table.

I sat down slowly, not quite sure where this conversation was headed. My dad filled the teapot and turned the stove burner on. If he offered tea, this would be a brief and comforting conversation. If he offered coffee, we would be here all night. I watched as he walked over to the cabinet that held both, and he quickly grabbed the tea tin. I quietly let out the breath I was holding in.

"Is chamomile okay?" he asked.

"Of course. Thank you."

It was quiet as we waited for the water to boil. Once it was ready, he brought the tea to the table and we sat in silence a bit longer. It was comforting to be able to just sit and enjoy each other's company in a place we both loved so dearly.

"How are you doing, pumpkin? I know it's been quite the week," he said.

I knew him so well, so I was waiting for the other shoe to drop. I knew he wasn't making tea and sitting because he wanted to know how I was feeling.

"I'm surprisingly okay. I feel at peace after reading everything from Mom, and although I still feel guilty, I know she would want me to move on."

"Good," he said, sipping his tea.

I played with the string on my tea bag and looked at him, waiting for him to say more.

"Is that all," I asked.

"No, actually. I've been thinking," he replied.

"Uh-oh, that can't be good," I teased.

"Funny." He smirked back at me. "Listen, I know you and Josh are just friends, but I was thinking it might be nice to ask him if he'd like to stay through the weekend and spend Christmas with us. It doesn't sound like his family is having a warm and cozy holiday. It's totally up to you, though."

"Dad, I think that's a wonderful idea, and you should definitely ask him. I think Mom would have done the same," I said, smiling. My heart was full knowing this was what he was thinking about during such a tragic time.

He stood up and pulled me in for a hug. I was so happy to be home.

28

WAKING UP IN THIS HOUSE WAS GETTING EASIER FOR ME EVERY DAY. I missed my apartment and all the things I had accumulated over the seven years in the city, but this truly was home. It was early, so I went downstairs and made myself a cup of coffee, grabbed one of my mom's afghans, and sat outside on the porch swing. There was something about being wrapped up with a hot drink while taking in a fresh blanket of snow.

I was about halfway through my cup when the mudroom door opened and out popped my dad with a fresh pot and his own mug.

"Can I top you off?" he asked, holding out the coffee and some sugar packets. "I know you'll want this, too."

I smiled and nodded. I missed how well he knew me and how easy it was to be around him. Seeing him visit me in the city just wasn't cutting it anymore. I wondered if I would be able to convince him to come back with me.

"Dad?" I said.

"Yes, pumpkin?"

"I miss it here and I miss you. I wish I would have visited more."

"I know," he said softly. "I know. But the past is the past and you can only look forward now. Use what you've learned and make different decisions now. Nothing is holding you back."

We spent the next hour drinking our coffee and talking about Mom. We laughed and we cried and then we laughed because we cried. It was a wonderful feeling. Before we knew it, the sun had come up, and we could hear Josh in the house talking to Gnocchi. I swore he was going to adopt a cat when he got back to the city.

"Let's go inside and get changed. I've been craving Tammy's western omelette and home fries. Hope Josh is ready to eat everything in the entire restaurant," my dad said, his eyes sparkling at the thought of food.

I was definitely this man's daughter.

"Paul. Leah. What a pleasant surprise," Tammy said, as she came around the side of the counter to hug us. "Josh, I didn't know you were still here. Please, come take a seat."

"Thanks, Tammy. Leah and I already know what we want, but Josh over here might need some time," my dad teased Josh, which was becoming quite the habit.

"Not a problem. I'll have Justin come over with waters and coffee, and he can take your order whenever you're ready," she said with her signature smile. "Josh, you take all the time you need."

"Thank you," he said. "Is everyone in this town so genuinely nice?"

"Yes," the three of us replied in unison before erupting into laughter.

"I'm not understanding how you could ever leave this place," he said, which made me sad.

Seven years ago, I thought I was running toward something. I knew I wanted to go to NYU and get a degree that would bring me to a great job. I wanted more than this small town could offer. Looking back at everything I'd done and accomplished, I realized I was actually running from everything I had known. I was scared I was going to end up stuck, but I was never willing to try to do both. If only I weren't so stubborn, I might still be with Caleb. And I almost certainly would still have my mom.

Justin rounded the corner with our coffees and waters, then took our orders. My dad ordered the western omelette with home fries. I ordered my favorite breakfast dish of all—two eggs over easy, extra runny, on top of corned beef hash, with a side of French fries and rye toast. I didn't care what anyone said—small town diners have the best corned beef hash, and I'd debate anyone on that until my last breath.

"How are you so tiny? You eat like a sumo wrestler," Josh said and laughed at my order.

"Hey, I like to eat. Sue me," I responded with a wink.

The food came out in no time, and we all dug in like it was the last supper—or breakfast. I couldn't tell you why, but the food tasted like home. There was nothing that compared to breakfast at this diner with my dad. Nothing. And it was at that very moment, I vowed to never take it for granted again.

"So, Josh," my dad began. "I've been thinking about Christmas. I wanted you to know we'd love to have you stay with us if you don't have other plans."

"Oh, I don't know," he said, then looked directly at me as if to ask for my permission.

Permission granted. "It's fine by me, Josh. I think it would do you some good to have a home-cooked Christmas meal here in Grace Valley. We can head back to the city on Monday," I said, answering his silent plea.

"I don't know what to say. This is so kind of you both," he said.

"Say yes," my dad told him. "The more the merrier."

"Yes. I would love to spend Christmas with you both. And Gnocchi, of course." He laughed. "Thank you."

We finished eating and were getting our things together to head back home when my dad asked if he could take me somewhere.

"Why don't I head over to the bakery and pick up the cookies and the cake?" Josh offered.

"That's mighty kind of you, Josh," he said, handing him some cash. "Do you mind swinging by the butcher while you're out? I ordered the Christmas roast, and it's already paid for."

"Sure, no problem. You guys take your time, and I'll just meet you back at the house, then."

"You two are so weird," I said, looking back and forth between them. "Where are you taking me, Dad?"

"You'll see," he said and led me out the door.

The town green was still covered in lights and decorations, and it would stay that way until the new year. Even this early in the morning, you could see the magic this town held. My dad led me around the side of the building and around the corner to the back entrance of his grocery store. I hadn't set foot in here in seven years, and I couldn't tell you the last time I had used that door.

"What's going on? Why are we here?" I asked him.

"I want to show you something, but we need to go in from the door in my office." He spoke without looking at me.

When we got into his office, he stopped at his desk and opened the drawer to get something. He pulled out a set of keys and walked to the door I had always assumed was a storage closet. He must have noticed my confusion because he looked at me and said, "This is the door that connects the grocery store and the building next door."

He motioned for me to go through the door and he quickly

followed. The hallway was bright, the walls painted tan on the bottom half and white on the top. The floors were dark gray linoleum that matched the metal doors. It was odd that the hallways between two stores were so well taken care of, but knowing it was my dad who owned this entire building made it a little more believable.

He walked down the hall and began to unlock another door. I noticed a small sign above the peephole with the letters LCA. My mother's initials. He opened the door and walked into another office identical to his minus all the paperwork.

"Are you expanding?" I asked him, not sure why he would need to do that.

"Patience is not your strong suit, is it, pumpkin?" he teased. "This was your mother's place. We were fixing it up to become her art studio."

"Her art studio? I don't understand. She was an Italian teacher."

"Yes, she was, but as you know, she was enjoying making her pottery, and she had gotten very good at it. She would come here every day after work and make something. She always had so many projects going on at once, and she was so happy in here. She was going to offer classes to the children in Grace Valley," he told me.

My eyes welled with tears as I took in everything he told me. That was so like my mother, and I wasn't at all surprised, but I was saddened by the news. The more he spoke of it, the more I realized that none of these children were going to get to experience this with her. It was hard enough knowing I had lost my mother, but I had forgotten that an entire town had just lost one of its most special residents.

"What do you plan to do with the space now that she's gone?" I asked him, afraid of what his answer might be.

He looked at me and then around the room at all the artwork

she had created. I didn't know how long she had been at it, or how she had ended up here in the first place, but it was magnificent. I always knew my mother was creative and talented, but I never could have dreamed she would have been able to create all this.

"I haven't given it much thought, but for now, it stays just like it is," he said matter-of-factly. "This place was her pride and joy— after you, of course—and I can't put all her things away and rent it out. Not yet. Maybe not ever."

I could see his eyes start to fill with tears. I didn't want to pressure him or make him feel worse, so I let him be for a minute. I walked around and touched everything I could in an attempt to feel her again. She was in there with us; I knew it. I also knew what this place would become, but I let it sit in the back of my mind and set my attention back on my dad.

"I think keeping it as it is sounds wonderful. It's a nice place to sneak off to when you need a minute to think or want to be close to her. Maybe one day you'll find a different use for it, but for now, I think she'd want you to leave it, too."

He pulled me in for a big hug, and we stayed like that for a while. I made a mental note to come back here every time I visited so I could spend some alone time in the place my mom felt the most comfortable. I had hoped that being in there would cause some of her creativity to rub off on me and help me with my own job. I had so many ideas but wasn't sure how to execute them. Cameron made it clear I was the right person for every job he put me on, but I still wasn't confident of that myself. I had a lot of work to put in to become the best, but I knew I was up for the challenge.

"Are you ready to get out of here and start putting the house together for Christmas?" I asked my dad. "The fact that there's no Christmas tree is really bringing me down. I doubt Dooley has any left, but I do know mom has the fake one she used to put up on the porch. We could always use that as a last resort."

"I'll call him on the walk home," he said. "But don't think this means you can become the parent."

"Okay, Dad." I laughed and we locked up and started walking back home.

29

CHRISTMAS EVE WAS ALWAYS ONE OF MY FAVORITE NIGHTS growing up. Partly because I was able to stay up really late to make it to midnight mass, but also because the town put on a show every year. It was short but always ended with a live nativity scene. One year, there weren't any babies in town, so Dooley tried to hop into the scene and be baby Jesus—diaper and all. It was hysterical. He was the type of man you could always count on for a good laugh, a shoulder to cry on, or in this case, a Christmas tree.

I slipped my arm through my dad's and rested my head on his shoulder. Looking at him and actually seeing him as an individual had so much more meaning than looking up to him as a child. For the first time in years, I could see how quickly his age was creeping up on him. That wasn't to say he looked old because he looked amazing for a man in his fifties, but I could see how life, specifically recent events, had taken a toll on him. He looked down and smiled before placing a tiny kiss on the center of my forehead. Forever a daddy's girl.

"Are you gonna call Dooley or what?" I teased.

"Yes, boss," he said, saluting me like a soldier.

I giggled as he pulled his phone out of his pocket and dialed Dooley's number. It was nice to see him happy again despite the week we had just been through.

"Hey, Dooley," my dad said. "I need a favor."

"Let me guess. You need a tree?" I could hear Dooley's response through my dad's excessively loud speaker.

"Told you," I mumbled and nudged my dad in the ribs with my elbow.

Laughing, he nudged me back and winked. "You two think you're so funny."

Dooley's laugh bellowed through the phone, and I knew him so well I could almost see his dimples getting deeper as he threw his head back in laughter. Man, I missed these people and times like this.

"As a matter of fact, Paul, I have two trees set aside for you," Dooley told him.

My dad looked at me and raised his eyebrows. I could see his crow's feet were a bit deeper than the last time I saw him and wondered if stress had finally caught up to him. I didn't want him to think I was worried about him, so I smiled and kept walking, not listening to their conversation any longer.

"So, what did he say?" I asked.

"That Dooley. He's something else. He said that, for the past seven years, he's been setting aside two trees just in case your mom changed her mind and needed one last minute."

"Oh, Dad. That is such a Butler thing to do," I said, tears filling my eyes. "I say it often, but we are so lucky to have all these amazing people in our lives."

"What do you say, kid? Want me to walk you home and then I'll head over to pick the trees up?" he asked.

"I think I'd like to go with you, if you don't mind. We can take Josh, too. He hasn't been to the meadow yet, and I'd love to show him a bit more of Grace Valley before he leaves," I told him. "I'm sure this is going to be his first and last trip here."

"I think that's a great idea, pumpkin. He can help me load the tree into the truck. This old body isn't getting any younger, you know."

"I'm gonna get you to live near me. I will and you know it!" I told him. I wasn't ready to leave him, especially alone.

He just smiled at me, and we continued our walk home in silence, breathing in the scent of winter. When we arrived at our property, I could see the smoke billowing out of the chimney and smiled inwardly at how quickly Josh had acclimated to country living. I never would have thought he would be the type to throw a log on the fire or help carry Christmas trees; he had people to do that for him. But a few days breathing in that country air had changed him.

"We're back," I called when we walked through the front door.

"I'm in the den with Gnocchi," I heard Josh call back.

My dad and I looked at each other and smiled. Of course he was with Gnocchi. Next thing I knew, he was going to try to take him back to New York.

"Hey, do you want to come to Dooley's farm with us to grab a Christmas tree? I thought maybe you'd like to see the meadow and all their decorations. They really go all out."

"You don't say," he teased. "I'd love to go. Sounds fun."

"Dad, do we still have the toboggans?" I asked, hoping they were still around somewhere.

"I think we do in the garage. Do you want to come help me get them down, Josh? If you could help me carry in the ornaments, too, that would be a tremendous help."

"When did you start storing Christmas stuff in the garage?" I interrupted. "I thought mom wanted everything in the house."

"Your bin is still up in the attic with the rest of the decorations. We only moved a few things to the garage to make room up there. I think she was hoping you would come back and we could store your apartment things up there."

I stood there frozen, embarrassed and crushed.

"Umm, no problem," Josh cut in and then turned to me. "Are you coming, Leah?"

"No thanks. I think I'll stay in here and gather some things. Don't get lost in there," I said winking, and shut the door behind them.

The last place I wanted to be was inside the garage that housed more memories than things. I was just starting to feel normal again, and I didn't want to end up reverting. I threw on a pot of coffee and started putting some things into a bag to bring to the meadow. A blanket, extra work gloves—Lord knows Josh won't want to get his precious hands scratched up—a few disposable coffee cups, and a baggie of cookies for Dooley. When the coffee was finished brewing, I poured some into two thermoses and put those in the bag, too. We would definitely need the warmth, and I always needed the caffeine.

My heart was beating out of my chest by the time my dad and Josh came back into the house. I hadn't been to the meadow in years, and the last memory I had of there was when Caleb and I said our final goodbyes. I wasn't ready to relive those memories, but I couldn't live in fear for the rest of my life, either. Besides, today wasn't about me, it was about my dad and keeping the memory of my mother—and the true spirit of Christmas—alive in our hearts and our home.

"Trucks warm, pumpkin," my dad said, looking across the kitchen at me. "You ready or do you need some time?"

"Sorry, I was just thinking. I'm ready," I replied and lifted the bag to show him. "I packed some coffee for us."

"You two and your coffee. I don't know how you can drink that much," Josh said, shaking his head.

"You should have seen my mom," I said with a laugh. "She could drink her weight in coffee."

"Come on, you two. I'd like to get the tree before New Year's," my dad teased, and led the way out of the house toward the truck.

The drive to Dooley's was quick but bumpy. I had gotten so used to city traveling I had forgotten what it was like driving around on these roads. Most of them were paved, but the Butlers refused to allow anyone to touch the gravel road that led to the farm from town.

"It's part of the Butler Farm charm," Dooley would say any time anyone suggested a change. I hated to admit it, as I clutched onto my chest as we bounced along, but I did love that rocky little road. Despite quite a few spills, bloodied knees and banged up elbows, I learned how to ride my bike there.

"Well, I'll be," Dooley said, walking out of the barn and throwing a rag over his shoulder. "I never thought I'd see the day."

My dad rolled his eyes at him and playfully hit him on the side of his arm before closing his window. Dooley laughed his loud, belly laugh and nodded for us to follow him. I grabbed the bag out of the bed of the truck and told Josh to go on ahead and I'd meet them up there in a minute. He obliged and I paused for a moment, taking it all in.

For the first time, I really stopped and allowed myself to be grateful for everything I had been given and for all that was to become. If I had learned anything since my mom passed, it was that time was fleeting and everything happened for a reason.

I smiled as I looked around and saw the fence sparkling with lights. Becky had truly outdone herself this year. I wondered if she decided to make it bigger and better because mom was gone or if it was just a coincidence, but I loved it. I noticed they added a sleigh to the roof of the barn and somehow made Santa look like he was floating in the air next to it. Leave it to Dooley and Becky to have the horse barn be the main attraction in this tiny town. I laughed to myself and walked up to the barn to meet everyone.

"Hey, Leah! I didn't know you were going to come," Jackie said, peeking her head out from behind the hay bales.

"Jackie!" I reached out and pulled her in for a big hug. "I didn't know you would be here, either. I figured you'd be helping your mom with some final Christmas orders."

"Yeah, I was gonna help her, but she said this was my last high school Christmas break and to enjoy it. So I'm just hanging around the barn with my dad."

"That sounds like a perfect way to spend a day," I told her.

I always admired how much of an old soul Jackie was. When the other kids were out partying and getting into trouble, Jackie was at home, hanging out with her parents or helping someone in town with whatever they might have needed. She was so much like her mom, and it warmed my heart to see that, even as she got older, her love of family remained strong. If only I had some of that when I was her age.

"I brought the toboggan," I said. "You wanna go for a ride while they put the tree in the truck?"

"Definitely! Let me grab my gloves. Do you want me to put your bag in the office?" Jackie asked.

"Sure. I'll meet you out back."

The snow was the perfect powder for sledding. Not too heavy but thick enough that if you were to crunch some in your hands, you could form the perfect snowball with one roll. Connecticut was only one state away from New York, but somehow, even the snow seemed different. The air was still and clear. It was quiet but you didn't feel like you were missing anything. I glanced over to Josh, who had looked up at the same time, and we caught each other's gaze. It was getting harder to look at him knowing that once we got back to the city, whatever it was that was happening this week would be over for good. Just as I was about to say something, Jackie came bouncing out of the barn, putting on her gloves. That girl had so much energy!

"Josh," she called. "You coming with us? I won't take no for an answer, city boy!"

"Yes, ma'am," he said with a smile.

"You are your mother's daughter, Jackie," I said with a laugh. I grabbed one of the toboggans from Jackie and started running toward the top of the hill. "Race ya!"

"Oh, come on! You totally cheated!" Jackie yelled to me, trying to keep up.

I jumped and landed bottom first on my toboggan. *I'm gonna feel that later.* The wind whipped my face, causing my hair to fly haphazardly and smack me in the back with every bounce. I felt like a kid again. When I reached the bottom of the hill, I was thrown off my toboggan and right into a massive pile of snow. Jackie quickly joined me and we laughed uncontrollably as if we really were kids again.

"Come on, let's do it again," Jackie said, pulling me from my snow hole. "Let's race Josh this time."

We must have ridden down that hill a dozen more times before we called it a day. I was thankful to have brought extra gloves and a blanket because I was soaking wet. Sledding in jeans was not my smartest idea. My dad, Josh, and I drove back home in silence, but I knew that each of us were contemplating the memories we had made tonight. Memories that would be with us forever.

30

I'VE ALWAYS HEARD PEOPLE SAY THAT THE ROAD SOUNDS DIFFERENT once you're close to home, and I never really understood it until that day. Pulling into our driveway and unloading the tree felt different than it ever had before, and it wasn't because I was home and my mom wasn't. There was something about the air, about the movements and the sounds and the smells. It was home. It was the place where I was allowed to fully be myself and was embraced for it. Yet, in two days, I would be leaving it all behind again to live in a world I knew I didn't truly belong in.

"Pumpkin, can you go heat up the soup I left in the fridge?" my dad asked from underneath the trunk of the tree he was setting down on the front porch. "We can put up the tree when we're done eating."

"Okay," I replied, smiling as I watched them walk back to the truck to get the second tree.

I loved that Dooley knew my dad so well and had saved two trees for him. It made my heart smile knowing there were so many people looking out for him while I was gone. And I was happy to have two trees to decorate and bring a little cheer back to this sad house.

I unlocked the door and put the soup on the stove like my dad asked. It was peaceful inside that little farmhouse, and I found myself thinking of Caleb once again. At this point, all I knew was that he was getting married, and I didn't know if I would ever see him again. I needed to get over him—and fast. I was glad I would be in this house for the rest of my trip and wouldn't have to see anyone else from town to cloud my judgement.

The soup was hot by the time the guys came back in, and I poured us each a bowl as they took their boots off and washed their hands. French onion soup was a staple in this house, and it was the perfect treat on this bitter, cold day. I broke off a corner of the sourdough bread that my dad had stashed in the pantry and dunked it into the soup. I didn't want to forget this taste ever.

"Shall we?" my dad asked when he was finished, placing his bowl in the sink.

"Definitely," Josh said. "I couldn't tell you the last time I decorated a Christmas tree. Or anything for that matter."

I went up to the attic to pull down the box of ornaments my dad said still lived up there and met the two of them in the den. Gnocchi was curled up next to the fireplace, purring up a storm. Occasionally, he would steal a glance at Josh, and it made me chuckle. I wished my apartment allowed pets because I wanted to take him back with me. But at the same time, I didn't want to leave my dad completely alone. I knew he found comfort in having Gnocchi with him.

When I got back downstairs, I was greeted by Nat King Cole's velvet voice singing Chestnuts Roasting on an Open Fire. His version of "The Christmas Song" was my parents' favorite, and I loved watching them dance in front of the fire every time it played. We started decorating every year to that song, and they would dance before they strung the lights. I held my hand out to my dad, and he twirled me and held me close. I knew my mom was with us in that moment.

After the song finished, I sat down on the den floor and opened the bin I had brought down. I rubbed my fingers over the ornaments and smiled at the memory that each one held. The Precious Moments graduation ornament my mom bought when I graduated middle school was still in the box, and it looked as though it hadn't ever been opened despite being hung on the tree every year. I laughed at the ornament of snoopy playing tennis that I had gotten the year I played tennis in high school. *Played* is a funny way of saying I made the team and then didn't really finish the season. The cat sleeping in the pink bed was from when we got Gnocchi, and we thought he was a girl. Oops.

The phone rang, startling all three of us. Of course, Gnocchi slept through the noise. My dad put the string of lights down and picked up the phone in the kitchen. I couldn't hear everything he was saying, but he sounded both lighthearted and professional. His demeanor shifted when he peeked his head into the den and told me to come into the kitchen.

"What's up?" I asked.

"It's your Nonna. Would you like to speak with her?" he asked me.

My hands started to sweat and my chest tightened. I took a deep breath and extended my arm toward my dad. He placed the phone in my hand and a kiss to my forehead.

"It's just a phone conversation," he said and walked back to the den to help Josh finish stringing the lights.

"Hello?" I said quietly into the phone.

"Leah? Is that really you?" Nonna said from the other end of the line. Her accent was thick but her English was good.

"Yes, this is Leah," I said, palming my forehead. I was so nervous.

"This is your grandmother. I am so sorry we are speaking like this for the first time. How are you, mi amore?"

"I'm doing okay," I told her. "How are you?"

I was awkward with my responses, and I felt terrible about

being so abrupt, but I didn't know what to say or what to do. It was the most uncomfortable I had felt in a very long time, including the coffee spilling incident with Caleb at the train station.

"My heart hurts, mi amore. Your grandfather and I tried to get to America to attend your mother's funeral but we couldn't come. Your grandfather's health has not been too good, and it wasn't safe for us to travel. I'm sorry we could not call sooner."

"I understand," I told her genuinely. "We both understand."

"Leah, I know we don't know each other, and I know you just recently found out about us, but I want you to know that your grandfather and I would really love to get to know you. Would you consider coming to Italy to visit?" Her voice shook at her question, and it made me feel connected to her. It almost seemed like I was talking to my mother again.

"Nonna? Can I call you that?" I asked.

"Of course you can."

"Nonna, I would love to visit you. Maybe my dad and I can plan a trip next summer. I'll have to see how work is then, but we should be able to make that happen," I told her.

"Oh, wonderful!" she exclaimed.

I didn't know her well enough to anticipate her next words, but the way she responded was so much like my mom that I burst into tears.

"Don't cry, mi amore. It is far better to start late than to never start at all. I cannot wait to start this new relationship," Nonna said.

We said our goodbyes and I went back into the den to see Josh tangled up in the string of lights and my dad elbow deep in a box of garland. It was exactly the view I needed after that emotional phone call.

"How did the call go, pumpkin?"

"Great! She invited us to visit next summer," I told him.

"I'll mark my calendar now," he said, always on my side.

We finished decorating the tree in silence with the exception of the Christmas music quietly playing in the background. It was different than the fun and exciting time we had growing up, but this was a different time and the mood seemed to fit. I noticed Josh seemed to be quite the decorator as he placed each ornament exactly three inches apart and did so with a very delicate touch. It made me giggle watching him take such pride in his very first tree decorating event. The phone rang again and we all jumped.

"Now, who could that be?" my dad asked and got up to answer it.

"No, sit. I'll get it," I offered.

"Hello," I said into the phone.

"Hey, Leah! It's Becky," boomed from the phone.

"Hi, Becky. What's going on?"

"Dooley and Jackie told me that you three stopped by earlier for a tree. I was hoping that since you got the tree, you'be celebrating Christmas Eve. Tell me you are," she pleaded.

"Well, my dad had Josh pick up a bunch of food from the grocery store and the butcher this morning. So, yes, we absolutely are!" I exclaimed, suddenly as excited as her.

"Oh, Leah, you have no idea how happy this makes me," she said. "I was so worried your dad might spiral after your mom passed, but I think you're bringing him much more than a little Christmas cheer."

"I know what you mean. I was worried about that, too. He seems to be handling things very well, and I know he might crumble from time to time, but I think knowing I'll be visiting him much more often helps," I said.

"I agree. So, listen, I don't want to be rude, but what do you think about Dooley, me, and Jackie coming over for dinner with you guys? I have a few desserts prepared that I could bring and then we could all go to midnight mass together at the church? Do you think your dad would like that?" Becky asked.

Of course, I thought the idea was wonderful and the furthest thing from rude. We spent most of my childhood Christmas Eve dinners with the Butlers anyway, and they were the closest thing to family we had. I turned my attention to my dad and Josh, who were standing identically and staring at the tree. Left hands around their mouths and chins, right hands gently touching their left elbows, and their heads cocked to the left, examining each pine needle. I laughed, pulling them out of their zone.

"Dad, Becky's on the phone. She wants to know if we want to have Christmas Eve dinner with them. She'll bring dessert," I told him.

"Absolutely! But only if they dress in their ugly sweaters. No sweater, no dinner," he said with a laugh.

"I'll let her know," I said and laughed in return.

This was going to be a great Christmas despite a really shitty month. Becky agreed to my father's demands and we settled on dinner at seven-thirty. I popped the roast into the oven and then we finished decorating the inside and outside of the house. I was quite proud of myself for successfully attaching Frosty to the roof without falling off. It was easier than I thought it'd be considering I didn't have to climb a ladder since the attic window opened right up to the roof. Too bad I wasn't a rebel in high school. I could have totally used that window to my advantage.

Josh surprised us all and made an eggnog from scratch which we sipped by the fire waiting for our guests to arrive. At seven-thirty on the dot, the back door opened and Dooley's voice bellowed throughout the downstairs.

"Ho, ho, ho! Santa's here!" he called, making us all laugh.

He ripped his jacket off and stood in the doorway to the den with his hands fisted on his hips like a superhero. I almost spit out my eggnog at the sight of his sweater. It was red, black, green, and white and had vintage snowflakes and Rudolph knitted on the front. Only on the bottom of the sweater where the ground was supposed to be was Rudolph's red nose and the words "Ho, ho, NO!"

"All right, Dooley. You win," my dad said and stood up to hug his best friend.

Becky and Jackie came in wearing matching elf sweaters, and I couldn't stop laughing at how closely they resembled the sweater I had put on Gnocchi. What were the odds that two women would come to a Christmas Eve dinner and match the cat?

I had on my *NSYNC Christmas sweater, which I still considered to be the coolest thing ever. Josh borrowed one of my dad's many sweaters and chose one with tassels and pom poms. It was a sight, for sure. And my dad went simple this year and wore a black sweater that had a Christmas tree with lights that actually lit up. This party was what we all needed.

Dinner was delicious, as always. The roast came out perfect, and the potato, carrot, onion, and brussel sprout combination my mom used to make was amazing. We ate and ate and then ate some more, and I don't know how we had any room left for dessert, but we did. When we finished eating, we retired to the den for some wine and to exchange gifts. It was weird being home with all these people who had become family and not having my mom with us. I really hoped she was looking down on us today.

31

Before we knew it, it was time to head to midnight mass. Growing up, mass was my favorite because it meant I got to stay up late and try to catch a glimpse of Santa before I went to bed. We would come home afterward and set out milk and cookies for him and carrots for the reindeer. We kept this tradition going all the way until my last Christmas at home, even though we all knew it was for our own sake. Somehow, I never caught that glimpse, but I've always kept the magic alive in my heart.

Mass was quiet this year. I'd like to think the town was still a bit somber because of the loss of my mom, but that made it surprisingly easier to get through. The choir was beautiful and when they started to sing "O Holy Night," my mother's favorite, I saw a single tear roll down my father's cheek and land on the book of hymns he was holding.

At that moment, I knew my mother was with us.

We saw Tammy when we were leaving and stopped to chat for a bit. I assumed this was the first midnight mass she had seen my dad at since I left for college considering he had told me they stopped celebrating. She glanced at Josh and then looked at me before acknowledging my dad.

"Paul," she said, cradling his hands in hers. "I hope this is the beginning of new and wonderful traditions. She will always be with us; I can feel her here tonight."

"Thank you, Tammy. It's hard but I can feel her, too," he replied, somehow managing to maintain his composure.

He was so strong. I didn't know how he did it, but I vowed to learn from his strength. I could do anything with him by my side.

"Where's Caleb?" Jackie asked, peeking around from behind me.

"He's at home packing. He has to be back for some meetings Monday, so he's catching a train out of here tomorrow," Tammy told her.

"On Christmas? Don't they get a break?" Jackie replied, astounded.

I knew he just wanted to get back to warm Tennessee to celebrate Christmas Day with his fiery little fiancée. I'm sure he didn't want to be stuck in Grace Valley when he could be cuddled up next to her. Becky must have sensed my discomfort and stepped in to save the day.

"Well, we should be heading home now. Santa comes bright and early in the Butler household," she said. She winked at Jackie, who seemed to be picking up on her mother's subtle hints. "It was wonderful spending this evening with you all. Please swing by tomorrow."

"Sounds great, Beck. Thanks," he said, hugging her tight. "Merry Christmas."

The rest of us said our goodbyes and went in separate directions to our homes. We got back to the house and took Gnocchi's ugly sweater off, set out milk, cookies, and carrots and went to bed. That was the first night I fell asleep without crying. It was the first night I felt comfortable with the way my life was going.

I woke up to the smell of coffee wafting through the house and my heart felt light. I felt like I had as a little girl waking up on Christmas morning. I half expected to see my mom in the kitchen, dressed in her snowman bathrobe and putting the breakfast casserole into the oven. I quickly threw on some leggings and wrapped her sweater around my shoulders, then followed the scent of the coffee. Nothing makes me happier than a hot coffee first thing in the morning.

I took a peek into the den at the Christmas tree, just like I did as a little girl. I noticed there were a lot more presents under it than there were when I left it after sneaking downstairs at one a.m. to put my gifts under the tree. I made a mental note to buy Sara an extra gift when I got back to the city as a thank you for going to my apartment and not only collecting, but also wrapping and sending the gifts I had bought to give to my dad and Josh. Good thing I didn't return Josh's gifts!

"Merry Christmas, pumpkin," my dad said, rushing to cross the kitchen and enveloping me in a bear hug. That feeling was what Christmas dreams were made of.

"Merry Christmas, Daddy."

"Merry Christmas, Abernathys!" Josh exclaimed, still in his pajamas and rubbing sleep from his eyes.

"Merry Christmas, Josh," my dad and I said in unison.

"Let's eat and then we can open some presents," my dad said.

I could tell he was trying to make this as close to my childhood as possible. I wasn't sure if he was doing this partly because my mom was no longer here or if it was because I had missed seven Christmases with him and he felt like we needed to make up for lost time. Either way, I was happy that some things really were best left untouched. He had made the casserole that we ate every year, and I probably could have bet my life savings this was the first time he had made it since I left. We scarfed down breakfast and excitedly made our way to the tree. We were such kids!

The gift opening was pretty standard for adults. A sweater here, a scarf there, a money clip, some matching cat mugs, and a tie clip. I had bought Josh a new portfolio for his iPad since he was working so much more these days. My dad turned off the

Christmas music and quietly stood up, reaching around the back of the tree and pulling out a box.

"This one's for you," he said, handing the box to me.

"Dad, you've already given me so many wonderful things. You didn't need to get me so much," I said, appreciative but still feeling guilty.

"It's not from me, pumpkin," he said. He sat down next to Josh, who was sitting in front of the fire with Gnocchi purring on his lap.

I looked from my dad to Josh, who merely shrugged his shoulders, and then back to my dad again. I gently took the box from him and laid it across my lap. I was afraid to open it.

"Dad?" I asked. "Do you think it would be ok if I waited to open this one? I think I'd like to be alone for this."

He nodded understandingly. "Of course, pumpkin. I get it."

We spent the rest of the morning hanging around the house relaxing. It was nice not to have to do anything, but the work week started back up again on Monday. Even though Cameron told me to take off until the new year, I really wanted to get back into the office and do a little work on the Portugal project to see what was in store for me.

Part of me felt like I had just gotten to Grace Valley, while the other part felt as though I had been here for months. Josh stood up and announced that he was going to pack up his things, and my dad and I retreated to the kitchen for our last cup of coffee together before I went back to the city.

"You know, Leah. Your mom's studio could easily be turned into a travel agency for you," my dad said, catching me off guard.

"Dad, you know I love you and I've enjoyed every second visiting, but the city is my home now. I've worked too hard to leave now."

"I know, pumpkin. I just wanted to put it out there. Think about it. It wouldn't be difficult at all, and I know your mom would want you to use her space if you could."

"Thanks, Daddy."

THE DRIVE to the train station was quiet—painfully so. The last time I made this drive was seven years ago when I was leaving my parents, Caleb, and Grace Valley in search of a new life. A life I thought I had wanted and needed in order to feel fulfilled, but I had come to realize it was just chasing the fear I'd always had. I never thought I wasn't right for this town; I just thought there was more for me out there, and I couldn't possibly have found it in Grace Valley.

There I was, ready to embark on a similar journey but with a mindset polar opposite to the one before. Only this time, the pain in my heart was ten times stronger. We pulled up to the curb and reluctantly exited my dad's truck. I swung my purse over my shoulder as Josh picked up my suitcase for me.

"I love you so much, pumpkin. Come back soon, okay?"

"I will, Daddy. I promise," I said, meaning it. "I love you, too."

"Think about what I said."

I nodded and hugged him tight one last time.

"Josh, thank you for taking care of my baby girl. And thank you for celebrating the holidays with us," he said, shaking Josh's hand.

"Thank you, sir. It was a great weekend I'll remember forever."

"All right, you two. You'd better get going before you miss that train, and I have to head to The Flower Pot to meet Dooley to help him transport some flowers. A friend's work is never done," he chuckled.

"Love you, Daddy. See you soon."

He winked at me and walked back around his car, standing at the driver's-side door and watching us walk into the station. I smiled when we reached the door, and he nodded and drove away. It was beautiful and sad all at the same time. We made our way quickly through the station, and when we reached the ticket booth, we noticed that the train was going to be delayed by fifteen minutes. Matt wasn't at the coffee shop, so I decided to skip out on a hot drink, and Josh and I just waited quietly together.

The train came exactly fifteen minutes later, and we were up and ready to get on before it came to a screeching halt. I couldn't believe I was already heading back to the city and would be leaving the place that I knew in my heart was truly home. So much had happened in the short time that I was back, and so many feelings had been stirred up. Seeing Caleb was the most unexpected part of my trip, and it was also the hardest. I always thought the next time I saw him would be fine, but I couldn't help but imagine every part of my life with him in it. I had let him go and he wasn't coming back.

The train slowly started to roll and we were off. I looked out the window at Grace Valley one last time as tears filled my eyes. Was I seeing things? Was that Caleb running toward the station? I blinked, and when I opened my eyes again, I only saw an old couple sitting on the bench and watching a young boy jump up and down in the snow. All this fresh air had definitely gotten to me.

32

"Well, hello there, my dear," Walter said as I walked into the foyer of my building. It was the best welcome I could ever hope to receive.

"Walter," I said, smiling back at him. "I hope you had a nice Christmas."

"I sure did. The Missus and I celebrated with our children and grandchildren."

"Wait a minute! Why are you working?" I said, realizing it was still Christmas day.

"I'm not," he replied and held up a pair of ice skates. "I came back to get my grandson's skates. We're headed to Rockefeller Center for some skating and hot chocolate."

"Oh, well, I won't keep you then. Merry Christmas!"

I pushed the button on the elevator and dragged my suitcase inside, then pushed the button to my floor with my elbow. The door opened with a ping, and I stood, staring at my apartment. I hadn't been gone long, but it felt like ages. I opened the door and walked inside and immediately felt like I didn't belong. It was the weirdest feeling and one I hadn't experienced in a long time. I called my dad to let him know I had arrived safely and then unpacked my suitcase and took a quick shower.

Of course, there was nothing to eat, and anything that had been left needed to be thrown out immediately. I called and ordered Chinese and curled up on the couch. There was a Hallmark Christmas movie marathon calling my name. I was about an hour into the movie, and three-quarters of the way through my carton of lo mein, when my cell phone buzzed.

"Sara!" I said excitedly into the phone. "Merry Christmas!"

"Merry Christmas, my girl. How's your day?" she asked.

"It's great! I'm back in the city. Got back a couple of hours ago," I told her.

"Nice! I can't wait to see you. You wanna come to my parents' tonight for dinner? It's just my family so it won't be crazy," she offered.

"Thanks, but I think I'm gonna stay here and relax. I just overate Chinese and I'll probably get to bed early. I want to get to the office early tomorrow and get a jump start on some things anyway," I told her.

"All right. If you change your mind, let me know. I'll have my parents' driver come and pick you up."

"Do you know how snobby that sounds?" I asked, laughing.

"Well, if the Louboutin fits, I say wear it loud and proud," she said.

"You're a mess. Goodbye."

"Merry Christmas, Leah girl. I love you."

"Love you, too, Sara."

I smiled and shoveled another forkful of lo mein into my mouth. That couch had seen more Chinese eating nights than almost anything else. I didn't care, though. I kept on eating and watching and loving every second of it. I surprised myself when I went to throw the cartons away and started to look for Gnocchi. I had never done that here before and was immediately saddened at his absence. I needed to plan my next trip home sooner rather than later.

The unopened Christmas gift sat on the corner of my bed, and I still wasn't ready to open it. I gently placed it on the sitting chair in the corner of my room and turned the covers down on my bed. It was only nine o'clock, but I couldn't keep my eyes open any longer. I had hoped for as easy of a night's sleep as I had the night before.

I woke up to the sun beating into my room and nearly blinding me. In my exhaustion, I had forgotten to draw my room-darkening curtains and that New York City sunrise was a beast! I took it as a sign to get ready for the day and head off to work. I had no idea what was waiting for me in that office, but I was eager to get started on whatever it was.

For a city that never sleeps, it was eerily quiet that morning. Thanks to the many available taxis and the open roads, I made it to work in record time. The only people already at the office were Cameron and my assistant, Casey. She was almost always there, though. She was the textbook definition of a workaholic. She said she was happy with her current position, but I secretly hoped she was saving up all her knowledge to apply for a spot on the team one day. She graduated from NYU two years after I did, but had worked here since she was a sophomore. She knew the ins and outs better than anyone, and she deserved to be recognized.

I made a mental note to have a conversation with Cameron about keeping her as my assistant when I permanently changed roles in a few weeks. I went to the kitchen to make two coffees and went to tell Cameron I'd returned. He turned in his chair and smiled when he heard my voice, and I handed him his coffee.

"Leah, you've been promoted, not demoted. You don't need to fetch me coffee," he teased, the corners of his mouth turning slightly. "You're back sooner than I'd expected. How was your trip back home?"

I really liked that he referred to Grace Valley as home.

"It was hard, to be honest. But it was necessary, and it was worth it," I told him. "A part of me didn't want to leave. I'm worried about my father, but I'm planning another trip back home as soon as I can."

"You know, Leah. While you were away, I had a lot of time to think about things and about your time here at World City Travel."

"Oh my gosh, you're not firing me, are you?" I asked.

"Fire you? Never!"

"Oh, thank god," I said, letting out a huge breath.

"Leah, you're an extremely important part of this company, and I would never want to lose you. However, as I was saying, I started this company many years ago at the insistence of my wife. It was very small for many years, and we worked out of a tiny apartment in Brooklyn. My point is, if you ever wanted to move back home, I would help set you up. You would be able to take John's account with you, and I have quite a few small-town venues that are looking to open soon. I want you to know that there isn't another person in this company that I would do this for. You're special, Leah Abernathy. You have a gift and it shouldn't be shoved away somewhere."

I stood there, mouth open and speechless. If this was what Christmas miracles felt like, I wanted it to be Christmas every day. At the time, I wouldn't even know where to begin and I was just about to start International. Two dreams come true and I could only choose one.

"Cameron, I truly appreciate everything you've done for me. And this, this goes above and beyond anything I could ever dream of. But I think I need to politely decline—at least for now. I really want to get International up and running and expand my knowledge there," I told him, not sure I believed what was coming out of my own mouth.

"I understand," he responded. "The offer has no expiration

date, so just let me know if, and when, you're ready. Now, go get to work."

I was really starting to like this side of Cameron, and I was happy that a part of him was saved just for me. With him losing his wife, and me losing my mom, I felt as though we shared something not everyone else in the office had. It was nice being able to come to work and not worry about someone "getting" you. I walked back to my desk with a new feeling of purpose and sat down to text Sara. I was just pulling my phone out of my purse when she walked through the door and sat on the corner of my desk.

"Well, you certainly did arrive early today, didn't you?" she said with a laugh. "You are, by far, the hardest worker I know."

"Yeah, well, somebody has to be," I said, playfully swatting at her arm. "You look nice today."

She smiled and brushed a curl from her eye. "Thanks, love. I have a date tonight."

"With whom?" I asked, my eyes as wide as saucers. "And why am I just hearing about this now?"

"I wanted to tell you in person! It'll be our third date and trust me when I tell you this, I'm going to marry him."

"Holy shit! Tell me everything," I said, leaning closer to her. "And don't leave anything out."

"Believe it or not, I met him through my parents. He was an intern at my mom's firm and his father works with mine. They invited us to their house for some pre-Christmas cocktail gala and we hit it off immediately. He's not like anyone I've ever met before, and I feel like I can be myself around him," she said.

Her eyes sparkled and her cheeks turned a shade of rose I'd never seen on her before. Maybe this was actually the Christmas miracle. She was beaming and she deserved to be.

"So, when do I get to meet him?" I asked. Best friends always have the final say, anyway.

"Do you want to come to lunch with us? We're going at noon

but I don't know where yet. You can pick the place since you weren't here last week, if you want," she offered.

"I'd love to," I said. "Let's get sushi."

She smiled knowing I only picked sushi because she loved it. I was excited to meet this mystery man. I couldn't remember the last time she had introduced me to someone she thought had potential, let alone someone she actually considered sticking around for the long haul. And after only two dates, no less. But, I was a firm believer in fate and intuition, and if she said she felt he was the one, then he was.

My heart dropped at the thought of fate. I wanted so desperately to erase the memories I had with Caleb, but they kept coming to me stronger and stronger every day. I didn't know what to make of it all, but I had to let him go. After all, he was further away from me than I had thought and completely and utterly taken. I just hoped that Brittany knew how amazing of a man he was, and how lucky she was to hook him.

Noon crept up quickly and we were on our way to meet the mystery man. We walked into the restaurant and the most attractive man I had ever seen came walking toward us, a big smile on his face. There was no way he was an employee, and he was definitely not here for me, so he had to have been Sara's man. My suspicions were confirmed when he kissed her on the cheek.

"Hi, I'm Aiden," he said, his voice as smooth as butter.

My knees buckled and for a second I thought I was gonna marry him, too. I totally saw what she meant. We ate and laughed and truly enjoyed one another's company. I loved the way he listened when Sara spoke and laughed at her ridiculous jokes. It was as if they had known each other their entire lives. We parted ways at the door, and Aiden leaned down and gave me a hug. It was an unexpected but very welcomed gesture.

"So, what did you think?" Sara asked me as we walked back to the office.

"Two thumbs up from this girl," I said. "But you could have

told me you were dating People's Sexiest Man Alive. I almost broke a sweat in there."

"Oh my gosh, Leah. You're such a nerd," she said and laughed. "I told you he was amazing."

"He is definitely perfect for you, and I couldn't be happier for you."

"Hey, I wanted to ask if you were doing anything for New Year's Eve? I know you usually go to watch the ball drop with Josh, but since that shit the bed, I assumed you were free."

"Wow, subtle," I said, rolling my eyes playfully.

"Best friends don't do subtle," she replied.

"No, Sara, I do not have plans. Why? What does your crazy ass have in mind?"

"My parents are hosting an event. It's some pre-fashion week thing they're doing to ring in the new year and hopefully pull some more donations in for something or other. It's similar to the one they did last year during fashion week," she told me.

"I'm so in. That was by far the most fun I've had in this city. I still can't believe your parents give us their tickets every year."

"I guess to them, once you've seen one, you've seen them all."

I SAT on the corner of my bed and stared at my open closet. I had no idea what I was going to wear to the New Year's Eve gala. As dress after dress stared back at me, I became increasingly stressed about the coming night. I wasn't ready to meet anyone, but I also didn't want to be the third wheel. I threw myself backwards onto my bed and let out a huge breath. Something shiny caught my eye, and I noticed the unopened gift still sat on my chair. I sat up and reached for it, holding it as if it were a bomb about to detonate.

My heart began to pound, and I slowly pulled out the card that was carefully tucked under the ribbon. The card read:

. . .

MY DEAREST LEAH,

My one wish for you is that you find eternal happiness with whatever you do. I love you more. Merry Christmas.

Love, Mom.

SHE ALWAYS TOLD me that a mother's love was stronger than anything else on earth, and even with her gone, she still got the last word. I smiled through tears and opened the small box. Inside was a silver, bar bracelet with the inscription: *All roads lead to home*. I smiled and reached for my cell phone.

"Hello?" my dad's voice rang through the other end of the phone.

"Daddy, I'm coming home."

THE END

EPILOGUE
CALEB

Christmas Day

"THANKS SO MUCH, BILL," I SAID, SHAKING HIS HAND. "I'M REALLY looking forward to this opportunity."

"As am I, Caleb. I'm happy to welcome you to the Grace Valley School. We are the lucky ones to have you," Bill Palmer responded.

I wasn't expecting this conversation to go the way it had when he mentioned me stopping by during the Christmas Festival. I had been looking online for teaching jobs closer to home since the night Brittany and I broke up. Never in my wildest dreams had I thought it would lead me home.

"There are a few things I'll need you to do before you can transfer roles and certifications here, but you have time. You enjoy the rest of your holiday here with your mom, and we'll touch base again after your school year is up in Tennessee," he said, shaking my hand again. "Merry Christmas, Caleb."

"Merry Christmas to you, too."

I couldn't believe I was going to be Bill Palmer's replacement as the Principal of Grace Valley School next year. It was a dream come true, and although I loved teaching Social Studies, I was excited for my new venture. I needed to tell my mom right away and walked directly from the school to her diner. I knew she was busy setting up for tomorrow morning's opening since it was Christmas and the staff was off.

"Mom," I called, racing through the front door.

"Caleb, what's wrong? Is everything okay?" she asked, panic streaked across her face.

I took the silverware out of her hands and placed them on the table beside her. I held both of her hands in mine and the door opened behind us.

"Hey, hey, hey! Merry Christmas, Patterson familia!" Dooley's voice rang through the diner. Did he do anything quietly?

"Hey there! Merry Christmas," I said.

"Merry Christmas, boys," my mom said, dropping my hands and motioning for Paul and Dooley to place the flowers by the bar. "Caleb was just about to tell me something."

"I hope it's good news," Dooley said with a smile.

"I just had a meeting with Bill Palmer, and I'm gonna be the new Principal at the high school," I blurted out. The speech I had intended on making was thrown out the window.

My mom's jaw dropped and she jumped up and down like a kid. "You're moving back?" she practically screamed.

"I'll be back for good by the end of May, and I'll start up at the school in September," I told them.

"Congratulations!" Dooley and Paul said in unison, followed by laughter in unison, which then caused us all to laugh.

"Thanks, guys," I said.

"What about your girl?" Dooley piped. Leave it to him to ask the question no one else wants to.

"Uh, we broke up at the festival. I'm surprised Mom didn't fill you all in," I said.

"Not my news to tell, Caleb," she responded.

"I'm sorry to hear that, Son," Paul said. "Sometimes things happen for a reason, though."

"I know. I think I knew all along she wasn't right for me, but it was seeing Leah again that solidified it for me. I knew we were over, and she was with that Josh guy, but it made me realize I didn't feel the same way about Brittany as I had felt about Leah. It wasn't fair to string her along," I admitted.

"Honey, they're just friends," my mom said.

"You sure? Because they looked pretty serious at the festival, and I saw them kiss with my own eyes," I countered.

"Trust me," Dooley chimed in. "They're over."

"Caleb? Are you still in love with Leah?" Paul asked me.

"Yes, sir, I am."

"Well, then you better go get her because her train's about to leave," he said.

I ran as fast as I could to the train station, but the doors of the train closed as soon as I got there. I ran my hands through my hair as the train started pulling away, and I saw her sit down in her seat. Just like that, she was gone.

I had lost her again.

ENJOY THIS BOOK?

I'd love to hear about your thoughts and reactions. Please leave a review using the link below. Stay tuned for book two of the Grace Valley series, Full of Grace.

https://www.amazon.com/reviews/create-review/error?&asin=B08N47FKRV

ACKNOWLEDGMENTS

First and foremost, thank you to everyone who is reading this right now. Your support throughout this journey, and what's to come, is incredible. It means more to me than I can ever put into words.

Dave. My ridiculously supportive husband who worked full-time remotely and still took care of our babies so that I could have blocks of time to write this book. You are my best friend, and I couldn't do any of this without you. I love you.

Sabrina and Alexandria. My babies. My little muses. My favorite girls. This book is for you. You've taught me that I can do anything. Being your mommy lights up my world and my heart. I hope that I can make you both proud. I love you the most.

Mom and Dad. Thank you doesn't seem to be enough. Through all of the ups and downs, you have supported me, loved me and guided me. You've seen my path and the direction I needed to take long before I ever did. The proof is definitely in the pudding and I hope you like it! I love you.

Jenna. You're my favorite sister. No matter how far our life journey takes us, we will always be there for one another. I love you

Nacolle. I don't know where to start. My writing partner in crime. My late-night freak out texting companion. You want me to succeed more than anything and I'm not sure I deserve your friendship. But I will cherish it forever.

Sarah Sego. You are the single most positive person I know, and I owe so much of this to you. You're next!

Melanie Cherniak. AKA Elsa Kurt. Thank you for answering every single one of my questions and then some. You believed in me from the very first word I typed, and I can't wait for you to see the finished product!

Amanda Cuff. The world's most amazing editor and proof-reader! I am so glad that God brought you into my life! You have become such a wonderful friend and I can't imagine this book life without you in it.

Ashley Munoz. Book formatter extraordinaire. You jumped into this project without any hesitation and I am forever grateful to you.

Matt. Thank you for the memories and for being a part of this. I wonder if that bench is still at our high school. Hopefully you will make an appearance in book two. I promise to get you some bagpipes for that one!

Rebecca Donovan. Thank you so much for your amazing writer's seminar where I learned so much about where I needed this book to go. Your patience and understanding is unparalleled and I can't wait to work with you again!

And last but certainly not least, The Hallmark Channel. Seriously, I wouldn't have written this book if I wasn't so head over heels in love with every single movie you've ever made. Feel free to turn this book into another one of your movies!

And to anyone I missed, thank you for everything! Writing this book has been nothing short of amazing and I owe it to each and every one of you.

ABOUT THE AUTHOR

Bethany is an author, wife and mother to two little girls. When she isn't writing or spending time with her family, you can find her whipping up something in the kitchen, enjoying a hot cup of coffee, or with her nose stuck in a book.

Find her on her website at
www.bethanysurreira.com

Made in the USA
Middletown, DE
07 November 2021

51354710R00139